"Why are you defending that man?"

Her grandfather peered down at Lacey, looking so much like the robust man who'd raised her that for a minute she forgot about his ill health.

"I don't have a good feeling about things, Lacey. I don't know where you are most of the time, or who you're with." He swallowed hard. "Mostly, I'm afraid you're not telling me the truth." He handed her a sheet of paper. "Please print this in Wednesday's paper and prove to me that I'm imagining things, that I'm wrong in my suspicions. I need that from you now."

Lacey forced herself to face him. This was the man who'd given up so much of his adult life for her and her brother. In that instant she knew she had no choice.

Family had to come first. She had to print the editorial the way her grandfather wanted—or admit she was falling in love with Seth Taylor.

And that would surely kill the man standing in front of her.

Dear Reader,

Writing a Christmas story for Superromance has been one of the highlights of my career. That this book is a sequel to my earlier novel, *Cop of the Year*, with several of the characters from that book appearing in this one, was an added bonus. And it was truly enjoyable to tell you, once again, about life in a typical high school in the nineties.

Because It's Christmas is a principal's story. I've often wondered why anyone would want to be a principal—the job is thankless, open to a barrage of criticism and lacks many of the rewards of classroom teaching. Therefore, it was a challenge to get inside Seth Taylor's head....

This book has affirmed my belief in two of the most important things in my life—the love between a man and a woman struggling against the common *and* extraordinary roadblocks in their relationship, and the true joy educators find in influencing the lives of youngsters. Miracles happen at Christmas, but they also happen every day in a high school classroom. And of course, the magic between two people who were meant to be together is nothing short of miraculous. I hope my Christmas story adds love and happiness to your holiday.

I'd love to hear from you. Please send letters to Kathryn Shay, P.O. Box 24288, Rochester, New York 14624-0288.

Kathryn Shay

BECAUSE IT'S
CHRISTMAS
Kathryn Shay

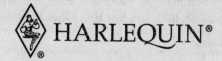

HARLEQUIN®

TORONTO • NEW YORK • LONDON
AMSTERDAM • PARIS • SYDNEY • HAMBURG
STOCKHOLM • ATHENS • TOKYO • MILAN • MADRID
PRAGUE • WARSAW • BUDAPEST • AUCKLAND

ISBN 0-373-70815-7

BECAUSE IT'S CHRISTMAS

Copyright © 1998 by Mary Catherine Schaefer.

Printed in U.S.A.

To all the secretaries, aides, custodians, teachers and administrators at Gates Chili High School

CHAPTER ONE

BARKER ISLAND PRISON loomed before Lacey Cartwright like a modern-day Alcatraz. Located on a
desolate piece of land about two hours west of New
York City, the island epithet was appropriate because of the prison's remoteness. Lacey took a deep
breath, reached for the door handle of her car and
shook off the horror she felt every time she thought
of her younger brother Kevin incarcerated in this
hellhole.

What must it be like for him to be cooped up
here? In the dim twilight, as she exited the car and
approached the entrance, she could still see five-
year-old Kevin looking up at her and pleading as
she put him to bed, *Don't shut the door, Lace. I
can't stand being closed in.*

She gazed ahead of her. Even the outer doors of
the monolith were huge—steel things that she could
barely open; frustrated, she yanked at them until
they gave way.

"Ma'am." The grizzled man with blank eyes at
the security desk nodded. He wore a drab gray uni-
form with Hanley, Corrections Officer, printed on
his name tag.

She nodded back.

"Name?" He followed the procedure even

though she'd been here so often in the last six months she knew he recognized her.

"Lacey Cartwright."

"Inmate?"

My baby brother. "Kevin Cartwright."

The guard retrieved a wire-mesh basket from a sturdy shelf and handed it to her. Going through the familiar routine, she removed her jacket and deposited it inside the container, along with her purse. Purposefully she avoided Hanley's eyes because the first few times she'd come here, taken off her coat and surrendered her belongings, she'd seen a leering look on his face that had made her skin crawl. She barely glanced at him as she held up a manila folder. "I'd like to keep this."

Hanley nodded as his beefy fingers took the slim file. He checked it and returned it to her.

Without a word, he pointed to the steel archway— a state-of-the-art metal detector. Sucking in a breath, Lacey walked through it. She heard the loud snick of the inside steel-core door unlocking. She dragged it open and took a seat in the waiting room.

She'd stuck a copy of tonight's *Bayview Herald* in the folder, thinking she'd check it during the usual wait for Kevin to be summoned. When she shook open the newspaper, she came face-to-face with the person responsible for her brother's imprisonment.

Seth Taylor.

From the front page, he stared up at her, his grin broad, his wide shoulders relaxed, his eyes twinkling at the camera. The assistant editor's headline, Taylor Voted Educator of the Year, screamed across the top of the article. As editor, Lacey hadn't wanted to run the story, but she'd had no choice—it was big community news. She'd sent her assistant to cover it.

Lacey *had* managed, however, to finish an incisive editorial on student violence at the high school. Its principal, Seth Taylor, wouldn't be happy to see that published on the School Page of the paper.

She studied his picture and remembered when she'd gone to see him eight years before to plead for her brother. Taylor hadn't been smiling then.

Please, give him another chance, Lacey had begged him.

I can't. Not only did he hit two students this time, he attacked a teacher. Jerry Bosco says Kevin punched him. I have no choice.

Kevin says he didn't hit Bosco.

Taylor had stiffened and she thought she saw a hint of doubt cross his face. But he'd said, *I have to support my staff, Ms. Cartwright. And I won't tolerate violence in my school. Kevin has been given several warnings. I'm sorry...*

Lacey sighed. Taylor's hard line with her brother had been the beginning of a downward spiral that had taken sixteen-year-old Kevin from Hillside School for Troubled Teens to Barker Island Prison to serve a five-year stint for grand theft and assault.

And precipitated her grandfather's heart attack.

And brought her back from her job as a reporter on the *L.A. Times* to run the *Herald.*

Damn, if only Taylor had been more compassionate, things might be different today.

Her negative thoughts were interrupted by the creak of another iron door. A second somber-faced guard with a scar running from his ear to his jaw glanced into the room. She'd seen this guy, too. Cramden. He said little and stared hard at all visitors as if he could read their minds. "You here for Cartwright?"

"Yes." Lacey stood, dropped the paper on the chair and braced herself.

"Come on."

Upon entering the visitation sector, Lacey spotted Kevin sitting at one of the tables. Other than the guard, no one else occupied the room. Lacey suspected the cold, windy October weather on top of the remote location had kept visitors away.

Pasting a smile on her face, she approached her brother. "Hi, buddy."

Kevin lazed back in his chair, the perpetual sneer hardening his mouth. "Hi, sis."

"How are you tonight?"

He folded his arms over his thin chest. In the six months he'd been here, Lacey would bet he'd lost at least fifteen pounds. "Just peachy. It's been a wonderful day at Barker Island Resort and Golf Club."

After a brief hesitation, she reached across the table to touch him. This particular prison was a newer facility, and as a medium-security jail, it had been designed with open visiting areas. All that separated Lacey from Kevin was a half wall, so she could squeeze his arm.

Kevin drew back, but before she dropped her hand, he lifted his left one to briefly cover hers. "Sorry. I'm a jerk."

"I don't blame you, honey." She glanced around

the room. "This is a horrible place. You're entitled."

"How's Grandpa?" Kevin asked.

"Good. He's still ticked off that the doctor's limiting his visits to once a month."

Kevin's face sobered. "He shouldn't come at all. Any change in his condition?"

"He's doing okay—recovering well."

"Thanks to you." Lacey shook her head but Kevin protested her denial. "Yeah, it is. If you hadn't come home to take over the paper when they railroaded me into this place, Grandpa would be in a lot worse shape."

"I wanted to come home. I wanted to be here for you and him."

She saw Kevin's hands fist on the small ledge before him. "You got your own life."

Not anymore. The selfish thought came out of nowhere and Lacey quickly banished it. "They built a new indoor track at the high school," she said, to change the subject. "It's opening to the public next weekend. I'll be able to run all winter."

Kevin's smile was genuine. "I'm glad for you, Lace." He glanced at the folder she carried. "What'd ya bring me?"

Lacey's stomach clenched. "Those forms I told you about last time. For the Graduate Equivalency Degree program."

The expression on Kevin's face degenerated to pure contempt. "I don't want them."

"Just read them, Kevin. Please."

"Why?"

"Because when you get out of here, you'll need at least a high-school diploma."

"I tried to get a high-school diploma, and that bastard kicked me out."

Lacey sighed. Kevin's undiluted hatred of Seth Taylor exacerbated their grandfather's animosity toward the man, and sometimes her own.

"You have a second chance, Kevin. Please just look at them."

Kevin shook his head. "Give up on me, Lacey. I'm not going anywhere in life."

Reaching over the half wall, she took her brother's hand again, though this time he flinched at the contact. She remembered how his little palm used to slide eagerly into hers. "I love you," she said, choking back emotion. "I'll never give up on you."

For a moment, a look of such intense despondency shadowed Kevin's face that Lacey wanted to weep. Then the sneer reappeared. "Well, I've given up on myself." Kevin stood abruptly. "I gotta go. Bye, Lace."

Lacey watched her brother signal the guard, who opened the heavy door. It clanked shut behind him with finality. She cringed. Clutching the folder on degree equivalency programs, she stood and made her way out of the visiting room.

In the waiting area, she reached down and picked up the copy of the *Herald* she'd left on the seat. Taylor's smiling face mocked her.

Damn you, Taylor, she thought as she headed for the guard station. *Damn you.*

PHILIP SQUATTED and stretched out his arms to the boy.

The child teetered, his brown eyes glowing, his chubby cheeks rosy with delight. "Pa...Pa...Pa," he said as he took his first steps.

Tears clouded Philip's eyes. "Come on, boy. You can do it. Come to Papa."

One more...two more...three more steps, and the baby gripped Philip's large hands.

Philip scooped up his grandson. "Good boy, Kevin. Good boy."

"Grandpa..."

Philip started, then came awake. "What..."

"Shh, Grandpa, it's me. Lacey. You fell asleep in the recliner again."

For a minute, Philip let himself sink back onto the chair. His granddaughter was leaning over him, concerned. She looked so much like her mother, except for her thickly lashed light brown eyes, which she got from the Cartwrights. But her wavy blond hair, slender build and peaches-and-cream complexion resembled her namesake—the Lacey's.

Kevin was the spitting image of Tom, Philip's only child. God, Philip missed them all so much.

"Grandpa? Are you all right?"

He smiled at the only family he had left—Lacey. She'd been ten when her mother died giving birth to Kevin, fourteen when Tom was killed by a drunk driver. After his son's accident, Philip had left his position at the *New York Times* to buy the *Herald* so that he could work in town and raise her and her brother; he'd loved every minute of it. Still, when the time came, he'd done a good job letting Lacey go. He'd smiled when she went off to college—his alma mater—and practically burst with pride when she got her first reporting job at the *L.A. Times*.

Until his heart attack. After that he'd become weak and needy. And he hated himself for it.

"How are you, honey?"

"Fine."

She wasn't. She looked tired. And upset.

"How's Kevin?"

"Good."

Philip waited until Lacey hung up her coat. "What did you talk about?"

"Not much."

"Did you bring him the GED information?"

"Yes." Lacey gave him a brief account of the conversation.

Philip sighed and thought about probing for more information about his grandson. But the lines around Lacey's mouth and the tautness of her features made her look older than her thirty-four years tonight, so he backed off.

"Dani called while you were gone."

Lacey's smile was like unexpected sunshine in February. "Sorry I missed her."

"She and I talked."

"Don't start, Grandpa."

"She's right, Lacey. You need to go back."

Lacey stood. "I'm not going back and leaving you alone."

His heart constricted, not from angina this time. How could he be doing this to the girl he loved so much?

How can you not?

Damn, he hated this dependence. He'd rather be dead than be an albatross around her neck. He remembered so vividly when he was her hero... *Papa, look, the science project we worked on, I got an A... Papa, I'm going to be the editor of the high-school paper because they said I knew so much... Grandpa, I got into UCLA, just like you...*

Now she was sacrificing her career for him. It was hell getting old.

"Lacey, I can't let you do this anymore. You've been home for over six months."

"It's my choice, not yours. I'm going to get some hot chocolate. Want some?"

He studied her. Chocolate was one of her few weaknesses and indulging in it was a telltale sign that she was not doing well. "Honey, I..." But what could he say? That he didn't need her? He did. Though he was financially secure, he was physically and emotionally unable to support himself any longer.

He thought about what Celia Trenkler said today when she'd come to clean the house...

"If you aren't happy, Philip, do something about it."

"I can't fix my heart."

"It's your head that needs fixin'. You can do something about that..."

Damned woman. Why did she stick her nose into his business, anyway?

"Grandpa? Do you want some cocoa?"

He eased forward and wrestled himself out of the chair. Standing, he looked down at his beloved granddaughter. "Sure. I'll make some popcorn to go with it."

And just like when she was little and needed comfort, she nestled her hand in his—it was still smaller—and they headed for the kitchen.

Six fights at the high school last week saw one student hospitalized and the other teenagers involved suspended.

The administration clearly lacks the ability to control the school environment so that this kind of violence doesn't erupt. Perhaps if there was better supervision kids wouldn't have the opportunity to raise their fists. It seems obvious to this reporter that the staff is not teaching the students to respect each other. Surely this value should be instilled along with instruction on reading and writing.

The administration needs to find more effective answers to the problem of violence in the school. Suspensions help no one. Getting rid of the kids isn't the answer.

What do you think?

Seth Taylor slapped last night's edition of the *Bayview Herald* down on his desk and glanced at the phone. What the hell? He didn't have anything to lose. He dialed the paper's number and drummed his fingers on the newsprint until she answered.

"Lacey Cartwright."

"Ms. Cartwright? This is Seth Taylor."

She waited a telling moment before she responded. "Yes, Mr. Taylor. What can I do for you?"

The formalities were odd, he thought. Though it was only thirty miles outside of New York City, the Long Island village of Bayview Heights still had a small-town mentality for the most part, and people were low-key and informal. Almost everyone was on a first-name basis.

Except the principal of Bayview Heights High School and the editor of the *Bayview Herald.*

"I'd like to talk to you about yesterday's editorial."

Again, a meaningful pause. "All right."

"The time and place at your convenience."

"I have a meeting with the superintendent tonight at six. It shouldn't take more than an hour. Why don't I come by your office around seven?"

"Fine. I'll see you then."

Stifling the urge to slam down the receiver, Seth glared at the phone after he hung up, then grabbed a pen and pad to make a list of things he wanted to discuss with Ms. Cartwright. What did you tell a woman who hated you? Frustrated, he threw the pen onto his desk and searched for the folder on the school's Christmas activities. He tried to concentrate on the student council report, but his mind drifted. Tossing the notes aside, he rose and crossed the office to stand in front of his wall of memorabilia. It usually made him feel better, but tonight it had the opposite effect.

The picture of his eighteen-year-old son only made him miss the boy more. He'd tried to call Joey earlier, but couldn't reach him. Seth smiled. He could picture Joey in his dorm room at UCLA, looking older and more mature in the college atmosphere than he had at home.

Seth wished he didn't have to wait until Thanksgiving to see Joey again. But the boy had been adamant about sticking it out until the holiday. Seth had bitten his tongue to keep from telling Joey that it was more for him—Seth—than for Joey that Seth wanted to fly his son home in October. But Seth had to let go sometime. To stop the dull ache in his heart that came every time he realized Joey was grown up, Seth focused his attention to the newest plaque on the wall.

Educator of the Year. Now that was ironic. He'd recently received the prestigious Phi Delta Kappa award—at a time when he was seriously questioning his career in education and what good he'd done in his twenty-five years of service. Seth fought the pessimism rising within him. Lately, he'd felt he hadn't accomplished enough. And, of course, he'd made some mistakes—big ones, especially in his first year of teaching. His naiveté—and his belief he could effect positive change in even the most difficult student—had led Seth to defend a boy despite criticism from other teachers. The student, Tim Johnson, had abused Seth's trust with tragic repercussions.

Which brought him full circle to the problem at hand. Turning, he went back to the desk and scanned again the editorial on student violence—written by the sister of another boy Seth had been unable to save.

Over the years, Seth had put his failure with both Tim Johnson and Kevin Cartwright into perspective.

Despite the former *Herald* editor's attacks—Philip Cartwright had not pulled his punches—and now his granddaughter's witch-hunt, Seth had hung on to the fact that he'd done what he thought was best for the school at the time. Lately, though, with these midlife doubts about his success in helping kids, his decision didn't seem so clear-cut. He wondered if, because of the incident with Johnson, he'd acted too harshly with Kevin. He sighed heavily.

"What was that sigh for?"

He looked up at the smiling face of Cassie Lansing, one of his best teachers, who was scheduled for a budget meeting with him. She was his greatest success. She'd been a tough streetwise kid eighteen years ago in this very school. When he'd had her in his English class, he'd turned her around, and she'd gone on to become an English teacher, just like him. When he'd taken over as principal of the high school twelve years ago, he'd talked her into coming back to town to teach in their newly formed At-Risk Program. Often, just watching her work her special brand of magic with the kids was enough to confirm he'd done some good.

She plopped down on a chair and stared at him, waiting for an answer.

Finally he said, "The sigh was because of your budget numbers, Cass." He picked up the folder from his desk. She wasn't going to like his cuts, and he hated disappointing her. "You've got to trim the budget for your department."

"I can't trim it any more," she told him implacably.

"Order four sets of novels instead of five. Two

poetry books instead of three. Make the kids buy their own notebooks.''

''Why are you nickel-and-diming us?''

''Nickles and dimes make up the budget.''

Cassie frowned as she stared at him. ''Seth, something's wrong.'' She hesitated. ''You're behaving strangely these days. And this stuff—'' she nodded toward the folder ''—was never a big deal to you.'' Before he could respond, she added, ''Mitch thinks there's something wrong, too.''

Seth watched as Cassie leaned back and rested her hands on her rounded belly. It took some getting used to seeing tough-guy Cassie softened by falling in love with Mitch Lansing, the cop who had worked in her class last year. Now she was married to him and almost seven months pregnant. Seth was finally adjusting to the changes in her.

''I'm only reacting to Leonard Small's demand that taxes go down. He's got an ax to grind with the high school and we're being attacked for overspending.''

''Board members always have an ax to grind. You know that. So what else is bothering you?''

Seth considered confiding in Cassie. She was a loyal supporter and unabashedly trustworthy. So he asked, ''Have you seen Lacey Cartwright since she came back to town?''

Smiling, Cassie dropped her hand to the tattoo on her right ankle—the one she'd gotten during her days as a street kid. ''I spoke to her briefly when she got back in April. I told her how sorry I was about her grandfather.'' She paused, looking rueful.

"But things got so hectic, and we haven't gotten together for a proper reunion yet."

"You should."

"I know. She was great to me after I decided to dump that chip on my shoulder." Cassie rolled her eyes. "Even if she was prom queen and head cheerleader."

"It was an unlikely friendship the two of you had."

"Well, she told me once she hated how the other kids ostracized me. She'd seen her brother suffer through it in elementary school."

There it was again. *Kevin Cartwright.* The boy who haunted him like Caesar's ghost. "I never knew she related to you because of Kevin. I didn't have much contact with her when she was in high school."

"That's because you were too busy with punks like me, Mr. T."

Seth grinned at the old nickname.

"Why did you bring up Lacey?" she asked.

"Because of the editorial she wrote in yesterday's paper." The thought of it sparked his anger again, so he changed the subject. "Speaking of punks... have you heard from Johnny?"

Cassie had gotten one of her students, Johnny Battaglia, on the right path, just as Seth had done for her. Then, when Mitch had come to the high school, he too had taken Johnny under his wing. A New York City gang had been trying to lure Johnny back into its fold and Mitch and Cassie had given the boy the support he'd needed to say no. Johnny was now eighteen and in college and was like an adopted son to the couple.

Cassie's smile was proud. "Yeah, he's doing great at Columbia. Mitch's brother says he's invaluable at the clinic. He's also—"

The door swung open and Seth's secretary burst in. "Seth, there's another fight in the orange hall."

Bolting out of his chair, Seth flew to the door. When he felt Cassie behind him, he turned. "Stay here, Cassie. You could get hurt—the baby could."

Cassie stepped back.

Dozens of students blocked the hall, making it almost impossible to penetrate. As Seth elbowed his way through the crowd, he saw several adults keeping kids back. When he reached the scene, he found two teachers in the fray, both women, one on the floor on top of a girl, one backed up against the drinking fountain trying to maintain a hold on another girl. There was blood on the linoleum.

Seth stepped in.

TWENTY MINUTES LATER Seth walked back into his office, needing to be alone, discouraged by yet another eruption of teenage violence. Cassie had left but his least favorite teacher waited in the outer area for a meeting Seth had forgotten about.

"You've got to do something about this fighting," Jerry Bosco whined, his small eyes narrowed behind wire-rimmed glasses.

Yeah, like I did with you and Kevin Cartwright?
"Come into my office," Seth said, quelling his resentment of the man. Every time he looked at the guy, Seth wondered if he'd made a mistake in be-

lieving Bosco eight years ago when he'd accused Kevin of assaulting him.

When the science teacher was seated, Seth took his place behind his large mahogany desk and wasted no words. ''Jerry, something's got to change with you.'' He held up Bosco's most recent classroom observation report. ''Alex's notes on the lesson he observed show no innovation using the teaching methods you discussed with him.''

''Alex Ransom doesn't know squat about teaching. He was a damn gym teacher before he became junior class vice principal.''

Seth held his anger in check. Bosco was running scared for good reason. ''Alex is a competent administrator. People here like and respect him. You're the problem, Jerry.''

Bosco's bushy eyebrows rose. ''If this is the tack you're taking, I want a union representative with me when we talk.''

''Fine,'' Seth said, slapping his hand down on the desk. ''Get a union rep in here.'' He gave his calendar a quick glance. ''A week from Monday at 7:00 a.m. I'll tell you both then what I intend to do.''

Red-faced, Bosco stood, his pudgy stomach heaving. ''We'll be ready for you, Mr. Taylor. As will the union lawyers.''

Frustrated, Seth sighed as Bosco stormed out the door. The situation with Bosco was bound to come to a head. His attitude and his archaic and ineffective teaching methods had to be dealt with. This just wasn't a good time.

Before he could catch his breath, Seth's secretary looked in again. "Can I talk to you?"

Seth smiled. Sue Watson was a godsend. She'd kept his office running smoothly for the twelve years he'd been principal at Bayview. "Of course."

Poised, almost unflappable, Sue smoothed the front of her classic blue sheath as she sat down. Her gray hair was meticulously cut. But her usually happy brown eyes were troubled. "I know it's been a bad morning, but I promised myself I'd do this today if it killed me, and you're booked up this afternoon."

Alarmed, Seth leaned forward. "What is it, Sue?"

"I'm resigning, Seth."

Poleaxed by the news, he sank back against the leather chair. "Resigning? When?"

"As soon as we get a replacement." She paused. "I wanted to tell you first, before giving you written notice."

Seth blew out a heavy breath. "Why? Aren't you happy here?"

"No, I guess I'm not." One of the things Seth liked best about Sue was her honesty. Her gaze swept the office. "I've been a secretary in this school for twenty-five years. It's not the same now as it was. It's tougher. Like that latest fight. I heard Joan Jackson went to the hospital after getting slammed up against the drinking fountain. And all the bad press is even more discouraging. I'm too old for this."

The phone rang, interrupting them. "I'll get it," Sue told him. "We'll talk more later." She picked up the extension on his desk.

"It's for you. It's the State Education Department."

He took the phone and his secretary left. Still stunned by her news, he said into the receiver, "Taylor."

"Seth, this is Mike Thomas from State Ed."

Seth had been meeting with the representative from Albany about the Board of Regents' new requirements. The Board—which was responsible for all New York State instruction—had recently introduced an entirely new and more rigorous curriculum and had upgraded the tests students needed to pass in order to graduate. Though Seth agreed with the changes, this kind of revamping caused anxiety among teachers, parents and administrators.

"Hi, Mike. What can I do for you?"

"Well, we've been talking about you here lately. The guys upstairs have been discussing the need for an additional member of the advisory staff to get these Regents' requirements in place. Since you were so effective in our initial meetings with the school principals, I thought you might want to apply."

Seth remained silent.

"You interested in leaving Bayview Heights?" Mike asked.

Images of Lacey Cartwright, Jerry Bosco and the two female teachers who'd intervened in the hallway fight fast-forwarded in front of Seth's eyes. "Yeah, Mike, I might be interested. Tell me more."

CHAPTER TWO

AT PRECISELY SEVEN O'CLOCK that night, Seth looked up from his computer, then stood when the slender blonde reached the doorway. "Mr. Taylor," she said stiffly.

"Ms. Cartwright." He nodded to a plush chair opposite his desk. "Sit down."

As she seated herself—he did too—she glanced at the newspaper on his desk, open to her "What do you think?" column on the School Page. Tracking her gaze, he asked, "No one should give out any reports on what's happening here at the high school without running it by me. Where did you get this information?"

Lacey Cartwright sat up a little taller. "My sources are confidential."

"So is the number of fights at the high school. Where did you get the statistics?"

"What does it matter where I got them? The facts are accurate—and damning."

"When they're presented in such an inflammatory manner."

She cocked her head and her delicate jaw tensed. "I thought you asked me to stop by here to discuss the editorial. If you're simply going to attack me, I'm leaving." Lacey got to her feet.

Seth's temper rose as he stood again, too. He didn't try to disguise the anger in his voice. "Sit down, Ms. Cartwright. I'm not through with you."

Her eyes widened. He saw that they were the exact whiskey color of her brother Kevin's. The reminder of who she was, why she had such an interest in the high school, calmed him. He dragged a hand through his hair and opened his mouth to apologize, but she cut him off.

"I'm not through with you, either, Mr. Taylor." She glanced around his office. "Or with this school."

Maybe it would help to get to the root of the problem, though each time he'd tried to discuss the issue with her grandfather in the past, the older man had exploded. Seth released an exasperated breath. "Please sit down."

Reluctantly she did.

He followed suit and steepled his hands. "Your attacks on the high school are because of Kevin, aren't they?"

"No, they're not." Her voice was strained but controlled.

"You and your grandfather still blame me for what's happened to him."

"That's another story."

"You do, though, don't you?"

Lacey forced herself to stay calm as she studied Taylor. He still exuded the aura of someone comfortable with himself. He'd always been like that. He'd been a teacher at Bayview Heights High School when Lacey attended here, though she'd never had him in class. She'd been a straight-A student and he'd taught all the unmotivated kids. *Reluctant learners,* they were now called.

Like Kevin. "You know how I feel about what happened to Kevin," she said impatiently. "I made it very clear to you eight years ago when I came back from California to help straighten out the trouble he'd gotten into. This editorial has nothing to do with my brother."

Taylor hunched over his desk and clasped his hands in front of him. "I put Kevin on permanent suspension because of the number of fights he had while he was a student here. Particularly the last one where he attacked a teacher. The district was going to pay for home tutoring. When Kevin refused to cooperate, the courts recommended Hillside."

Lacey stared at him hard. "Are you trying to convince me, or yourself, Mr. Taylor?"

A shadow crossed his face—regret? guilt? Lacey couldn't tell. She listened as he continued. "I'm trying to convince you. I know that what I did was best at the time. But it wasn't an easy decision. I told you that then."

Wearily Lacey shook her head. She hadn't planned on getting into this.

Seth added, "And I feel bad about your grandfather's heart attack last February."

Cold seeped into her bones at the reminder of Philip Cartwright's condition. Though she knew blaming Taylor wasn't completely fair, it was hard to separate the chain of events—begun by this man—that had devastated Lacey's family from the man, himself.

Lacey's shoulders sagged with the weight of it all,

especially when she remembered how Philip had given up a prestigious position to come home and take care of her and Kevin when her father had died. That unselfish action, along with his unstinting care, had earned him her absolute loyalty. "Look, Mr. Taylor," she said, trying to restore the conversation to its original topic. "I know you've gone around on these editorials with my grandfather."

"Yes, I have. And I haven't been happy about yours since you took over the paper. They're biased."

"My grandfather's editorials were based on fact. So are mine. I resent your accusations."

He flicked the paper with his fingers. "And I resent yours. Do you have any idea how hard it is to run a high school like this?"

She shook her head. "In some ways I probably don't."

"Maybe you should spend some time finding out instead of consistently printing dirt about us."

Though she resented the slam, she refused to react to it. "Maybe." Bending down, she gathered her briefcase and purse. "Or maybe *you* should spend some time figuring out a way to make this place safe."

With that she stood, turned and walked out the door.

THE NEXT DAY, Seth had just sat down to lunch when Jerry Bosco plopped the *Bayview Herald* onto the cafeteria table. "Have you seen this?" the teacher asked.

"Yes," Seth responded, refusing to let the man rile him.

"Apparently the press agrees with me. Perhaps you should concentrate on disciplining students instead of teachers," Bosco said smugly, then walked away.

Seth picked up the *Herald,* folded open to Lacey Cartwright's column. He wouldn't read it again. Instead, he tossed it into a nearby wastebasket.

Carolyn Spearman sat down with her lunch. "Hi."

He smiled at the senior class vice principal. "Hi."

She angled her head at the trash can. "You letting that get to you?"

"No." She stared at him until he said, "Yeah, I guess."

"Schools always take a lot of heat from the community."

"Yeah, I know. This is more personal, though. Eight years ago, the editor's brother was suspended from this school for fighting. Given the reference in the editorial to dealing with student violence by 'getting rid of the kids,' this was clearly a vendetta against me."

"So, meet with the editor. Tell her about the Safety Task Force you've set up to begin next week."

Seth smiled at his practical, no-nonsense VP. "I met with her last night. I didn't have a chance to tell her about the committee before the accusations started flying."

"I'm sorry. Want some good news?"

"I'd love some."

"Seventy students signed up this morning for our first meeting on this year's Christmas Good Deeds Project," she said, referring to the high school's annual drive to provide Christmas gifts and food for needy families in the community. "That's ten percent of the school."

Seth smiled. "Lacey Cartwright should print *those* statistics. Great job, Carolyn."

"It's not me. You set this whole thing in motion by giving us the time and resources to mobilize the kids."

"Still, you and the staff do the work."

"Thanks." He saw the glimmer in her eyes. "Since we're doing such a great job, the student council has a request."

"All right."

"It'll cost more money."

"What doesn't."

"You know that new day care that just opened for underprivileged kids on Franklin Street?" Seth nodded and took a bite of his sandwich. "Our students want to add it to their list of organizations that we support."

"Won't we be spreading ourselves too thin?"

"Not kidwise. Those seventy will enlist more of their friends to do the actual work. We *will* need another couple of adults for this group, and ninety percent of the staff is already committed."

"Okay. I'll take charge of the day care, then. We'll find someone else to work with me."

"We could get the community involved."

Seth preferred that this remain an entirely school-run project. "We'll see."

"We should also get more publicity for these activities. It's great what the kids do this time of year."

Seth thought about his students working in soup kitchens, delivering toys and food to needy families, surprising a school member with a gift, doing Kris Kringles with each other, decorating the building. Originally, the teachers thought he was nuts when he wanted to make the holiday season "an event" at the high school. But Seth believed that kids— even those who didn't celebrate Christmas at home—could benefit from helping less fortunate people at the holidays. And camaraderie was at an all-time high.

He glanced at the *Herald* in the trash. "You know, Carolyn, you're right. We *should* have more publicity. And I think I know exactly how to get it."

"HEARD YOU TRYIN' to call that sister of yours tonight, Cartwright. She sure is a looker. She gonna visit more during the holidays?"

Kevin avoided looking into Cramden's fat face and fisted his hands tightly at his sides until they hurt. Without answering, he made his way to his cell.

Kevin wanted to smash the guard's face. For as long as he could remember, he'd wanted to smash things. People. Objects. Anything. *Kevin, do you remember the first time you felt like hitting and punching someone?* The question had come from one of a long line of psychiatrists he'd seen. Kevin had been seven. Even then, he'd thought the doctors were stupid sons of bitches. He'd shrugged, made up some answer and looked at the jerk with innocent eyes.

The best of the shrinks was the lady that tight-ass Taylor had made him see. She'd been this foxy black woman with braid things in her hair. The school psychologist. She'd tried to get him to talk, but mostly he remembered just wanting to rip her clothes off.

In the end, they'd given him drugs to "curb his violent tendencies." When the medicine made him groggy, Kevin only pretended to take the pills.

Inside his one-man cell, he shuddered when he heard the heavy metal door clang shut. He had to count to ten to keep himself from panicking, from giving in to the claustrophobia that attacked him every time his cell was locked.

"Sweet dreams," Cramden said as he walked by, banged his baton on the bars and laughed. It was a mean sound, an ugly one.

As Kevin lay down on his narrow, metal shelf of a bunk, he thought about all the mean and ugly sounds that haunted a prison in the dark hours. His first night here had almost driven him mad. He hadn't known then how the veterans initiated new prisoners, how they waited till lights-out and screamed, "Hey, fish, how ya doin'? Like your new accommodations? Wanna know what's it's gonna be like here for you, little fishy?" They'd outlined a litany of obscenities for almost an hour. When Kevin didn't break, he guessed he'd passed some kind of test because they didn't do *that* to him again. They did other things, things he couldn't bear to even think about, but they left him alone at night. All he heard now was an occasional hollering and shaking of the bars by some jerk who was flipping out or the fanatical cries of somebody calling out to God.

God? Who was he kiddin'? There wasn't any God. Not in prison, anyway.

"Hey, Cartwright? You awake?"

Kevin lay still. His next-door neighbor in cell-block D was Donny Sharp. He was an okay guy and had helped Kevin out some, but Kevin didn't trust him, of course, and most of the time didn't want to talk to him.

"Cartwright?"

Tonight he decided to answer. He felt lonelier than usual. When he'd finally gotten a turn tonight at the one phone in this twenty-eight-man pod where he was housed, Kevin hadn't been able to reach Lacey. "Yeah?"

"You get that stuff to Markham?"

"Yeah. Came in with a delivery and I put it in his sheets."

"Black Eyes says you doin' good, man."

Kevin snorted. Black Eyes ran the Market; you went to him if you wanted something from the outside that you either couldn't get from a visitor—only about half of the two hundred prisoners had visitors—or if you wanted something that was banned. Much of the contraband was delivered through laundry distribution, and since Kevin had been assigned to work in the laundry area, he'd been approached. Kevin hadn't really wanted to get involved with Black Eyes, mainly because there were two groups in this place, and they were always dissin' each other. Black Eyes, a thirty-year-old guy with alabaster skin and the darkest eyes Kevin had ever seen, headed one faction. And Brazil, a bulky Latino with a Rambo tattoo on his arm, headed the other.

But Kevin had learned fast that you had to take a side. You wouldn't make it through your stay if you didn't. And Kevin kind of liked the irony of doing illegal things in prison. He laughed at the thought. He was more of a criminal in here than he'd ever been on the outside.

"What so funny, boy?" Sharp asked.

"Life, Donny. Life is real funny."

"You crazy, you know that?"

"Yeah, so they tell me," Kevin said.

He remembered his grandfather staring down at him. His words had been hollow then. *You're just like everyone else, son. You just need some help behaving. That's all.*

Kevin scanned the eight-by-eight cell, his eyes having adjusted to the darkness and a small sliver of light coming from the guard station.

He was just like everyone else, all right, Kevin thought bitterly as he rolled over and blocked out the images of his family. Here.

AS LACEY FELL into a smooth stride on the newly finished indoor track at Bayview Heights High School, she thought about Kevin. She'd missed his phone call last night, and he'd sounded so sad on the answering machine. Her heart broke listening to it. It was ironic that in some ways he'd let her get closer to him after he'd gone to prison than he'd allowed for years before.

Life was full of these kinds of ironies, she thought. For instance, she'd lost her parents at a young age, but she'd been given the chance to know and love her grandfather. Later, her job at the *L.A. Times* had been exciting and interesting, but the pace in the big city had been wearing. In Bayview Heights, some aspects of putting out a small-town newspaper were less exciting, but life was slower, easier, and she had time to run every day.

She missed running with Dani—Danielle S. Kendall. The two of them had started out together as cub reporters at the *Times,* and Dani was still there, writing some incisive articles on urban violence.

And you're covering high-school fights.

Stop it. You made your choice. Besides, it's not forever.

As she circled the spanking-new track, Lacey felt the familiar aura of peace come over her and she tried to settle into it. Usually, she just cleared her mind and let the endorphins flow. But today she kept thinking of her conversation with Dani yesterday afternoon.

As usual, Dani wanted to know when Lacey was coming back to California. Dani had warned her against sacrificing her life for her family. Lacey shook her head and closed her eyes. No one understood what had brought her back home. It was love.

She loved Philip Cartwright. He'd given up so much for her and Kevin. Personally, he'd forgone any semblance of a private life for a healthy, attractive man of fifty-six. Professionally, he'd given up a career that many people felt would have earned him a Pulitzer Prize. Lacey wanted to give something back to him. She believed in family loyalty and taking care of those you loved. And of course, she had to be near Kevin when he needed her the most.

As she rounded the track, she noticed someone else had come to run. Not many people in Bayview Heights were up this early on a Saturday morning. His back to her, the runner stretched, the long lines of his body encased in a navy blue nylon sweat suit. As she neared him, she crossed lanes to be on the outside. Dedicated runners usually greeted each other, recognizing a kindred spirit.

When Lacey got closer, her heart rate speeded up.

This wasn't a kindred spirit.

This was Seth Taylor.

He turned just as she closed in on him.

Surprise flickered across his face. In the morning light filtering through the high gym windows, she could see evidence that he was not sleeping well—Lacey saw the same signs in her own mirror—a pale cast to the skin, brackets around the mouth. She slowed, touched by the vulnerability she saw in him. "Good morning."

"'Morning."

She sped up again, but as she rounded the corner, she thought of how Taylor—a former track coach—had pushed for this facility. Indoor track was a new varsity sport in New York State; most high schools used their existing gyms for practices and meets. But Seth had campaigned for a whole addition to the school, believing the more space for activity, the healthier the kids would be—physically and emotionally. Lacey had considered getting behind the endeavor in her editorials, but Philip had been appalled at the idea of her supporting Taylor. The measure had passed narrowly in a close budget vote eighteen months ago, anyway, so it didn't matter. The construction had been completed this fall.

Circling the track, she kept her eyes straight ahead, though it was impossible not to notice him when he came into her peripheral vision. He ran like a pro. Some runners had a natural, graceful, loping stride, their long legs eating up the ground, their arms swaying at their sides.

Lacey had it, too.

He'd removed his sweat suit and wore simple navy jock shorts and a white T-shirt. His dark blond hair was shorter than when he was a teacher. She remembered the girls drooling over him. *Sexy Mr. T.* Several of her friends had contemplated moving down a level just to get into his English class. Women teachers were always in his room. Surreptitiously she watched him.

He was still attractive, if you liked a lean runner's body.

Lacey did.

When she realized the direction of her thoughts, she was so horrified that she missed taking a curve soon enough and she stumbled. The action broke her stride and her foot twisted. Righting herself, she kept going for another quarter mile. When her ankle began to ache, she slowed to a walk. Another few paces and she limped off the track.

Damn. She recognized the injury.

From behind her, she heard, "Are you all right?"

Lacey turned. Though his words indicated concern, his voice was cool, his blue eyes narrowed.

"I twisted my ankle." She matched his impersonal tone, then took another step and winced.

"So I see. Sit over there." He pointed to a padded bench provided for runners.

"No, I'll just go home." Lacey knew from experience that her ankle would swell painfully.

"Sit. I'll get some ice."

His tone irritated her, but since her foot was throbbing, she did as she was told. Icing the ankle down would preclude later problems and she'd be back on it faster.

Seth returned in minutes with a blue, prepackaged ice pack. By then Lacey had removed her shoe and sock. Propping her foot on his bare knee, he felt her instep. "Does it hurt here?"

She shook her head, watching his long, lean fingers probe her skin. He had a scholar's hands, and the sight of them reminded her of his enthusiasm for reading and his love of literature. His students had often teased him about it.

"Here?" He flexed her toes.

"No."

"Good. It's just your ankle."

"I know, it's an old injury. I should have worn my brace."

His forehead creased. "Why didn't you?"

"I couldn't find it. And I didn't want to wake Grandpa by rummaging around downstairs."

When Seth still seemed puzzled, Lacey said, "He

sleeps on the first floor now. It's easier than climbing that winding staircase.''

The sad look she'd seen at his office the other
night when he talked about her grandfather's illness
crossed his face again. It made him appear older.
But he simply nodded and adjusted the ice pack.

"Listen, I can do this," she said, trying to escape
the tension between them. "I don't want to interrupt
your run."

"Sit still. How'd you hurt this just now?"

Lacey felt her face flush. "I was thinking about
something else and lost my stride."

"There isn't anything wrong with the track is
there?"

"No." She scanned the arena, taking in its half-
mile track, stations for vaulting and shot put, plenty
of spectator seating. "It's beautiful."

"Yeah, isn't it?" He sounded like a proud father.

"It was a great idea."

He stared at her unblinkingly. His eyes were slate
blue, rimmed with black. "I could have used the
Herald's support in trying to convince the voters to
approve the budget for it."

Lacey's whole body stiffened, and Seth wished
he hadn't let the comment slip. She'd been relaxed,
doing what she obviously loved doing—running.
He'd seen her covering miles around town several
times in the last few months. And of course, she'd
been a track star in high school years before he'd
taken over the team. There were a couple of trophies
with her name on them in the display case in the
front of the school.

Finally she said, "I should have supported it, I guess."

"Why didn't you?"

"I had my reasons."

"Mind telling me?"

Lacey shook her head, sending to the floor the tie-thing that held her hair. Seth picked up the band. He ran the silky material through his fingers. When he looked up, she'd shaken her hair out. It fell in thick flaxen waves around her shoulders.

He watched as she threaded her fingers through the heavy mass and twisted it up in back. It was a thoroughly feminine gesture that intrigued him. Then she held out her hand for the tie. He gave it to her. Their fingers brushed. The contact jolted him and he inched back, still holding the ice around her ankle with one hand. He stared down.

That didn't help. He focused on the ice pack. But it wrapped a beautifully shaped ankle, attached to a sleek, muscular calf, topped off by a long, lean thigh.

Oh, damn, he thought as he felt his body respond. *This is just what I need.*

To counteract the untenable reaction that had shot through him, he said with as much edge in his voice as he could muster, "Maybe you should try to concentrate on some of the good things at Bayview High."

"Maybe you should do more significant good things."

Their gazes locked. He broke the stalemate. "I have a challenge for you."

She arched an eyebrow.

"Come to the high school. Spend some time there. See some of the good we're doing."

"Like?"

"Like *ten* percent of the kids are involved in some pretty unselfish Christmas projects. Our first meeting is Monday at three o'clock in the library. Watch them work. See what they do. Report some of that on your School Page. Then I can handle your propaganda."

"My editorials are *not* propaganda. They are thoughtful, intelligent attempts to keep the community informed."

"About the bad things at Bayview Heights High School."

Lacey drew in an angry breath. Before she could comment, he leaned over, bracing his arms on the bench on either side of her. "What do you say, Ace Reporter? Are you woman enough to accept my challenge?"

CHAPTER THREE

ACE REPORTER? Had the man really thought that was *funny*? But the challenge worked. She'd agreed to come to the high school to see for herself what was going on. The *good* that was going on. Now, as she stepped through the front doorway at two forty-five on Monday afternoon, she stopped dead in her tracks.

Snow White—clearly a guy in drag—was trailed by seven perfectly garbed dwarfs. A huge box of M&M's followed. A string of witches, vampires and werewolves—appropriately scary—were right behind them.

As she stared at the figures heading for the buses, Lacey remembered today was Halloween. When she'd been in high school, kids never dressed up for the day. It wasn't cool. This was kind of nice, she thought as she made her way to the library's large meeting room. And healthy. She enjoyed the menagerie in the halls all the way to the library.

Once inside the meeting room, she slipped into a chair at the back, hoping to remain unnoticed. The costumes here were just as vivid and inspired. Up front, a very realistic Tin Man was trying to get the attention of the students. Sitting in the first row were

Dorothy, the Cowardly Lion, Glinda the Good Witch and a couple of munchkins.

"All right, you guys, listen up." The Tin Man began to give directions for the task at hand. Lacey scanned the room. Off to the side were the teachers. She smiled. Their concession to Halloween was that each was wearing a special shirt as a costume. One man wore a medical scrub tunic with a surgical mask hanging down. Another teacher wore a Mickey Mouse top with big black ears askew on her head.

Lacey's gaze landed on Cassie Smith. She'd chosen a huge football jersey that was snug across her bulging middle. On the back it said, Smith-Lansing. Number 1. Seeing her old friend, Lacey was swamped by memories—good ones—of this school and the years she'd been a student here. Suddenly, a feeling of discomfort assailed her at the tack her grandfather—and then Lacey herself—had taken with the paper's editorials about this place.

There was no sign of Seth Taylor. Administrators were too busy to participate. When Lacey had been in school, she remembered teachers heading up the activities and the administration being pretty invisible except when discipline was required.

Lacey focused back in on what the speaker was saying. "As you all know, Ms. Spearman, the senior class vice principal, is in charge of Christmas Good Deeds this year." All the kids clapped when a woman dressed in a cat shirt with cat ears peeking out of her short dark hair waved at them. "Before we show you the groups we've assigned you to," the Tin Man continued, "Mr. Taylor wants to say a few words."

As if on cue, the door flew open behind the Tin Man and in bounded Seth Taylor. His dark blond hair was mussed and his cheeks red from hurrying. He wore a meticulous navy blue suit, white shirt and tie. Over the latter, he had on a blue and red super-hero jersey. The Tin Man joked, "Okay, super guy, it's all yours."

Seth took the mike. "In case you didn't know," he said, plucking at the T-shirt, "the student council gave this shirt to me this morning."

The kids laughed.

"Seriously, though, it's great to see all of you dressed up for Halloween. What was our participation this year, Mr. Ransom?"

A black-leather-jacketed biker called out from the teacher group, "Seventy-five percent."

The kids cheered loudly and Lacey copied down the statistic in her notebook and next to it wrote, "Great morale builder."

"Now, on to Christmas. Thanks for volunteering to work on the Good Deeds Project. Today's meeting will focus on families and organizations we support. After Thanksgiving, we'll get into soup-kitchen volunteering, and Kris Kringles. I'll give the mike back to the student council president...er...the Tin Man, but I just wanted to tell you how thrilled I am at the turnout for a very important activity."

The students applauded, and some whistled. They seemed to like Taylor. Of course, Lacey thought, the atmosphere is cheerful today anyway, and might be influencing their attitude toward him.

But they gave him a superhero shirt.

Filing away the thought, Lacey watched as the student council leaders projected a sheet on an overhead screen with the assignments for each student. They already had the students divided up and linked to families or organizations. There were eighteen groups altogether.

"The groups will stay as they are, except we need a few volunteers to work with the Franklin Street Day Care Center. Mr. T. okayed our request last week and is willing to be one of the staff supervisors. He's looking for another adult to help him. He needs four students. Who wants to go with him?"

Hands all around the room shot up, including the Tin Man's. Because of Taylor, or the day care? Lacey wondered. Ms. Spearman stood and picked out four teenagers.

"Time to break up into groups," the Tin Man said. "Just one warning, guys. If you find out you can't hold up your end of the deal, tell me or Ms. Spearman right away. Otherwise you could be leaving a five-year-old without any toys on Christmas morning."

Lacey sat back, impressed. The kids were organized, enthusiastic and mature. What a wonderful thing for teenagers to do for other people at Christmastime.

As the students found their groups, Lacey wandered over to Cassie's and stayed far away from Taylor's. When Cassie looked up from her list and saw Lacey, her gray eyes lit up. She struggled out of her chair, spilling her folder and purse all over the floor. "Lacey, it's so great to see you here." In seconds, Lacey was enfolded in an enthusiastic embrace.

Lacey hugged Cassie back, deluged again by memories of her adolescence. It was hard to connect this mature, responsible adult with the kid Cassie used to be. Lacey had heard Cassie was pregnant, but still the leap was hard to make. As Lacey held on to her friend, she felt a strong nudge against her stomach. Cassie's baby had kicked her. A wave of longing shot through Lacey; it brought tears to her eyes.

Drawing away, Cassie said, "Welcome back to Bayview. Listen, I've got to get this group moving, but can you stick around? I'd love to talk afterward."

"Of course I can. Mind if I stay and take notes? I'm here for the paper."

A flicker of unease crossed Cassie's face. She'd never been able to hide her feelings, Lacey remembered. It was one thing that had gotten her into so much trouble. Her old friend's reaction brought back the discomfort Lacey had felt earlier for all the negative press she'd given the high school. People were doing good work here, as Taylor had said.

Lacey watched Cassie and her partner, Zoe Caufield, turn the entire show over to the kids. As she scanned the room, she noticed other staff members doing the same. Her gaze hooked on Taylor. He was answering questions and smiling broadly.

Soon the groups broke up and the students trailed out. Lacey watched Cassie say goodbye to the teenagers, then stand and approach her. Before Cassie could say anything, though, big masculine hands grasped her shoulders from behind. "At least you were sitting down," the man said.

Cassie turned and Lacey could see love suffuse her friend's face. "Don't start, big guy."

Gently, the tall, dark-haired man tucked a strand of hair that had gotten loose from Cassie's braid behind her ear. The intimate gesture sent another wave of longing through Lacey.

Cassie grabbed the man's hand and tugged him toward Lacey. "Come on, there's someone I want you to meet."

The man indulged himself with one more small squeeze on Cassie's shoulder and turned to Lacey. Piercing green eyes focused on her intently.

"Lacey Cartwright," Cassie said, "this is Mitch Lansing. My husband." Lacey noticed the pride in Cassie's voice as she emphasized the word, *husband.*

"Nice to meet you, Mitch." Lacey had come to Bayview in April after Mitch Lansing had been hurt trying to keep a gang from infiltrating the high school. She had read back issues of the newspaper about the harrowing events.

"Ms. Cartwright." Mitch's voice was deep. "I've read the *Herald* with interest since you've taken over."

And not liked what you've seen, she thought. His tone gave him away. Lacey hadn't realized she was making so many enemies.

Just then, Taylor approached them. Clapping Mitch on the shoulder, he said, "Hi, Captain."

Mitch smiled. "Nice shirt!"

"Lay off. When the kids gave it to me, I was

going to stick it in my drawer." He shot Cassie a disgusted glance. "But your wife was there and insisted I put it on."

Mitch's hand went to Cassie's neck and curled familiarly around it. "Now, why am I not surprised?"

Watching the exchange between the two men, Lacey felt left out. Their ease with each other and their friendship was palpable. Warmth emanated from all three. Until Taylor's blue gaze turned to her. His eyes lost their teasing glint. "Ms. Cartwright. I see you made it."

"Yes. I said I would."

"What did you think of our meeting?"

In spite of her antipathy for the man, Lacey couldn't hold back her smile. "It was wonderful. I'm very impressed."

Shock registered on his face, but he regained his composure quickly and said, "As you should be. Countless hours go into the Good Deeds Project. That's why we start on Halloween every year. It takes a good two months to pull it off." He reached inside a folder and drew out a couple of sheets. "I asked Carolyn Spearman to work up a description of the project—how it's organized, how we get the names of the families and institutions to help, where the money comes from." He handed her the document. "I'll be glad to answer any questions—" he glanced at his watch "—but I've got to meet with Mitch for a few minutes. Can you wait?"

Lacey looked at Cassie. "Yes. Cassie and I were going to talk, anyway."

Cassie smiled at her, but it turned into a scowl

when she faced her husband. "This is about the Safety Task Force meeting next week, isn't it?"

"Yes." Mitch's tone was firm. "The task force *I'm* on and you're *not.*"

"I don't like being excluded from this, Mitch."

He arched an eyebrow. "And I don't like that you're participating in *this.*" He waved his hand around the library. "You shouldn't be taking on anything extra with the baby due so soon."

When she opened her mouth to speak, he said, "Cass, we agreed. You'll do the Christmas thing, but evening meetings are out. End of discussion." He turned to Seth. "Let's go before I change my mind about the Christmas project." He looked at Lacey. "I hope the school gets some favorable coverage for this activity, Ms. Cartwright."

Tension, thick and ugly, filled the room. "I intend to give the high school exactly what it deserves, Captain," Lacey said. She looked at Taylor. "Like I always do."

"Damn! That woman's determined not to cut us any slack," Seth said as he threw his folder down on his desk—after he closed the conference-room door tightly. One side of the room opened to the library, the other to his office; a large window afforded him a perfect view of Lacey Cartwright and Cassie settling down in one of the couch groupings.

Mitch took a seat at the long, oval table but said nothing. Seth jammed his hands in his pockets and silently counted to ten as he stared at the women. When he was more under control, he turned to Mitch. "Sorry."

"Don't apologize to me. I'd be ticked off at her, too."

"Want some coffee?" Seth asked. Mostly for something to do, he drew himself a cup.

"No thanks. Since Cassie's got to stay off caffeine, I'm staying off it, too." He smiled indulgently. "Another good reason to wish the kid would get here soon." Mitch glanced out the window and continued, "Ms. Cartwright hasn't given the high school what it deserves, Seth."

"No, she hasn't."

"I suspect she knows it, too."

"Really? Why?"

"She got the same look on her face that Cassie gets when she's not sure of what she's arguing about with me."

"You're pretty good at reading people."

"Comes from years on the police force." Mitch scowled. "It's hard to believe Cassie and Ms. Cartwright were friends. They seem so different."

"Lacey Cartwright stuck by Cassie when none of the other kids at school would give her a chance to get her act together."

"So you'd think she'd know how important it is to give people a chance."

"She does. That's why she hates me so much. You know the story of her brother?"

Mitch shook his head.

Seth had just finished filling him in on the Kevin Cartwright story when a discreet knock on the door put the discussion to an end.

His secretary poked her head in. "Seth, it's State

Ed. again. Mike Thomas called twice while you were at the meeting.''

He nodded apologetically at Mitch; picking up the receiver of the phone on the table, Taylor said, "Hi, Mike.''

"Seth. I just wanted to tell you that if you're going to apply for the Regents' job, you'd better do it right away. It's been posted and they intend to have it filled by the first of the year. You'd have to come to Albany for a couple of interviews, so you should get on it.''

"Sure. Can you send me the…application?'' Seth asked, hesitating in front of Mitch.

"It's on its way. Don't put your decision off, Seth. I'd really like you on board.''

"I won't. Thanks for calling.''

After he hung up, he met Mitch's gaze. "Shall we talk about the task force?''

Mitch didn't answer at first. Then he asked, "Like you said, I'm pretty good at reading people. What's going on?''

Seth considered lying, but Mitch's direct, honest gaze forestalled an untruth. "A lot of things, I guess.''

"Like?''

"For one, some empty nest syndrome.'' Seth smiled sadly. "It's hell having Joey gone.''

"That's pretty normal. Is that all?''

Seth toyed with the coffee mug that sat in front of him. "Mitch, when you left the New York City Police Department, was it hard to do something else?''

"No. Mother Nature made the transition easy for

me. I was getting too old to be involved in big-city law enforcement.'' At forty-seven, Mitch was a year older than Seth. "Coming to Bayview Heights was a good move for me." He waited. "Why?"

"Sometimes I wonder if I'm not too old to keep up with the kids at Bayview."

Mitch nodded to the phone. "You thinking of leaving?"

"I'm thinking about it."

"Why?"

Staring out the conference-room window, Seth could see Cassie and Lacey sitting close, smiling. He wondered what they were talking about. "I've been in some sort of funk lately. I'm considering other options."

Mitch was silent.

"Sometimes I wonder just what I've accomplished as an educator," Seth confessed. "I know I've made some mistakes. Big ones."

"Cassie says you were Bayview's savior."

Seth snorted. "Cassie's biased."

"Maybe. But then, so are you. Sometimes it's hard to see whole picture when you're inside the frame."

A chuckle escaped him. "That sounds like one of Cassie's classroom posters."

Mitch laughed. "It is. That doesn't make the sentiment any less true." He angled his head toward the window. "Look at Cassie. She's living proof of what you've done, Seth."

"My greatest triumph."

"Along with several others. Like Johnny Battaglia."

"Cassie turned Johnny around."

"Yeah, but you gave her the tools to do it. Twice."

"What do you mean?"

"First, when she was sixteen, you helped her out of the mess her life had turned into. For which, by the way, I'm eternally grateful. Then you spearheaded a program at Bayview where she could do the same for other kids." Mitch shook his head. "You know, I've always envied teachers. You have a domino effect on the world—you help one kid, that kid goes on to do good things for other people. The positive impact of a teacher's actions is unlimited."

Seth watched Lacey Cartwright and remembered her eyes, so like her brother's. "The reverse is true, too."

"Well, I suppose you could view it like that. If you were looking for a reason to leave here."

"Don't tell Cassie just yet. It will only upset her."

"I don't like keeping things from her." Mitch, too, glanced out the window and smiled as he watched his wife. "But I'll keep the confidence for a while. Until you decide. She'll go ballistic when she finds out you're thinking about resigning."

"Yeah, well, her old buddy there would throw a party to celebrate the event."

"Maybe." Mitch studied the two. "But I'm not so sure. Let's see what happens with this Christmas project."

"IT'S SO GOOD to see you," Cassie repeated after she'd settled onto the couch with Lacey across from her.

Lacey nodded to Cassie's pregnant belly. "Looks like you've been busy."

Cassie's throaty laugh and vibrant glow warmed Lacey. "I have." She glanced toward the office. "He's wonderful." She placed her hand on her stomach. "And I never thought this would happen to me."

"I know. You said you never wanted kids."

"And you wanted a dozen."

"I still do." The confession slipped out and Lacey could feel herself blush.

"Any serious relationships in California?" Cassie asked.

"One or two. They didn't work out."

"Are you going back there?"

"I'm not sure."

"How's your grandfather?"

Lacey filled her in on Philip's health. "The prognosis is good if he doesn't overtax himself. He's seventy-six, so he should have been slowing down anyway."

"I always loved him. He was so interested in you and Kevin. It was hard to believe he was that much older than most parents of teenagers."

"He said we kept him young."

"For what it's worth, Lace, I think it was really unselfish of you to come back here for him."

"After all he did for us, how could I not?"

"A lot of people wouldn't have."

"I believe in loyalty."

Cassie drew in a deep breath. "What about loyalty to your alma mater?"

God, Lacey was getting tired of this...conflict. "You mean, the editorials in the *Herald?*"

Cassie nodded.

Laying her head back on the upholstery, Lacey stared up at the ceiling. "When I took over the paper, it seemed like a good idea to pick up where Grandpa left off. I read all his back stuff, and took the same tack. I didn't think I'd be in Bayview Heights that long, and I didn't want to upset him."

"Did you believe what you wrote?"

"Of course I did."

"But?"

"But I may have presented only one side." She scanned the room. "There are some good things going on here." Glancing toward the office, she said, "Despite Seth Taylor."

"*Because* of Seth Taylor. None of this would be happening without him."

Lacey smiled. "You haven't changed a bit. You always loved the guy, defended him."

"He helped save my life."

"Well, he ruined mine."

"Did he?"

"What do you mean?"

"I mean that he's not responsible for what happened to Kevin." When Lacey started to object, Cassie held up her hand. "No, let me finish. We're each responsible for our own actions, Lacey. Even if Seth made a mistake with Kevin—which I'm not sure he did—*he* didn't send your brother to prison."

"Maybe." Lacey could feel her eyes mist. "It's just that seeing Kevin in that place is so hard."

Reaching over, Cassie grabbed her hand. "Of course it is. But Seth didn't put him there, honey. I think it's time you let go of that idea."

Lacey didn't answer. Suddenly, she wanted to let go of it. She was tired of it. Looking at Cassie's belly, Lacey wished with all her heart she had a normal life without all the responsibility and resentment she felt. At one time, *her* life had looked charmed and Cassie's had been on the skids. Now it was reversed. Though Lacey couldn't be happier for her friend, she wondered what it would be like to have a man like Mitch Lansing so crazy about you that he couldn't keep his hands off you. What would it be like to carry the child of the man you loved?

Would Lacey ever have that?

LACEY STARED at the two men headed toward them. Mitch Lansing was taller than Taylor and built like a football player. But despite his height and girth, Mitch didn't overwhelm the principal. Taylor had removed his suit coat and his muscles were well-defined in the silly superhero jersey. It gave him an aura of strength and dependability.

Mitch clapped him on the shoulder and said something a moment before they reached Lacey. Cassie stretched her legs and yawned as she peered up at them.

"Looks like someone's ready for a nap," Taylor said to Cassie. The warmth and affection on his face stirred something inside Lacey. For one crazy moment she wondered what it would be like to have him turn that look on her.

"Naturally," Cassie said, disgust lacing her voice. "I can't even make it to dinner anymore."

"Better take care of my godson." Taylor stretched out a hand, helped her up from the couch, then patted her belly as she stood. "Right, buddy?"

"Stop. We're having a girl. That's all there is to it."

Mitch dragged Cassie close. "I wish it was twins," he said.

"Oh, God. You're a glutton for punishment." Cassie turned to Lacey, who had also risen. "I'll call you about dinner next week."

"I'd like that."

Mitch said coolly, "Ms. Cartwright. Enjoy the rest of the day."

A little taken aback by the curtness in his tone, Lacey simply nodded in response.

After they'd left, Taylor pointed to the couches. "Let's talk here. It's more comfortable."

She sat back down and he took a plush chair across from her.

"These furniture groupings are a good idea." Lacey ran her hand over the nubby fabric. "We never had anything like this twenty years ago."

"School's changed in the last two decades. But then, you're well aware of that, aren't you?"

Her eyes narrowed. Right back into it, she thought. All right, then... "Speaking of which," she said quickly, "what's this task force Cassie mentioned?"

Taylor eased back in his chair, crossed his ankle

over his knee and linked his hands behind his head. The *S* on the jersey stretched across his chest. "Some of us—despite what you think—*are* worried about the increase in the number of fights at the high school. Personally, student violence has always been of special concern to me. We also know that around the upcoming holidays, students cause more difficulties in school."

"Really? Why?"

"Not everyone comes from a functional home. Their *dys*function is more pronounced during the holidays. We want to nip this in the bud, so I've formed a committee of teachers, community members, students, the school psychologist and a guidance counselor to brainstorm what we can do to prevent the outbreaks."

Lacey said, "Sounds like a solid idea. Why didn't you tell me that when we met about the editorial on violence?"

"Would it have made any difference?"

"Yes, of course it would."

"I wonder."

"What do you mean?"

"You're pretty bent on burying us. The *Herald* rarely prints anything good about the schools."

"We put in almost everything the district PR guy sends us on the schools."

"I stand corrected. You do okay with the middle school and the elementary buildings."

"How could I mention the task force if I didn't know about it?" As she spoke, an idea jelled. "As a matter of fact, how can I report on it if I don't know how it works?"

Seth watched the color suffuse her fair skin. It highlighted her cheeks prettily—and warned him right away that she was up to something. "What are you getting at?"

"Let me be on the committee."

"You're kidding."

"Afraid?"

That got his hackles up. "Of what?"

"You invite me here to parade out the good stuff. Afraid to let me watch how you tackle a problem?"

Seth knew he shouldn't do it. But there was challenge in that sultry voice and in those sparkling eyes. "You really want to be part of the task force?"

"Yes."

He stared at her, a notion curling inside him. Maybe he could beat her at her own game. "You know, we're short a few adults for the Christmas project."

Frowning slightly—presumably at his non sequitur—she answered, "I heard."

"If you've got time to be on a committee, you could volunteer to help out there."

"What do you mean?"

Seth hunched over and locked his hands between his knees. Besting her had become important. "Here's the deal. You can be on our task force and report how we confront problems here. I'm not worried about what you'll see. And I'll keep an eagle eye on how you write the article. If it's unfair in any way, you're off the committee."

"I can accept that."

"That's not all. You've got to go the other way, too." Lacey cocked her head. "You've got to be part of the Christmas project. Be the other adult supervisor for my group at the day care. Work with these kids for the next two months, experience the good we do. And report that with as much conviction as you do our problem with student violence.''

She liked the challenge, he could tell by how her face glowed. "Do you realize this would mean spending an inordinate amount of time with me?" She smiled smugly. "Are you man enough to take it?" she asked, parroting the question he'd put to her when he'd challenged her to come to the Good Deeds Project meeting.

Oh, he was going to enjoy this, Seth thought. Flinging his arms out to his sides so the T-shirt he wore flashed in front of her like a red flag, he said haughtily, "Hey, superheroes can take anything you dish out.''

CHAPTER FOUR

THE NEXT MONDAY, Lacey planned her day so that she could get to the school for the three-thirty meeting she had with the Christmas Good Deeds group. She and Taylor working together! She shook her head, not even wanting to think about what she'd committed herself to. She had more than a niggling suspicion that she'd been tricked into this, but she'd won on the Safety Task Force—its first meeting was tonight—so she'd help out with the Christmas project graciously. In spite of Taylor, she was looking forward to it. She smiled when she thought of the kids at the day care. What fun that would be.

Since she had a half hour to kill, she turned to her computer. Lacey loved to surf the Internet, finding its diversity distracting. She also did a great deal of research on the school law section—and had gotten many ideas for her School Page.

Lost in thought, she realized that instead of clicking on her on-line server, she'd called up the folder next to it. These were Philip's files, none of which she'd needed for the paper. The menu for a folder entitled SJT was on the screen. Lacey was about to quit it when a name caught her eye. "S. Taylor. Biographical Information." Lacey scrolled down. "S. Taylor. Teacher. S. Taylor. Principal." Then a final file, "Correspondence with Private Investigator."

Lacey leaned back in her chair. She believed strongly in the right to privacy. Though Philip had said nothing about staying out of his files, she felt uncomfortable accessing them. But these were about Seth Taylor. It was too great a temptation. She clicked on the first icon.

As the file came up, she heard the front door open. Her office was behind glass windows, much like the newspaper offices in old movies and TV shows. Swiveling her chair around, she peered through the slatted blinds; the high-school-girl receptionist was smiling at a visitor.

When Lacey saw her grandfather in the outer office, a wave of sadness swept through her. He hadn't been down to the *Herald* since his heart attack. She reached the doorway just as he did.

"Grandpa," she said, fixing a calm smile on her face. "How nice to see you."

At first, he didn't answer, just scanned his surroundings. When he faced her again, she could see moisture in his eyes. "It's—" he cleared his throat "—it's good to be back."

"Come on in." Grabbing his hand and squeezing it, she tugged him inside.

He entered the office where he'd spent more than twenty years of his life. Lacey remembered coming here to visit him, sitting in his chair, how patiently he'd taught her to use a typewriter.

She watched him as he stared at the wall of accolades he'd received—in Bayview Heights as well as New York City. Then he took a seat, not at the desk but on the other side of the room. Lacey's heart ached as she watched her beloved grandfather come face-to-face with what he'd been forced to give up.

"How did you get here?" she asked, knowing he still couldn't drive.

"Celia came to clean today. She asked if I wanted to get out for a ride. I thought I'd drop in on you while she did some grocery shopping."

Lacey glanced at the clock.

"You in a hurry, honey?"

"I have an appointment in half an hour."

"Where?"

Lacey drew in a deep breath and felt as if she was sixteen again, when she'd skipped religious instruction to meet a boy her grandfather had specifically forbidden her to see.

"Lacey?"

"I'm going to the high school, Grandpa."

He cocked his head. "The task force meeting isn't until tonight."

"Yes, I know."

"What's going on, Lacey?"

"Well, when I finagled my way onto the task force, I agreed to do some other things at the school, too."

Philip threw back his head and laughed. "I hope whatever it is will be as beneficial to us as your being on the task force."

"What do you mean?"

"We'll be able to use the task force against him." At Lacey's questioning look, he added, "There will be fodder for a lot of editorials from that committee."

"I think the committee's a good idea."

"I do too, honey. But don't you see, they'll have to air their dirty laundry and you'll be there to watch it." He closed his eyes and smirked. "I didn't think Taylor was stupid enough to let you on the task force."

Lacey didn't respond.

"Where are you going now?"

"I agreed to work on one of the committees for their Christmas Good Deeds Project, too. The first meeting is today."

Philip stiffened. "What will you do with that information?"

Instead of answering, Lacey stood and walked over to the window.

"What is it, Lacey?"

She turned around and faced him. "I think the student Christmas activities deserve some good publicity, Grandpa."

Philip's eyes narrowed on his granddaughter. "Did Taylor talk you into that?"

"Not exactly. In any case, I want to do it."

"Why?"

"Because I think what's good about the high school warrants coverage, too. It's only fair."

"Fair? Do you think it's fair what that man did to us?"

"Grandpa…he didn't really do anything to us. At least not intentionally."

"What are you saying?"

"Even if Taylor is responsible for kicking Kevin out of school," she said softly, "that doesn't mean he put him in prison."

Philip stood abruptly and started to pace, as if unable to believe what he was hearing. "Have you forgotten what your brother looks like in that place? Didn't you hear the fear in his voice on the phone last night? Something's going on in the laundry, I think. Some kind of trouble. And Taylor's responsible for all of it."

"Is he?"

"I can't believe this. Listen to yourself." He crossed to her and grasped her shoulders. "Do you know what they do to young men in places like that? They…" Philip let the unspeakable words trail off.

She felt the color drain out of her face. "Stop it, please," Lacey begged.

"What's going on in here?" Celia Trenkler said from the doorway. "You were shouting, Philip. That can't be good for your blood pressure."

"Don't interfere, Celia." He turned back to Lacey. "We need to talk about this."

"All right. But I've got to go. We'll discuss it later." In slow, precise movements, she hugged him, then gathered her things. After speaking to Celia, she crossed to the door. She pivoted to face him before she left. "It was good to see you in the office, Grandpa," she told him, her voice threaded with tears. "I'll talk to you later." Then she fled out the door.

"You're going to lose her Philip," Celia said, "if you don't watch out. And it'll be your own fault."

"I'll never lose her," he said in a low, even voice. "I'll do anything to stop that from happening."

SETH GLANCED at the clock. She was late. Maybe she wasn't coming. Damn her if she thought she could dupe him—if she thought she could ignore the Good Deeds Project, but come to the task force meeting tonight. He refused to give credence to his disappointment that she hadn't kept her word.

"Mr. Taylor, can we start?" Nick Leonardi, student council president, aka the Tin Man, asked from one of the tables in the converted storeroom, now set up for meetings.

"Sure. Ms. Cartwright's late. Let's start."

The door burst open. In rushed the woman in question. Her cheeks were red and her hair was wild around her face and shoulders. It looked about twenty different shades of gold in the fluorescent lighting. "Sorry I'm late," she said, addressing the group.

"That's okay," Nick said. "Thanks for agreeing to help."

"Have a seat," Seth told her.

When she looked at him, he knew right away something was wrong. Her eyes were deeply shadowed, giving her a vulnerability that kicked into his protective instincts.

She took the chair farthest away from him, unbuttoned her coat and took it off. Underneath she wore a soft pink sweater that added to her aura of fragility. Lacey looked at Nick.

"I'm Nick Leonardi, president of the student council."

"Hi," Lacey said, just as the girl next to her snorted. All eyes focused on the student.

"I'm Darcy McCormick," she told Lacey, then

shot a venomous glance at Nick from under kohl-rimmed eyes. "All-around bad kid."

Seth intervened. "Darcy, Ms. Cartwright was Mrs. Lansing's best friend in high school."

Darcy's gaze whipped to Lacey. "No sh—kidding?" The girl eyed her carefully. "You? And Mrs. Lansing?"

Seth watched as Lacey smiled warmly at the girl. He wondered what Lacey thought of Darcy's partly shaved hair and totally black ensemble.

"Yes," Lacey said, not batting an eye. "And everyone was surprised then, too. But honestly, we were—we *are*—good friends."

"Then you must be really neat." This came from a sweet-faced girl sitting next to Seth. "Everybody loves Ms. Smith, I mean, Mrs. Lansing. I'm Hope Ford. This is my sister Hannah."

"Obviously," Lacey said. "Are you two identical?"

Both smiled the same smile. "Yes," they chimed in unison.

Seth checked the clock. "Okay, we only have the room until four. Who was voted chair?" he asked.

"Who else?" Darcy tossed back her head. "Mr. Clean-Cut President."

"Geez, McCormick," Nick snapped. "Get rid of the chip on your shoulder at least for today, will you?"

Seth groaned inwardly at their sparring. He hoped he was doing the right thing with these two. "The day-care center, ladies and gentleman?"

"Right," Nick said. "Any ideas for what we should do first?"

One of the twins offered a suggestion. "Go over there?"

Darcy rolled her eyes. "No, we should get a list of the kids, their ages and talk about what we're going to do for them before we visit."

"I agree." Nick sounded surprised. "We also need to find out what our budget is."

They all looked to Seth.

"I'm still figuring that out. I'll have it by next week."

Lacey asked, "Money is donated by local businesses, isn't it?"

"Yes." Seth stared at her. "Why?"

"No reason."

"Who wants to call the day-care center and get the names, ages and stuff?" Nick smiled charmingly at the twins.

"We will," Hannah said.

"When do we meet again?" Darcy asked.

"I've got football practice every day after school for the sectionals," Nick told them. "Coach said he'd let me out of practice occasionally, but I'd rather not miss too many."

"Wouldn't want your muscles going to flab," Darcy said.

The twins giggled nervously.

Seth decided to referee. "Obviously, we have to go to the center during the day. How about if we meet next Monday after we've gathered all the information, then take our first trip over there Friday." He looked at the calendar in front of him. "That's the fourteenth and the eighteenth. You have a sectional game Friday night, Nick, so you wouldn't miss practice. Can you do the visit, and still make the game?''

Nick scowled at Darcy. "Sure." He smiled at Hope and Hannah. "Is that okay with you two? Does it conflict with any of your band stuff?"

Four adoring eyes latched on to Nick's dark good looks. "Oh, no, we'll be there."

Out of the corner of his eye, Seth saw Darcy scrape back her chair. "Don't bother asking me, lover boy. Everybody knows all At-Risk kids do is get in trouble after school. I can be there." She glanced at Lacey. "Ciao. Bye, Mr. Taylor." Her thick army boots rasped across the floor as she left.

Nick turned to Seth. "What'd I do?"

"Nothing, Nick. Darcy will come around."

"Sure." He looked at Lacey. "This schedule okay with you, Ms. Cartwright?"

Dragging her appointment book out of her bag, Lacey checked it quickly. "I'll be there. I'll have to shuffle some things, but I want to attend both days."

Nick smiled at her. "Good. I'm off, then."

"Oh, wait, Nick, we'll walk out with you." Hope and Hannah scrambled after him.

Lacey and Seth were left alone.

"I feel like I've been caught up in a war zone," Lacey said.

Seth chuckled. "You have. Jocks versus punks, I think would be an appropriate way to describe this particular battle."

"Too bad they ended up on the same committee."

"It was no accident," Seth said. "I arranged it. They're both on the Safety Task Force, too."

"Why would you do that?"

"Because they need to learn to work with each other. I'm going to help them do it."

Lacey's gaze narrowed on him. "I saw other kids volunteer for this group. Another administrator picked them."

"I...um...talked to Carolyn beforehand and told her my plan."

"Are you always so sneaky?"

"When it's good for Bayview Heights, I am." He smiled at her. "After all, I got *you* on both committees." The shadows in her eyes deepened. "What is it?"

She shook her head. "What is what?"

Bracing his forearms on the table, he leaned over. "You're upset. You were when you came in."

"No, I'm all right."

"Tell me."

She seemed to think about that a minute, biting off her raisin-colored lipstick. Finally, she said, "My grandfather came to the office just before I left. It was the first time since...it was hard for him to be there, that's all. It was hard for me to see it."

Seth felt the familiar sense of guilt curl through him. "I'm sorry."

She didn't say anything.

"And then you had to leave for this meeting?"

She nodded, her frown telling him the rest of the story.

Slowly, Seth got up and moved to the end of the table. He sat down very close, but didn't dare touch her. "Philip wasn't happy about your working on this committee, was he?"

"No."

Seth plowed a hand through his hair. "Look, Lacey," he said, and her eyes widened. At his use of her name? "I didn't think this through very well. I shouldn't have coerced you into helping with the day care. It was inconsiderate of me. I'll get someone else to supervise with me."

"No!"

"No?"

"Well, no. I gave my word."

"I'll let you out of it."

She smiled sadly, and Seth's gut clenched. "Actually, I want to do it. The paper should cover this, anyway, and…"

"And?"

"I…I…want to go to the day care. I want to do something for them."

"Why?"

"I like kids." Her chin lifted. "Something wrong with that?"

Seth shook his head. "You don't have any kids of your own, do you?"

"No."

He surprised himself by asking, "You ever been married?"

"No."

"Come close?"

This time there was shock on her face. Before she could answer, the door burst open and the group scheduled to use the room at four o'clock hustled in. The relief in Lacey's eyes was telling.

"Looks like our time's up." She stood and shrugged into her coat. Seth stayed where he was.

He watched her fuss with her things, say a quick goodbye and hurry to the door.

When she reached it, he called out, "Lacey?" She turned back. "See you tonight at seven."

"Okay." And she was gone.

After a moment, Seth got up, said hello to the members of the other group and left the room. Deep in thought, he headed back to his office.

If there was anything that would gum up the works right now, it was falling for Lacey Cartwright. It was bad enough that she looked so appealing in her pink sweater, her cheeks glowing from the cold, her hair wild around her shoulders. He felt the same response zap through him as that day at the gym when he'd held her foot. Forcibly, he squelched his reaction. It certainly wouldn't help their situation, he repeated to himself as he walked down the halls.

Still, the picture of her in fragile pink, her eyes clouded with hurt, stayed with him for a long time.

LACEY ENTERED the principal's office at six forty-five that evening. Not having asked where the task force meeting would be held, she'd come a little early, hoping to catch Seth. She'd had plenty of time anyway; after the Good Deeds Project meeting, Lacey hadn't gone home to her grandfather's house on Bay Road. Instead, she'd called and told him she'd be eating out. She'd had a solitary dinner at Pepper's Diner because she wasn't ready to face Philip.

As she pulled open the outer-office door, she was grateful to hear voices coming from within. Crossing to the doorway, she stopped cold. A shapely brunette in tight jeans and an even tighter sweater leaned over Taylor's desk. Her giggle was sexy, if you were into Marilyn Monroe types.

Apparently, Taylor was. He was staring up at the woman with an appreciative male look on his face. For some reason, it bothered Lacey.

"You really didn't have to do this, Monica."

"Well, since you wouldn't come for dinner, I brought dinner to you." She scowled prettily. "You work too hard, Seth. I'll bet you haven't left here since you arrived at what, six this morning?"

"Six-thirty," he said absently as he scooped up the foil containers on his desk and stashed them in the paper bag. When he turned to throw away the trash, he caught sight of Lacey.

"Oh, hi, Lacey." Taylor's skin was almost as light as her own, and he blushed just as easily as she did.

"I'm sorry to interrupt." *God, had that come out bitchy?* Carefully modulating her tone, she said, "I wasn't sure this was the right place…where the meeting was." Damn, she was stammering. Well, she was embarrassed to have walked in on Taylor's…assignation!

Seth smiled warmly at her. "This is the right place. The conference room is all set up. You can go in through here." She glanced at the door on the other side of his office. The closed door. "I think most people have already arrived." He gave his attention to the brunette who'd finally straightened. She was tall and even more voluptuous standing upright. "This is Monica Matthews. Monica's got a son who's a senior here and she runs the beauty shop in town."

"You're showing your age, Seth. It's called a hair salon." Monica's sultry gaze focused on Lacey. "And you are?"

"Lacey Cartwright," Seth answered for her.

"I'm the—" Lacey began.

Frost quickly replaced the warm sensuality in the other woman's eyes. "I know who you are. I read the *Herald*." Monica looked at Seth questioningly.

Lacey's spine stiffened in reflex.

"Well, let's all go inside." Seth ignored the woman's implied question. "We'll make formal introductions there."

Lacey hesitated. How many others on the committee were going to resent her being here? Damn, she was tired of fighting everybody. In L.A., she'd stepped on some toes as any hard-hitting reporter would. But she hadn't felt this kind of personal animosity from anyone. An overwhelming sense of loneliness accompanied her as she followed Taylor and his lady friend into the conference room.

Nine people gathered around the table. "I see you found your places," Seth remarked as he picked up a name tag and attached it to his lapel. "I took the liberty of arranging the seating plan. I separated teachers, students, community members and so on. Since we'll be sharing in small groups, I thought the diversity was important."

Monica found her designated place at the end of the table, next to a somber Mitch Lansing. When Lacey caught Mitch's eye, he nodded to her.

Seth said to Lacey, who was rooted to the doorway, "Lacey, your seat's here."

Right next to him. Drawing in a deep breath, she

moved to her chair. He pulled it out for her, and after she sat down, so did he. Woodsy cologne wafted over to her. Had he applied it for Monica Matthews?

Taylor scanned the room. "Good. Everyone's here. First, thanks for agreeing to be on the committee. Each of you was selected for the differing viewpoints you bring to the group. Before we get to the agenda, I think we should introduce ourselves and state our relation to this building—why we're here, in other words." His smile was warm. "Let's be informal. I'll start. I'm Seth Taylor, which all of you know. And I help run this place." Chuckles went around the room. "Nick, you go next."

Lacey breathed a sigh of relief. She'd be last. Nick Leonardi introduced himself. Next to him, Zoe Caufield told who she was, and that she taught At-Risk kids. Mitch and Monica were after her.

The scowling, balding man next to Mitch spoke up. "I'm Jerry Bosco. I teach biology. I'm here as a building representative—the union put me on this committee."

Lacey was stunned to realize she hadn't recognized the man who'd testified against Kevin. Instead of looking eight years older, he'd aged at least two decades. And he seemed just as surly and unhappy as he'd been when she was a student here.

"Don Hopkins," another man said. "I own the hardware store and have two kids in elementary school."

The introductions continued—another scowling man, Leonard Small, a friend of her grandfather's, was a board member and the one who had given

Lacey the statistics on student violence. Alex Ransom, the junior class vice principal, was also there.

Darcy McCormick told her name quickly, as did the school psychologist Barbara Sherman, and the guidance counselor, Linc McKenna. Lacey had spoken to Linc when he'd called her about setting up some kind of internship at the paper for students interested in journalism. By the time the introductions came round to Lacey, she was in a state of high anxiety. What would she say about why she was here? Could she take their animosity?

She cleared her throat. "I'm Lacey Cartwright. I run the *Herald.* I'm here at my own request to see how you handle problems at the high school."

Mumbling around the room made her shift in her seat. Seth reached over and squeezed her arm. "Actually, I encouraged Lacey to be on this committee and another one—the Good Deeds Project." Well, that was almost true. "I think it's a fine idea to have her see how we deal with problems in the building. I'd like you all to welcome her."

There was dead silence. Monica Matthews broke it. "It's no secret that Ms. Cartwright's written a lot of negative things about this school."

"Lacey please," Seth said. "Let's use first names. We need to be informal and friendly."

"*Lacey,* then," Monica said. "I wonder if she's going to get in the way of our progress. Will we feel comfortable airing our real concerns? Will we be afraid to say what we think because of what she'll print?"

Bosco leaned forward. "Or maybe that's why you

asked her, Mr. Taylor. So we'd whitewash this whole thing.''

Seth stared hard at Bosco, then glanced around the table. "What do the rest of you think?"

Zoe Caufield spoke up. "I'm not afraid to say what I think with Lacey here. We know we have a problem with fighting. So does she. I think it'll help us understand each other better if we talk about the issue openly."

Seth looked to the kids. "Nick, Darcy, what do you think?"

Nick said, "It's cool. I'll say what I think."

"Me, too." Darcy carefully averted her gaze from Nick.

Mitch Lansing sat back in his chair. "We're all adults here—" he smiled warmly at Nick, then Darcy "—or young adults. I think we can be honest about the issue." He focused in on Lacey and she had to force herself not to squirm. "Lacey says she'll give the high school the coverage it deserves. I'm confident that we deserve good press for the humanitarian things we do, as well as for how we tackle problems."

Seth's gaze swept everyone at the table "Anyone else?"

Silence.

"All right, then. Before we get started tonight, I'd like to reiterate what I told all of you in the memo I sent out about our general timeline. My goal is to meet every Monday night from now until Christmas, and by the twenty-second of December to have a plan to implement. Anyone have a comment about that time frame?"

When no one did, he said, "Good. Let's get to it. Put your name tags on." He stood and pulled up a screen that had been covering a blackboard. There was an agenda written on it. "The first thing I'd like to do tonight is brainstorm reasons why there is violence at the high school. Then I'd like to form subcommittees to focus on the areas we're going to investigate. For purposes of this exercise, let's not include the anti-drug efforts we implemented last year. Those should remain a separate area." He checked his watch. "And let's see if we can be out of here by nine o'clock.

"In front of you, you'll find a sheet of paper asking two questions. First, why is there a problem with fighting in this building? Second, what do *you* think should or can be done about it? Write down anything that occurs to you. You should know that I'm going to ask you to share what you write."

Lacey watched Seth steamroll through the directions. She'd never seen anything like it. Most committees she'd observed got off to such a slow start, she usually wanted to scream. But he'd plunged right in. The room was quiet while everyone focused on writing down their thoughts, giving her time to digest what had happened earlier.

He'd defended her. He'd reached over and squeezed her arm because he knew she was nervous. After she'd bulldozed her way onto this committee, he'd made it sound as if he supported her participation in it.

Surreptitiously, she watched him out of the corner of her eye. She'd never noticed he was left-handed. A shock of dark blond hair fell over his creased forehead. He'd loosened his tie and unbuttoned the top button of his shirt. His neck was corded with muscles and he swallowed hard a couple of times as he wrote. The gesture made Lacey realize the vulnerable position he was in. It must be hard to admit you had problems in a place you'd obviously devoted your whole life to. Steering herself away from that line of thinking, she took in a deep breath and turned to the task at hand.

FORTY MINUTES LATER, Seth smiled with satisfaction at the blackboard—covered with ideas and suggestions. "Great job, Darce," he said to the young girl he'd singled out to write the suggestions on the board. "You can sit back down. Now, let's highlight the areas we might want to pursue."

Linc McKenna, the guidance counselor, spoke first. "It looks to me like there are four or five groupings here. For instance, the inability of youngsters to control their anger, lack of social skills and face-to-face confrontations all suggest a need to set up some kind of counseling groups for the kids who have problems."

Barbara Sherman, the psychologist, added, "I checked with other schools like you asked, Seth. They run anger-control groups. We could look into that further."

"A subcommittee you and Linc should head, then," he said, smiling.

Zoe Caufield, the teacher, focused on what the staff could do, since the concerns indicated there needed to be better supervision in the halls and large congregating areas. "Why don't you and Alex head that subcommittee?" Seth asked her.

"I'd like to be on that one," Bosco said. "We aren't social workers and I don't want teachers committed to things that we aren't ready to deal with. Personally, I'd like to see armed guards in here."

Seth caught Alex's glare and Zoe's scowl.

"I doubt we need to go that far," Seth said. "But we could use more hall monitors and security guards."

Board member Leonard Small piped up with, "Staffing is not our job. Our hands are tied there."

Leaning back, Seth crossed his arms over his chest. "But maybe you could look into it for next year's budget, Leonard, and see about recommending additional help to the Board of Education."

Small frowned but nodded.

Two more subcommittees, one on community input and one on the role of students, were up for grabs. Don Hopkins and Monica volunteered for the community subcommittee. Seth looked at Darcy then Nick. "You two should be on the student subcommittee. We're investigating peer mediation right now with the student government, but other kinds of student groups might be appropriate for Bayview."

"You want us to work together again?" Darcy asked.

"Makes sense, doesn't it?" Seth said. "I'd like to be on that one, too." He looked at Lacey. "Want to be on the student subcommittee with us?"

Her eyes widened. He didn't need X-ray vision to figure out what was going on in that pretty little head of hers. Another committee? With you? Did she think he was keeping tabs on her? Was he?

"All right," she said finally.

Seth smiled approvingly at her, then glanced at his watch. "Good. Let's look at the agenda and see what we've accomplished." He stood and went to the board. Checking off each item as he spoke, he said, "Tonight we brainstormed reasons why kids are violent, and proposed responses the school could take. Then we set up committees. Anyone want to add anything?"

Monica raised a hand. "I want to know what Ms. Cartwright is going to put in her paper about the task force."

Lacey cleared her throat. "I'd like to publish everyone's name, if that's okay. Then I'll report what we did."

"And criticize us?"

"No, I'll be impartial, Monica," Lacey said, staring down the other woman.

Seth liked her grit—particularly when it wasn't directed at him. Monica had made things very uncomfortable for Lacey.

"That's it then," Seth said. "Thanks for coming. See you next week. Same time, same place."

As everyone rose to leave, Seth watched Linc McKenna approach Lacey. The guidance counselor's smile was warm and interested. Casually, he took Lacey by the elbow and steered her toward the door, speaking too softly for Seth to hear. Seth recalled that McKenna, who was divorced, had quite a reputation with the ladies. Looked as though he was going in for the kill.

Well, maybe some diversion would keep Ms. Cartwright off Seth's back. If she had a man in her life, she might be too busy to make trouble for the school. But after Seth had bid everyone goodbye, he couldn't rid his mind of the image of McKenna touching Lacey's arm.

Back in his office, Seth sat down at his computer to write a memo recapping what had happened at the meeting. It was slow going, because he kept thinking about Lacey and...

"Seth?"

He looked up into the bright and very pretty eyes of the woman occupying his thoughts. "Lacey. I thought you'd left."

"I came back for a minute."

"Oh. Why?"

She grasped her purse and shifted uneasily. "I...um...I just wanted to tell you how impressed I was with how you ran the meeting."

"Really?"

She smiled, and Seth felt something inside him soften. "Yes, I've been on a ton of committees that take forever to get off the ground."

"Oh, well, good. I mean, I'm glad you were pleased with this one." Geez, he was stammering.

"And thanks for running interference. I forced my way onto the committee. You could have thrown me to the wolves but you didn't."

"I'd never do that, Lacey."

She cocked her head. "Why wouldn't you?"

Cautious, he shrugged. He didn't trust her enough to tell her he was having second thoughts about what he'd done to her brother, that the Tim Johnson incident may have caused him to overreact. He knew he couldn't confess that he didn't want anything else to happen to her family because of him. So he chose humor. "Superheroes don't do that to the good guys."

She smiled at the reference. "Well, thanks." She glanced down at his computer. "Aren't you leaving?"

"In a while. I want to sum up what happened tonight before I forget it."

She glanced meaningfully at the clock. "You really do have a superhero complex, don't you?"

"Nah, I'm just an average guy in real life."

"Well, good night."

"Good night." Lacey turned to go. "Lacey?"

She faced him.

"Thanks for coming back to tell me this. It helps."

"You're welcome." And she was gone.

Swiveling his chair away from the computer, Seth linked his hands behind his head and propped his feet up on the desk. "Now, I wonder what that was all about?" he said aloud.

CHAPTER FIVE

The bad news: the high school is having a problem with violence.

The good news: concerned administrators, students, teachers and community members have formed a committee to do something about it.

The bad news: there was another fight this week at the high school.

The good news: the committee has a four-step plan almost ready to implement, and sub-committees are meeting next week.

What do you think?

LACEY STARED at the School Page of this week's edition of the *Herald*. Philip hadn't been pleased at all. After Monday's confrontation, she'd talked with him about her feelings that the paper had been presenting only one side of what was happening there—the negative one. She'd also told him she planned to write both this editorial and a report on the Good Deeds Project for Wednesday's edition.

He'd been adamant that the *Herald*'s criticism was justly deserved. She'd been equally adamant that the teachers and students deserved more. They deserved to have the positive things happening at the school reported as well.

When he'd still balked, she'd told him if she was going to stay in Bayview and run the paper, she had to do it her way. That comment had done the trick; he'd stared at her for a long time, then let it go. But the hurt look on his face almost made her give in. She knew she'd let him down, and after all he'd done for her, she hated to disappoint him. But ultimately, she'd stood her ground.

She glanced down to the bottom of the School Page at the sidebar entitled Christmas Good Deeds Project. There, Lacey had given an overview of the whole project. Each week until the holiday, she told her readers, she planned to report the Christmas activities of the entire school in general, and her subcommittee in particular. Truthfully, she loved the idea and felt that including the small articles would be a real morale booster to the community, to the school…and to Seth Taylor.

Not that she was out to please him, Lacey thought. Images of his skill and aplomb in running the task force had filtered into her mind since Monday. She also remembered how he looked smiling up at Monica Matthews. She wondered if they were dating. Were they sleeping together?

Uncomfortable with the direction of her thoughts, Lacey nonetheless admitted she'd been wondering a lot about Seth Taylor all week. She glanced at her computer, then the clock. She had to meet Cassie at The Spaghetti House—one of their old haunts—for dinner in an hour. What the hell? She'd resisted going back to Philip's files the day of her first visit to the high school, but tonight, curiosity got the better of her. She booted up the file.

She started at the beginning. S. Taylor. Biographical information. It was in report form, neatly listed: Seth Jacob Taylor, born 1952, Binghamton, New York. Mother Anna Lewis Taylor, father, Mark Taylor.

She read on. His father had worked for General Electric, his mother was an elementary-school teacher. Mark Taylor had died when Seth was nine. Two younger sisters, Kara Taylor Lang, Patrice Taylor Cooper. Both married, two children each, now living in Phoenix and Seattle, respectively.

Seth's mother still resided in Binghamton. He'd attended school in the small Southern Tier city. The report listed his activities. Lacey chuckled when she saw he'd been editor of both his high school newspaper and literary magazine. He'd won the high school English prize and several athletic awards for track. He'd gone on to Geneseo State College where he'd continued running but he also played club hockey. He'd worked on the college's literary magazine, graduated magna cum laude. *Impressive.*

The report noted his marriage to Connie Grover, whom he'd met at Geneseo. They had a son, Joseph, born six years after their marriage. His wife had died of an aneurysm five years later. *How sad.*

According to this report, Seth hadn't dated for a long time after his wife's death. Then there was a list of women he'd taken out. The P.I. had been thorough. Lacey scanned down. Monica Matthews's name wasn't there. This section ended a year ago.

Quickly, Lacey booted up S. Taylor, Professional

Information. He'd come to Bayview Heights after traveling through Europe following college. She tracked the events of his teaching career—graduate degrees, committees he'd been on, when he became principal.

Then there was a separate professional section that stopped her cold. It included names. Dates. Specific events. One read: Student, Cassie Smith, and gave her address as of a year ago. Then there was a blurb on Taylor's role in her life. Lacey shivered. This was very personal, and very private. Poor Cassie.

The list continued, naming several students after Cassie. They were all in the same vein. J. L. Tyson, valedictorian, 1982. Location as of two years ago, present occupation. Then Seth's role—he'd apparently intervened in a suicide attempt and saved the boy's life.

There were teachers, parents and administrators named, too. All painstakingly documented with location, present circumstances, Taylor's role in their lives.

Lacey sat back in her chair. It didn't make sense. Why would Philip pay a private investigator to gather this good information on Seth? With the exception of Kevin and a few other difficult students, everything reported was an accolade.

She clicked on the last icon—correspondence with P.I. Scrolling through, she read Philip's initial request to dig into Seth's life, summaries of the P.I.'s responses and copies of his reports. The last letter, dated a few months before Philip's heart attack, read:

Dear Mr. Cartwright,
Enclosed is the latest report on Taylor. Unfortunately, there is little in the negative column. This represents almost six months of investigation...

Fascinated, Lacey scanned the rest of the document. Mostly, though, she was appalled at this invasion of Seth's privacy, and the privacy of all the other people whose lives he'd touched. Philip's obsession with Seth was much greater than Lacey had realized. Her heart sank when she admitted her grandfather was clearly looking for a way to hurt the high-school principal.

But he hadn't found it.

Lacey checked the clock. It was time to meet Cassie. She closed down the computer and grabbed her things. She'd changed into jeans, a designer sweatshirt and low-heeled black boots to be comfortable. Donning her suede jacket, she decided the walk to the restaurant would clear her head.

Outside, the early November air had turned cool. As she made her way along the few blocks, she was bombarded by conflicting feelings about what she'd read. Anger at Philip was among them. So was respect for Seth. Both emotions made her uncomfortable.

When she arrived at The Spaghetti House, Cassie was already there, studying the menu.

"Hi," Lacey said as she reached the table.

Cassie looked up and smiled. "Hi." She took Lacey's hand and squeezed it. "I'm so glad we followed through on dinner this time. I'd get up and hug you, but I had a hell of a time getting into this booth to begin with.'' She nodded to the other side. ''Sit down.''

Shedding her jacket, Lacey slid onto the bench opposite Cassie. ''You look wonderful,'' Lacey said. ''You...glow.''

Cassie rolled her eyes, but the smile remained intact. ''I know. Isn't it embarrassing? I go around grinning like an idiot.''

''Because of the baby?''

''Partly. And because of Mitch.''

Lacey quelled the spurt of envy she felt. ''He seems very nice.''

Cassie nodded. ''I was surprised when he told me you were on the task force.''

''I'm surprised I'm on it, too.''

''How did it happen?''

After Lacey filled Cassie in on Seth's maneuvering, Cassie laughed and shook her head. ''That sounds so much like Seth. He'll win you over yet.''

A vision of Kevin in prison gray assaulted Lacey. She must have frowned, because Cassie asked, ''What is it?''

''Nothing. Tell me about what happened last winter.''

Though Cassie regaled her with interesting stories, Lacey had to struggle to concentrate on her friend's anecdotes. Conflicting images of Taylor distracted her. She forced herself to focus on Cassie in time to hear, ''But he's so protective of me and this baby, it's driving me nuts.''

''It isn't like you to put up with someone telling

you what to do. I wondered about it the other day at the school.''

Shadows crossed Cassie's face. "I know it isn't like me. But I tolerate it for him." At Lacey's questioning look, Cassie continued, "Mitch didn't give his heart easily, Lace. He'd been through hell in Vietnam. He lost a lot. I couldn't bear for him to lose any more, to be hurt again. I'll give up anything to prevent that, even my independent streak—for a while anyway.''

The moisture in Cassie's eyes moved Lacey. "I think you're doing the right thing, then.''

Shaking off the tears, Cassie said, "Even if it kills me. He wouldn't let me drive here tonight. He heard it might snow. He dropped me off, then he's going over to play volleyball.''

"Where do they play?''

"At Hotshots. You know—that old warehouse they converted to a bar. Can we order now? I'm starved." Cassie's eyes lit up. "Still like jumbo pizza, thick crust with everything on it?''

"I haven't had that in years. Let's go for it.''

After they ordered, Cassie told her how she'd played volleyball until she'd become pregnant. Her eyes misted again when she confided in Lacey about the first time Mitch had kissed her, after a game. "Listen to me, I'm such a sap over him. Sorry.''

"No, Cass, I think it's great.''

"Well, I'm a sap over everything these days. I'll probably bawl my way through Thanksgiving and Christmas.''

The holidays. Lacey was dreading the first holidays with Kevin in prison.

"What's wrong?" Cassie asked.

Lacey started to deny anything was wrong, but suddenly she knew she had to share what she was feeling with someone or explode. "It's the upcoming holidays. With Kevin in jail, I'm not sure I can deal with them."

"Talk to me about it."

"It's so awful, Cass. Barker Island is new and only medium security, but it's a horrible place. Sometimes I can't even bear to think about it." For the next half hour, Lacey poured out all her worries over Kevin, her grandfather, and even some of her feelings about the paper. Cassie listened and commented appropriately. The catharsis felt good, but Lacey was exhausted when she'd finished. "Thanks for listening. Let's change the subject, though. I'm drained."

Just as the pizza arrived, Christmas music filled the restaurant. It came from behind Lacey. "A little early for this, isn't it?" she asked.

Choosing a large, cheese-dripping piece of pizza, Cassie told her, "It's a new cable channel." She indicated with her eyes the wall-mounted television set behind Lacey. "They started running Christmas movies right after Halloween." She stared up at the screen. "This one is my all-time favorite."

Turning, Lacey caught a glimpse of Jimmy Stewart and Donna Reed in *It's a Wonderful Life*. "A great movie."

Neither spoke much as they devoured the pizza. Cassie stared at the screen intently as she ate. Then she said, "That's it! I've found it."

"What?"

Cassie's look was wary. "Um, nothing, just an idea I'd been looking for."

"Something for school?"

"Sort of."

"What do you mean? And why are you squirming?"

"Pregnant women can't sit still too long."

"Cass, you're no better now at lying than you were in high school."

Cassie smiled. "It's about Seth Taylor." Her face became serious. "You don't want to hear it."

Lacey's gut clenched—she *did* want to hear it. "Tell me," she said.

Cassie shrugged. "If you're sure." At Lacey's nod, she continued, "This is Seth's twenty-fifth year at Bayview Heights. We're having a party to celebrate it. At first he had a fit, but when I told him it would only be a few close friends and family, he agreed."

"Sounds nice."

"There's more. Seth's been in a funk lately. I think it's a midlife crisis, teacher burnout combination. I want to do something special for him, something to show all the good he's done at the high school." She reached over and squeezed Lacey's hand. "I know you think he hurt your family, but he's done so much for the school, for kids."

I know, I just read about it, Lacey thought.

Cassie glanced up at the TV. "This would be a perfect thing to do." She nodded to the screen. "If we could get some of his old students to come to the dinner, show him how he'd affected their lives…"

In spite of the topic, Lacey smiled. "Like George Bailey. If he hadn't been there, what would have happened?"

"Exactly." Cassie frowned. "It'll be a bitch getting that information, though."

"When's the party?"

"December twentieth. Some of the people he helped are probably still in Bayview, and some might be coming home for Christmas."

"Probably."

"I really want to do this. I'll find a way to get this information. Maybe some back issues of the paper would help me."

"Could be." Lacey's tone was noncommittal.

After they finished their meal, Cassie yawned. "Damn, if I just wasn't so tired all the time."

Lacey smiled. "When is Mitch picking you up?"

She glanced at the door. "Right now. Here he is. Oh, God, Lacey, I'm sorry. I had no idea..."

Puzzled, Lacey turned to look at the door. Through it came Mitch Lansing, handsome and sexy in a forest green sweat suit and wind-whipped hair. Behind him, in his navy nylon sweat suit, his hair mussed, too, was Seth Taylor—looking just as handsome and just as sexy as Mitch.

SETH SWALLOWED HARD as he watched Lacey Cartwright slide out of the booth and stand. He knew Cassie was having dinner here with her and he'd followed Mitch over because he wanted to talk to Lacey about tonight's paper. What he hadn't planned on was a vision of her in jeans that showed off her long legs to perfection. He thought she'd looked sexy in running shorts, but the soft denim encasing those legs... He forced himself to look away.

"Hi guys," Cassie said as she tried to get out of the booth. "Anybody want to help free Willy out of here?"

Mitch threw back his head and laughed. "You don't look like a whale, love." He gave her his hand and grunted as she stood. "Well, maybe a little one."

Cassie donned her jacket and then hugged Lacey. "Let's do it again soon."

"Very soon."

After the Lansings said their goodbyes and left, Lacey shrugged into her coat. She eyed Seth's sweat suit. "You were playing volleyball?"

"Yeah. I let Mitch talk me into joining the team a few weeks ago."

"Oh. Good." She gave him a half smile. "Well, I'll be on my way."

With a nod of his head, he indicated the bar at the front of the restaurant. "Want to have a beer with me?"

The torn look on her face made him feel bad for asking. He knew they had no business socializing.

"Um, no, I don't think so."

Seth had forgotten what the sting of rejection felt like. "Oh, okay. Come on, I'll walk you to your car."

"It's at the office."

"Well, that's not too far."

"I can walk back by myself."

"I know. But I'd like to walk with you. I want to talk a minute."

She looked as if she was going to refuse, but she didn't. "All right."

Outside, a crisp November wind whirled around them. Night had fallen, but street lamps illuminated the sidewalks as they passed the older homes that lined the city streets.

"It's getting colder," Seth said as he zipped up his jacket.

"Yes. Mitch told Cassie it might snow."

Seth chuckled. "Mitch would say anything to keep her under wraps."

"I think it's sweet." Seth could hear the longing in her voice. She coughed to clear it.

"What? Having a baby or having a man hover over you?"

"The first mostly. But the second, too." She was quiet, then asked, "So, what did you want to talk about?"

"Tonight's paper."

Lacey's step faltered. "What did you think?"

"I think the editorial was fair, if not as positive as I'd like to see it." He smiled.

Lacey stopped walking. "I was objective."

"Yes, you were."

"And?"

"And I particularly liked the piece on the Good Deeds Project." He reached out and squeezed her arm, leaving his hand on her for a moment. "I appreciate even more that it's going to be a weekly column."

"I thought the kids would like it."

"They'll love it."

"Good."

They started to walk again. Finally, Lacey asked, "Was volleyball fun?"

"Fun?" He stuck his hands in his pockets as he shuffled alongside her. "Yeah, it was. That's something that seems to be missing in my life these days."

"Really? Mine, too."

"Being back here must be rough for you."

Lacey shook her head, and some golden strands of hair caught in her collar. Seth resisted the urge to untangle them. "That's not it. Fun was missing in California, too."

Seth nodded. "You know what I'd like?"

"What?"

"Some *kid* kind of fun."

Lacey smiled as if she knew what he meant. "Running just doesn't do it, does it?"

"No, running is a need for me."

"For me, too. What did you do for fun as a kid?" she asked.

He thought for a minute. "I loved to read."

"What?"

"The Hardy Boys. *Treasure Island.*" He gave her a quick sideways glance. "Superhero comics, of course."

"What else did you do?"

"Oh, I don't know. Climb trees. Eat warm cherries right off the branches. Jump in the leaves. How about you?"

She smiled. "I used to love to ice-skate."

He bet those legs were an asset there.

"Being an adult is a drag sometimes," she said.

"I know. And yet kids want to grow up so fast." He could hear the wistfulness in his own voice. "If there's one thing I could teach every student, it would be to enjoy being a kid. It's gone all too soon."

They fell into a companionable silence. As they passed the town library, Seth stopped. He looked out over the massive lawn. In the center of it were several piles of leaves, recently raked. It was unusual for the leaves to fall this late, even for downstate New York, but these were the last of the season. Seth angled his chin at them. "Now, if we were kids, we'd go over there and jump in."

"Yeah, but if we got caught, we'd have to answer to the cops."

"And the poor groundskeeper who raked them would have to do it again tomorrow."

Lacey laughed. "Listen to us. We sound like a couple of old fogies."

"Old fogies? I resent that. You have to be at least sixty to be a fogy."

She arched a mischievous eyebrow. "Yeah, well, I don't see you tackling that pile."

Catching her mood, he said, "That big one, right there in the middle?"

"Uh-huh."

Still, he didn't move.

"Scared?"

He struggled against the grin. "Me? Never?"

"Prove it."

His eyes narrowed on her. The teasing made her

look young and...cute. He wanted to keep her looking that way for a while. "Okay."

She started to cross her arms over her chest, waiting for him to take the dare.

"Oh no you don't," he said, and before she could object, he grabbed her hand and began to pull her across the yard. It took her a minute to realize what he was doing, then she matched his stride. Hand in hand, they loped to the leaves. Together, they dived into the middle pile. Once in it, like any ten-year-old boy, Seth picked up a huge handful and threw it on top of her. She sputtered and spit, then bent down, picked up her own pile and tossed it at him. They were on their third round when they heard, "Hey, you kids, get out of there."

Both froze.

"Caught," Seth whispered.

"Never." She reached over and grabbed his hand this time. "We weren't track stars for nothing."

They took off down the street before whoever had yelled started toward them. Sprinting at first, then slowing to a jog, they ran the few blocks to the paper. They weren't even breathing hard when they reached the *Herald*. But they collapsed, giggling, onto a bench in front of the building.

"That was close," Lacey managed to get out.

"Yeah." Seth looked over at her sprawled on the seat. Underneath the streetlight, her eyes sparkled and her cheeks were pink. Slowly, he reached out.

All mirth drained from her face as his hand came closer. "You've got leaves in your hair." He picked one, two, three big ones out of the blond strands. Then he took the ends of a lock and ran it through his fingers. "You'll have to wash this tonight." He stared at her hair and a gut-punching image of how this beautiful wavy mass would look spread across his chest almost took his breath away. Her coat had fallen open and he could see the full outline of her breasts beneath her sweatshirt.

Time and circumstance froze. She was no longer his nemesis at the paper, not the sister of a boy he'd been unable to save. She was only a woman—all woman.

He longed to kiss her, to take those full breasts into his hands, his mouth. He looked into her eyes. Desire was there, too. He might have done something about it if he hadn't also seen the fear.

It sobered him, made him draw back and stand abruptly.

No words were spoken as she stood, too. She didn't even look at him before she headed for her car. He let her go alone, not trusting himself near her. She didn't look back, either, thank God, because he wasn't sure what he'd do if she did turn to him, and bathe him with that whiskey-colored gaze that said, "I feel it, too."

As SETH MANEUVERED the roads to the Franklin Street Day Care Center a few days later, he wondered if seeing Lacey Cartwright would be as awkward today as it had been at their last two meetings. Though he'd never felt comfortable around her, he was downright edgy since the night they'd jumped into the leaves together. Since the night he *hadn't* kissed her.

He pounded his hand on the steering wheel. *Damn.* How had he gotten himself into this mess?

She's a beauty, that's how. Inside and out.

He could still see Lacey laughing as the fall leaves speckled her hair and clothing. It had been a deep, sexy sound that made him want to hear it again, under far different circumstances.

At the second Good Deeds meeting the following Monday, she hadn't been laughing. She'd been scowling as he told the group he could only get five hundred dollars out of the budget for the day-care project.

He'd lied about the money's source—he'd donated it himself. It wasn't enough to pay for toys and the small party for the kids, but it was all he could afford. Apparently, Lacey didn't think it was enough, either, because she'd reached into her purse, grabbed a checkbook and wrote out a check. "The *Herald* will match those funds," she'd said calmly.

"All right!" Darcy McCormick cheered, raising her hand for a high five. Lacey slapped it good-naturedly.

When the meeting was over, Seth snagged Lacey's arm after the kids left and she tried to run out. "Wait a minute. This check is a personal one, not a business one."

She stammered, "I…um…I don't carry the business checkbook with me. I'll transfer the funds."

"I don't believe you," he told her.

"Pardon me?"

"I think this money is from you."

"Now, why would you think that?" She cocked

her head. "Where did the first five hundred come from, Mr. Taylor?"

"The school budget."

"Uh-huh." He knew he was starting to flush so he stared down at the table as he got his belongings together. When he glanced back up at her, she said, "See you tonight, Santa," and left.

She read me far too easily, he thought, as he turned the corner onto Franklin Street. He didn't like it at all.

LACEY SAW Seth exit his car and head toward the day-care entrance. She tried to keep her gaze away from his long, purposeful strides, from the way the wind whipped his hair off his face. She groaned and put her head down on the steering wheel to avoid watching him.

This was a disaster. Attraction to this man spelled trouble loud and clear. For a minute she allowed the anger to surface. How *could* this have happened?

All right, she told herself, so she was attracted to him. She liked his looks, the way he carried himself; she admired his ease with the students, how he handled adults; and she respected his utter selflessness in his job. That didn't alter the fact that he was responsible for Kevin being in jail. She could use that reminder to keep her distance—even if it didn't quite ring true anymore. Because she had to keep her distance. A clear, painful image of her grandfather's face when she'd refused to kill the Good Deeds article assaulted her. For Philip's sake, she had to stay away from Seth.

She'd used her loyalty to Philip to steel herself

against Seth the previous Monday, when they'd spent time together on two committees. She'd been all right in the afternoon, but the task force meeting had been tough.

When she'd presented the information she'd found on the Internet on student shared decision making, the look of soft approval on Seth's face made her stomach somersault. "You checked the Internet for our subcommittee?" he asked.

"No big deal. I just went on-line, did a search and came up with this. I don't think all of it's usable, though." She handed a copy to each student and one to Seth.

After perusing it, Darcy spoke first. "I like the Helping Hands idea," the girl said, referring to a program where students were asked who—other students, teachers, staff—they would go to if they had a problem. Then a list was developed of Helpers who would be on call when a student was in trouble. Training of everyone involved would be implemented first.

Lacey smiled at Darcy. "It was my favorite, too."

"I like the Student Court," Nick said.

Darcy immediately responded, "You would."

"What's that supposed to mean?"

"It appeals to your need for power. For influence."

"What's wrong with that? I like influencing this school in a positive way. You should try it sometime, McCormick."

Seth intervened. "I like both these ideas. Can we get down to how we might implement them? A plan from our subcommittee needs to be presented to the task force next Monday.''

Again, Lacey had tried to leave quickly after they'd finished, but Taylor was very good at detaining people. ''Thanks for doing this,'' he said, holding up the folder.

Lacey remembered noting the lines of strain around his mouth. She remembered wondering how long he'd been at school that Monday. Had he eaten? Had Monica Matthews brought him supper again? When she'd realized the direction of her thoughts, she'd erected her protective barrier. ''Well, don't tell my grandfather about this. He'd have a fit.''

Seth had looked shocked at her candor—and hurt. Then he'd swallowed hard. ''No, of course I won't. I don't want to make more trouble for you with him than I already have.''

She'd stared hard at him, then said meaningfully, ''That's a given, Mr. Taylor. We can't hurt my grandfather.'' He'd nodded, and let her go.

Sighing heavily at the bizarre circumstances, Lacey got out of the car and hurried up the walk into the day care. The outer room was painted in primary colors with animals and their babies on every wall. The whimsical scenes made Lacey smile.

A woman looked up from behind the desk. ''Hi, I'm Mary Jarrett. I'm the director here.''

''Lacey Cartwright. I'm joining the school group.''

Mary smiled. ''You're with Seth.'' The phrase made Lacey uncomfortable. ''He was my English teacher twenty years ago,'' Mary chatted on. ''I did my senior project on day care for the underprivileged. It led to all this.'' She looked around the room.

Cassie could use Mary Jarrett's story for the tribute to Seth. ''Where's my group?''

''Two students wanted to go right to the nursery. The cute boy and the...unusual-looking girl. The twins headed for the playground out back. Seth is in with the toddlers. Come on, I'll take you to him.''

Before Lacey could say she'd rather be with the kids—or anyone but Seth—Mary led her to a room off to the side. Decorated again in primary colors, everything was pint-size. The children's work was displayed on the walls.

Five toddlers were in the room—one was painting in a corner with an adult, two were climbing the plastic jungle gym—well padded below—with a teacher supervising, one lay on a mat, cuddling a doll almost as big as she was. The last one sat in the lap of Seth Taylor, who occupied a big rocker. The gorgeous little boy, with fat blond curls, sucked his fingers and nestled into Seth's chest, absorbed in the book he held. As Seth read softly, one strong arm kept the child anchored to him.

Every defense Lacey had erected crumbled at the sight.

Mary tugged her over. Lacey went reluctantly. ''Hi,'' the woman said to Seth. ''Your partner's here.''

Seth looked up at her just as the child did. She noticed that the baby's eyes were light brown, like Kevin's. ''Who's this?'' she asked, reaching out and ruffling the boy's hair.

"This is Josh Cornwall." Seth gave her a grin that she thought could melt the snow outside. "And he likes to read, don't you, buddy?"

Mary laughed. "Still getting kids into the books, aren't you, Seth?"

He winked at Lacey and her knees liquefied. "You bet. Whenever I can."

Josh chose that moment to reach out to Lacey. "Up," he said.

Seth steadied the boy before he could fall, and Lacey leaned over. Chubby hands encircled her neck as she grasped Josh. Seth's fingers trailed down the boy's back, and then grazed Lacey's arms. Even through her corduroy dress, her skin tingled. "Don't blame you a bit, little guy," he said as he let Josh go. "She's a lot prettier than I am."

Ignoring the compliment, Lacey straightened and hugged Josh. One hand went to his silky hair and smoothed it down. The scents of baby shampoo and powder assailed her. She was reminded of Kevin, when he was little. Lacey had loved to help her father bathe and dress him. She closed her eyes to will back the moisture. Josh pulled his fingers out of his mouth and burrowed his face into her chest.

"He's getting your dress wet, Ms. Cartwright," Mary said.

Lacey opened her eyes. "It'll clean up."

Seth stood, watching them. "He looks tired. Want to rock him?"

Carefully she avoided Seth's gaze and nodded. Taking a seat, she settled the child on her lap and began to rock him as if she'd been doing it all her life.

Seth couldn't take his eyes off her as she cuddled the baby against her chest. Seeing her slender fingers smooth the boy's curls, listening to her croon to him, stirred something very potent inside of Seth.

Mary asked him, "Do you want to see the other rooms?"

After a few moments, he drew in a deep breath and tore his gaze away. "Yes, Mary, I'd love to see the other rooms." Without looking at Lacey again, he practically bolted out of the toddler area.

The phrase "running for your life" came to mind as he hurried after the day-care director.

CHAPTER SIX

THE FOLLOWING WEEK, on Thanksgiving morning, Seth sat at Mitch and Cassie Lansing's kitchen table as the couple prepared dinner. They'd invited Seth and his family for their holiday celebration. Seth's mother was spending the week in Phoenix with his sister, so he and his son gladly accepted.

Joey, home from school for the first time, was in the den, playing video games with Johnny Battaglia, the young man Cassie had helped turn around and who was now practically part of the Lansing family. Mitch's brother, Dr. Kurt Lansing, would join them after he finished work at the clinic.

Seth studied the large kitchen. Mitch's house was much like the man himself, big and orderly, with a lot of hidden warmth. As Seth watched him stir something at the stove, Mitch addressed Cassie. ''Sit down *now*,'' he told his pregnant wife. ''You've been rubbing your back all morning.'' When Cassie hesitated, he added, ''Or I'll carry you upstairs and make you rest in bed.''

''Try it, big guy,'' Cassie said sassily, but couldn't stifle a yawn.

He rounded on her and swooped her up in his arms. ''You asked for it.''

Seth glanced away, feeling like an intruder at the

intimate sight of Cassie snuggling into Mitch and whispering something into his ear. He heard Mitch laugh throatily as he headed out of the kitchen with his wife in his arms. "Say goodbye to Seth, love. You're taking a nap before dinner."

"Goodbye, Seth." Her words were muffled by yet another yawn.

Seth smiled at their gentle sparring. Both were strong personalities, agreeing on very little. But they were so outrageously in love that nothing else seemed to matter. With a force that surprised Seth, he realized he wanted a relationship like theirs in his life again.

He'd loved his young wife, Connie, who had died suddenly when Joey was five. Seth had been thirty-three; he'd been devastated for years by the loss.

Eventually, he'd dated and had one or two serious relationships since then, though he'd never remarried. He'd been so involved with Joey and taking over as principal of the high school that his personal life hadn't been a priority. Today, he wondered if he'd missed the boat. Without his consent, and against his will, a vision of Lacey Cartwright hit him with the force of a sledgehammer. He willed the image away.

Mitch returned, got coffee and took a seat at the table. "So, how's everything going?"

"Don't ask."

"Cassie says there was another fight at school yesterday."

Raking a hand through his hair, Seth shook his head. "You know, we've come to expect more trouble before every holiday."

"Loneliness is tougher at this time of year."

"The kids can't handle it very well."

"Looks like you're not doing so hot yourself."

Seth started to deny the fact, but knew better than to try to bluff Mitch. "Everything seems to be crashing in at once. Jerry Bosco's threatening to file a grievance for harassment."

"Jerry Bosco's an ass."

"I've got to deal with him, nonetheless. I'm going for a 3020A after the holidays." Seth explained the legal procedure he would use to fire a tenured teacher for incompetence.

"You'll have to be here to do that," Mitch said without much tact.

Seth didn't answer.

"What's going on with State Ed.?"

"I've got an interview for the position with the Board of Regents a week from Friday."

"I'm sorry to hear that."

Standing, Seth crossed to the window to look out. "My secretary is resigning, I've got problems with the staff and the kids are fighting just as much. Maybe the *Herald*'s right. Maybe the high school needs another principal. A younger one. Alex Ransom could fill my shoes easily."

"What does the *Herald* have to do with this?"

"Spending so much time in Lacey Cartwright's company has been difficult for me."

Mitch waited before he said, "She's a bitch."

Seth whirled. The words were out of his mouth before he could stop them. "No, she's not a bitch. She's a caring woman. She loves kids, she wants what's good for the school. She's fun and interesting, and—'' Seth halted when he saw a twinkle of something…knowing…in Mitch's eyes. A look that said, *I thought so.*

"What's going on out here?" Joey asked from the doorway before Seth could defend himself.

His son and Johnny shuffled into the kitchen. Glad for the diversion, Seth studied them. The boys couldn't be more different in appearance. Joey was tall, lean, blond and blue-eyed, with classic features. He was dressed in khaki slacks, an oxford shirt and a navy pullover sweater. Johnny was mostly muscle, with shaggy black hair and snapping black eyes. He wore dark jeans and a black shirt. His former sullenness, however, was gone.

Joey sat down next to Mitch, and Johnny went over to the refrigerator and took out two cans of soda.

Joining the men at the table, Johnny asked Mitch, "Where's Cassie?"

"Upstairs resting."

"How'd you manage that?"

"I hog-tied her."

Johnny grinned.

"You need a haircut," Mitch said gruffly, reaching over and ruffling the boy's hair.

"Look who's talking. Yours has never been that long."

Mitch laughed and leaned back in his chair, his eyes shining with unabashed affection.

"How's school?" Seth asked. He could remember a time not so long ago when Johnny had been about to drop out of Bayview Heights High School.

Now he was a freshman at Columbia University in premed.

"Good. Working at the clinic's better."

"He's going to make dean's list," Mitch said proudly.

Johnny rolled his eyes.

"You, too, I'll bet," Mitch said to Joey.

"Yeah, probably," Joey answered. "But I wish I could do what Johnny's doing. My journalism courses would be much more interesting if I could get some work experience along with school." He turned to his father. "I've been thinking about seeing if I can work at the newspaper in town the month I'm home between semesters. What do you think, Dad?"

Seth wanted to groan at the suggestion. He mumbled something noncommittal. The last thing he needed was for his son to get involved with the *Herald*.

Two hours later at the dining room table laden with a lavish Thanksgiving meal, Seth berated himself for his negative thoughts. He had good friends, a loving son and a nice life. What right did he have to complain? He vowed to enjoy the warmth and camaraderie around him.

"Before we eat, I'd like to start a Lansing tradition," Mitch said. He cleared his throat. "Since this is our first Thanksgiving together, I want everyone to share what he or she has to be thankful for. I'll start." He placed his hand on Cassie's belly. "I've got three things, actually." His gaze locked on his wife. "Cassandra, of course. And the baby." He turned to the boy on his right. "And Johnny."

Seth watched Johnny swallow hard, reach over and squeeze Mitch's arm. Showing emotion wasn't easy for either of them.

"I'll go next," Johnny said, smiling at Cassie then Mitch. "I'm thankful to be a part of the Lansing family."

Cassie's eyes teared and she blinked hard. "And I'm grateful for you both, too."

Kurt, who had arrived moments before dinner was served, spoke next. "I'm glad my brother is happy again." He lifted his wineglass in silent salute to the woman who'd made it happen.

When it was Joey's turn, he leveled his sky blue eyes on Seth. "I'm thankful for my dad."

Seth's throat closed up. "Thanks, son. The same goes for me. I'm thankful for you."

The emotional moment passed, and they all dug into turkey and the trimmings. Seth's mind zig-zagged to Lacey Cartwright.

What did she have to be thankful for this year? Anything? Kevin was in prison. Her grandfather was ill and angry with her. And it was all because of Seth.

PHILIP'S HAND trembled as he sliced the small turkey, and Lacey's heart constricted. She remembered those hands teaching her to type, catching a football from Kevin and hefting her new Christmas stereo up to her room. His frailty deflated the little holiday spirit she'd awakened with this morning.

"Looks good, honey. Though we should have gone out to dinner."

Stifling a groan at the thought of spending

Thanksgiving Day in some impersonal restaurant, Lacey said, "I love to cook, Grandpa. I don't do it often enough."

He harrumphed. "You've got other things to do. Celia and I can manage the meals."

"What's Celia doing today?"

"How should I know?" He looked up at Lacey. "Oh, all right. She's having her kids over."

"How nice."

"She invited us."

Oh, God, and you said no? They could have been in a house full of people. With kids. Maybe even babies. Glancing around their solemn home, Lacey bit her tongue to keep from voicing the accusation.

As if he'd read her mind, Philip said, "Couldn't imagine having dinner with the little rug rats her kids have now."

Lacey smiled. "Remember how Kevin used to smush mashed potatoes through his fingers?"

Philip's look brightened. "And the squash, too. We'd try and hide it from him, but Kevin always liked bright colors and his eyes zeroed right in on the orange."

Memories of her childhood flooded Lacey, but she dammed them up. Holidays were tough enough without trips down memory lane. They ate in silence.

"What time are we going to Barker Island?" Philip finally asked.

Lacey glanced at the antique grandfather clock that had stood guard over the dining-room table for as long as she could remember. "I thought we'd leave about two."

Philip gripped the fork. "I can't imagine..." His words choked him. "Thanksgiving...in a place like that."

Reaching over, Lacey touched his hand. "Don't think about it, then. Think about how we'll cheer him up when we get there."

The lie fell heavily between them. Both knew that nothing they did would cheer up the sullen young man they'd visit that afternoon.

After the meal that neither enjoyed, Philip insisted he clean up, but Lacey demanded he rest before they left for the two-hour drive to the prison. As she worked on the dishes, she stared out at the backyard, watching two squirrels scurry up and down the bare branches of a red maple tree.

Look, Lace, a squirrel.

Don't touch him, Kevin. He'll bite.

I'll bite back.

Lacey remembered thinking how odd Kevin's reaction had been. She remembered worrying about his comment. Later, there had been marked signs of aggression. He'd become a violent boy, and Lacey agonized over what more they could have done to help him. They'd finally traced part of the problem to a chemical imbalance and he had just been put on a new medication when he'd been kicked out of school.

When *Seth Taylor* had kicked him out of school. *Best remember that, Lacey. And remember what any connection with him would do to your grandfather.* She did, and it helped her not think about Seth today, not to wonder what he was doing, who he was having dinner with. His son? His mother? Monica Matthews?

Sighing, Lacey checked the clock again. She wished she could go running, but her ankle still hurt. She remembered the feel of Seth's long fingers on her skin. The gentle way he'd probed to see if she was hurt. With difficulty, she banished the thought.

Instead, she tried to figure out what she could do to make Kevin's Thanksgiving a little brighter. Not much, she decided, when she pictured Barker Island, as grim and foreboding as a medieval fortress.

KEVIN CRUMPLED the copy of the *Herald* that his grandfather had sent him and stared at the gray walls surrounding him. Instead of panicking at being locked in, instead of bawling like a damn baby at being in here on Thanksgiving, he thought about the editorial page of the newspaper he'd just read. What the hell was Lacey doing? Until now, she'd gone along with his grandfather's attacks on that bastard Taylor, on that stupid place that couldn't wait to get rid of him.

"You got visitors, Cartwright." Cramden stood outside his cell. "It's that juicy sister of yours and the old man."

Kevin forced himself to ignore the guard's taunting. His sister and grandpa were here. He gripped the steel post of the bed. He could handle Lacey's concern, her pity, but he didn't want to see his grandfather's face today. He'd look so sad, so disappointed. Kevin couldn't remember a time he hadn't brought that look to Philip's eyes. No matter how hard he tried not to.

They'd be worried, too, he thought as he rubbed the bump on his right temple. Hell, he hadn't deserved that, any more than he'd deserved being in this dungeon. Just because he'd gotten in the middle of some blowup between Black Eyes and Brazil.

"Come on, I don't have all day." Cramden's voice was gruff as he unlocked the cell and pulled open the door.

"Yeah, well, who gives a rat's ass?"

The guard started to close the door but Kevin shouldered his way out. "I'm comin'," he said sullenly.

He saw his grandfather as soon as he entered the visiting area. Kevin couldn't believe how much the old man had aged since the heart attack. His hair was whiter, and his shoulders stooped. For the first time, Philip Cartwright looked his age.

PHILIP WATCHED Kevin sit down on the other side of the half-wall barrier that separated the inmates from their visitors. "Hi, son." Philip reached out to squeeze Kevin's arm.

At first Kevin drew back. Then he allowed a brief touch.

Studying Kevin, Philip asked, "What happened to your face?"

"I walked into a post," he said simply.

"Kevin, if anything's happening I need to know—"

"Nah, Grandpa, nothin'."

Silence. Then Philip spoke. "What did you have for dinner today?"

"Fried squirrel," Kevin said sarcastically.

Philip felt his face fall.

"Sorry. The usual. Turkey." Kevin looked around. "Where's Lacey?"

"In the waiting room. She thought we should have some time together alone." Philip wished she'd come in with him, though. He no longer knew what to say to the boy he loved so much. "I brought you some more newspapers. I gave them to the guard."

"What's going on with the *Herald,* Grandpa? I read the editorial Lacey wrote a couple of weeks ago."

"I don't exactly know, son. Lacey seems to think we've taken too hard a line with the high school. She wants to give them some good press." *And it's got something to do with Taylor.*

He saw his grandson's hands fist. "Doesn't she remember what they did to me? It's that freakin' Taylor's fault I'm here."

Guilt tugged at Philip. "I know, Kevin. But Lacey's always been more forgiving than us."

Kevin stood up. "Yeah, well, tell her I don't want to talk to her if she's gonna take his side."

"You don't mean that. She'll be devastated. She drove all this way to see you. And it's Thanksgiving Day."

"I don't care."

"Please, son, sit down."

"No, I'm goin' back in." Kevin turned and stalked out.

Philip watched him go and winced when the door clanged shut. He stared at it for a long time after Kevin left. What was he going to tell Lacey? Could he bear to see her face when he told her Kevin wouldn't see her?

Oh, God, I have to do something, he thought. *Things are spinning out of control.* And it was Seth Taylor's fault.

Reaching into his back pocket, he dragged out his wallet and fished inside it. The private investigator's phone number was right where he'd put it before his heart attack.

He'd find a way to discredit Taylor, he decided as he stood and headed for the door. He'd find a way to make Lacey hate Taylor as much as Philip and Kevin did. Then there'd be no reason for his family to be torn apart.

LACEY LOOKED OUT the window of the *Herald*'s office at 6:00 p.m. the day after Thanksgiving and realized she needed to leave for home right away. How much snow *had* accumulated while she'd been immersed in the Net?

She'd come to the office today to try to forget her problems—mostly the slicing hurt she felt when Kevin had refused to see her yesterday. His intentional rebuff still brought tears to her eyes.

Shoving back the emotion, she shut off her computer and gathered her things. Bundled up in a heavy parka with a hood, she donned fleece-lined boots, a wool hat and gloves. She locked up and found her way to her Honda.

The wind had stung her cheeks and made her eyes water by the time she got inside the car and started the engine. She couldn't see through the icy windshield, so she climbed out again. As she hacked at the heavy layer of ice, she swore. Damn, she'd forgotten how she hated these Long Island storms. When one blew in, conditions could be treacherous, though it looked as if the snowfall was letting up.

She got back into the car and, squinting through the windshield, she drove slowly. Still, when she hit a slippery patch in the road, the car skidded. Turning into the skid, she gripped the steering wheel, muttered a prayer and managed to keep the Honda on the pavement. Thankfully, there were no other vehicles around.

Just as she reached the outskirts of town, which usually took five minutes but today had taken fifteen, she saw a car parked off to the side of the road, its hood up, its flashers blinking in the semidarkness. Next to it stood a man. Even though she couldn't determine his identity, Lacey drew parallel to the car. Bayview Heights was a small town and surely no mugger would have chosen today to find a victim. Besides, she couldn't leave *anyone* stranded in this cold weather.

As she lowered the window, the man jogged to her side of the car. It wasn't a man. It was a teenage boy.

It was Seth Taylor's son. There was a strong resemblance to his father.

"Man, thanks for stopping. Not a soul's come by but you." Dressed in a heavy ski jacket, he had on gloves but no hat.

"Can I help?" Lacey asked.

"I think my battery's dead. You wouldn't have jumper cables, would you? Mine are in my dad's Blazer."

"Yes. I have some."

Popping the trunk and the hood, Lacey got out and circled the car. She took the cables and a woolen hat from the trunk and rounded to the front. "Here, put this on."

The boy accepted the hat and covered his painfully red ears. "Why don't you get back in your car?" he suggested as he took the cables from her. "It's cold out here. I can do this."

"I'm okay." They hitched up the cables to both cars. "Want me to start yours?" she asked.

Joey looked faintly surprised that she'd know what to do. "Yeah, sure."

Lacey got into his small car. She turned the key. Nothing happened. She tried again. Still no juice. She got out.

"It's something else," she told Joey.

"Yeah, I guess." He frowned, the gesture reminding her of his father. Seth had done a lot of scowling at her.

"I can take you to a gas station."

"I think both of them are closed."

Lacey said, "I'll drive you home then. Lock up. Turn off the flashers."

She got into her car, and in moments Joey swung into the front beside her. He was a couple inches taller than his father—about six feet—and had to move the seat back. He flicked the seat belt closed as soon as he got in. "Thanks. I'm Joe Taylor."

"Yes, I know. I'm Lacey Cartwright."

"Yeah, you run the paper. How'd you know who I am?"

"It's a small town." She checked the mirror and pulled out onto the pavement.

"But you haven't been the *Herald*'s editor that long."

"No, I grew up here, though."

He rolled his eyes. "Don't tell me. You had my dad for a teacher."

She smiled at his youthful disgust. "No. I was in high school when he taught English, but I didn't take his class. Why?"

The boy laughed good-naturedly. "It's all I hear—what a great teacher Dad was."

She smiled weakly as she pulled onto the road.

Joey eyed her carefully. "You sure about taking me home? We could stop to call Dad."

"No, I'm out and you only live about ten minutes from us, I think."

Joey was silent.

Lacey smiled genuinely this time. "Joe, these are the nineties. I can handle a snowstorm, jumper cables and a little ice. You seem pretty chauvinistic for what—an eighteen-year-old?"

The boy chuckled. "I'm sorry. I was raised that way. Dad's got a real protective streak. The kids at college razz me about it all the time."

"Where do you go?"

"UCLA."

"No kidding? That's where I went."

"For journalism?"

"Of course. You?"

"The same. Maybe I could talk to you about working at the paper over—" Joey's words cut off as the car hit another patch of ice. The tires skidded again, only this time Lacey's Honda did a 180-degree turn. Her shoulders tensed and her heartbeat speeded up, but she grasped the wheel and turned into the skid.

When she righted the car, she looked at Joey. "You okay?"

"Yeah. You did great."

"We'd better not talk, so I can concentrate."

It took another fifteen minutes to get to the Taylor house. Though Lacey knew where Seth lived, she'd never actually been out to his place. The sprawling two-story cedar home was on the edge of town, standing alone in a copse of trees and backing onto a forever-wild park. As she pulled into the sloped driveway, she noticed the snow blanketed everything. It was a postcard pretty scene.

Lights blazed from inside and there were lights shining from the porch and lamppost. "Oh, man, Dad's gonna be ticked," Joey said as the car approached the front of the driveway.

"Why?"

"He, ah, told me not to go out this afternoon. He went to school for a few hours, but called and said the roads were bad."

"You went anyway?"

"I had to—"

Just then the door to the house flew open. Seth stalked out, his jacket flopping open. Joey exited the Honda, leaving the door ajar on his side. Lacey stayed where she was.

When Seth reached the car, Lacey heard, "Oh, thank God," and saw him give his son a bear hug.

It was obvious that Seth Taylor wasn't *ticked* at

all. He was petrified. "Get in the house," he said gruffly, but the underlying anxiety in his voice was marked.

Joey leaned into the car. He looked chagrined. "Thanks a ton, Ms. Cartwright."

"You're welcome."

When Joey trotted away, Seth poked his head in. "Lacey?"

Just hearing her name on his lips warmed her. "Yes."

"What happened?"

"I found your son stranded on Maple Street. His car died and we couldn't get it started with jumper cables, so I brought him home."

"Thanks." Yanking his jacket together, Seth asked, "You want to come in?"

"Excuse me?"

"I asked if you wanted to come in." He slid inside the car and shut the door. His wide shoulders spanned the bucket seat and his chest took up much of the small space. "The snowstorm looks like it's letting up now, but, um, the roads will probably be better in an hour or so..."

Lacey realized how lame the sentiment sounded and she smiled at him.

His grin was sheepish, then it turned into a scowl, as if he'd just thought of something. "Do you have plans tonight?"

"No."

"Any responsibilities?" He meant her grandfather.

"No." Philip had gone up to Leonard Small's cabin this morning for the rest of the weekend.

"Come in, then."

Lacey thought about the empty house on Bay Road and the loneliness she'd felt all weekend, especially after Kevin wouldn't see her. Because of this man. She should say no. For Kevin.

She blocked her brother out of her mind. "All right, for a little while."

Lacey turned off the engine and climbed out. Seth waited for her to precede him down the sidewalk that led to the porch. The distance was only about ten feet to the house, but by the time they made it inside, Lacey was thoroughly chilled. In the foyer, she hugged herself to stop from shivering.

Seth removed his jacket and hung it on a hook to the right. "Let me have your coat," he said. "The fire's going in the living room. You'll warm up faster there."

Shrugging out of her snow gear, Lacey picked her way around the wet floor and followed Seth Taylor into his home.

She was enchanted by his house. The main room was spacious without being cold. Paneled completely in cedar, it had a cathedral ceiling with two skylights, a fieldstone fireplace and plush, dark carpeting that felt thick under her socks. Two huge overstuffed beige sofas flanked the fireplace. One whole wall sported floor-to-ceiling shelves that functioned as an entertainment center, and a home for more books than Lacey could count. Recessed lighting was everywhere, casting the room in a mellow halo of light. Two leather chairs next to stand-up lamps formed a practical reading area. The whole room looked as if it had come out of a magazine on classy rustic living.

"This is gorgeous," she said.

"Thanks."

From his position by the fire, Joey spoke up, "Dad did the interior himself. You should see his study."

The comment drew Seth's attention from Lacey to Joey.

"Don't try to distract me, young man." Seth's voice was stern. "I'm furious with you for going out when I told you not to."

Sighing, Joey's blue eyes locked on his father, and Lacey braced herself for a tantrum like the ones Kevin had always thrown.

"I'm sorry I worried you," Joey said instead. "The roads didn't seem that bad, but I guess I shouldn't have gone."

Lacey crossed to the fire and stood next to it, watching the scenario with fascination. Seth went to Joey and put his arm around the boy. "I was crazy with worry. Why'd you go, son?"

"Sally Tyson."

"What?"

"Sally called and was hysterical. Bill broke up with her this morning. She asked me to come over."

Seth rolled his eyes. "Joey, you've got to get over this knight-in-shining-armor routine."

"I will, when you do, Dad," his son said teasingly.

Trying to look fierce, Seth scowled. "It was a dumb thing to do, just the same. You should have known better."

"I know."

Seth ruffled Joey's hair. "All right. Go change. You're wet."

Joey threw Lacey a boyish grin, then took the steps of the massive staircase two at a time. Lacey stared at Joey and wondered if her father, had he lived longer, would have been able to deal with a teenage Kevin so effectively. Philip was in his late sixties when Kevin got to high school. He'd been a good grandfather, but she wondered if...

"How can I thank you for rescuing my son?"

Lacey smiled. "No thanks necessary. He's a wonderful boy."

Pure bliss lit Seth's face. "Yes, he is. If a little too nice for his own good."

Lacey glanced out the window, suddenly uncomfortable. She bit her lip. "It's pretty here."

The small gesture zinged through Seth. Framed by the fireplace, with her disheveled hair, in a thick ski sweater and jeans and heavy socks, Lacey Cartwright looked young and very vulnerable.

And very desirable.

Seth stuck his hands in his back pockets and turned to stare out the window, too. Life was full of ironies. Grateful as he was that she'd been there to help his son, Seth knew that for his own good, and hers, the last person he should be with tonight was Lacey Cartwright. He'd had to fight not to think about her all weekend. He'd had to quell images of her holding Josh in the day care, cradling the little boy to her. But when he'd seen her in the car in his driveway, he lost the battle.

Now he looked over at her and said, "Please sit down."

Forgoing the sofa, she sank onto the floor, her back against the couch. Seth did the same on the opposite side.

She stared into the fire, the flickering light revealing sadness on her face.

"You're worried what Philip will think about your being here, aren't you?"

Lacey reached out to warm her hands in front of the blaze. A heavy sigh escaped her. "I don't think we should discuss this right now. My grandfather will always blame you for what happened to Kevin, and you'll always believe you did what was right."

Seth felt the familiar guilt well inside him. "I'm not so sure about that anymore."

"What do you mean?"

"Sometimes I have doubts about what I did with Kevin." There, it was out. For her to use against him.

"I don't understand."

"I've wondered a thousand times if I made the right decision. If I had listened to you that day you came to see me eight years ago, maybe things would have been different."

She studied him with troubled eyes. "Why didn't you?"

"You want the truth?"

"Of course."

"Kevin was a powder keg." Seth forked a hand through his hair. "He'd been in so many fights, done so much physical and emotional damage..."

"But he was going on new medication. And he

said he'd keep taking this one." She raised her chin. "It could have helped."

"If he hadn't hit a teacher, I might have agreed."

Lacey stiffened at the mention of Jerry Bosco. "Tell me you honestly believe everything Bosco said."

Seth frowned. He'd always prided himself on being a teacher advocate, especially since he'd had the experience of not being supported by an administrator in the past. And buried deep was the knowledge that *that* experience made him take a harder line with all students. "I...I'm not sure. Bosco had bruises. He testified that Kevin had given them to him. I felt then I had no choice."

"And now?"

"I guess I've learned there's always a choice." When she didn't say anything, he added, "Which is why I feel guilty..."

"What do you feel guilty about, Dad?"

Seth stiffened. Joey knew a little about Kevin Cartwright, but was unaware of Seth's doubts. That Lacey Cartwright could tarnish him in Joey's eyes unnerved him.

When Seth didn't respond, Lacey looked up at his son. "My brother, Kevin. He got in trouble and your dad feels bad he couldn't help him."

Joey shook his head. "That's Dad. He thinks he can save everybody. Fix everything." Joey scowled again just like Seth. "I'm sorry about your brother, though." He glanced from Lacey to Seth then back to Lacey again. "Do you blame Dad?"

The color drained from Lacey's face. The phone rang, and Joey cocked his head at the fact that she hadn't answered his question. When she still didn't respond, he went to get the call. Into the receiver, he said, "Yeah...oh, hi, Bill. Yeah, I talked to her. You what? Just a minute." Joey looked at his father. "Hang up for me when I get to my room, will ya, Dad? It's Bill. He wants me to call Sally to go sledding, and he'll come, too. It's an excuse to see her." He smiled at Lacey. "Sounds like a soap opera, doesn't it?"

She grinned. "'As the World Turns' in Bayview."

He rolled his eyes again and left.

Alone, the room seemed smaller to Seth. Neither he nor Lacey picked up the conversation about Kevin. When the clock chimed eight, he asked, "You hungry?"

"Yes, a little."

"I've got some soup simmering. Sound good?"

Lacey smiled and his heart rate stumbled. "Yes, it does."

She followed him to the kitchen to help. This room was also paneled in cedar, and Seth had painted the planks a soft beige and stained the wood a natural blond around the many windows. Copper pots and pans hung over a work island, and plants were scattered around the room.

"I love your home," she said again as they carried bowls into the living room.

"It's my haven."

"I haven't been in a house like this in California."

Seth watched her as they ate in front of the fireplace. "Do you miss it?"

She cocked her head and stared at the fire. "I miss the people. I miss the gritty stories. But, truthfully, I like being the boss. I get to pick and choose what I cover at the *Herald.*"

"I like being the boss, too."

"I just wish I knew more people here."

"Linc McKenna seemed pretty interested in getting to know you."

"He did?"

Seth nodded, sorry he'd brought it up. "Yeah. You'll do just fine."

"It takes a while to get back in the groove, I guess." She patted her mouth with a napkin then smiled at him.

Her lips were full and a little pouty and Seth's gaze was drawn to them. "A lot of women wouldn't do what you did—coming back here when Philip had his heart attack. I admire you."

She shrugged. "Family is important to me. Loyalty is a priority." She inclined her head across the room at the photos she'd seen on the bookshelf. "Your family?"

"Yes. My mother and two younger sisters. After my dad died, I was raised in a houseful of women."

"My mom died when I was ten. I was raised in a houseful of men."

Suddenly, the intimacy of the confidences was too much for Seth. He glanced up the stairs, wishing Joey would come back.

He was all too aware of what he was feeling for this woman, aware that to resist her tonight he'd need the strength of that superhero they'd been joking about. He stood abruptly. "I'll clean up," he said, his voice more curt than he intended.

Her eyes widened at his tone. "I'll help."

"No, stay where you are."

Lacey frowned as he left the room. He was anxious to get away from her. She knew why. They'd shared too much in the two hours she'd been here. Any emotional connection with him was stupid. Understanding him would lead to pain and frustration.

And acting on the physical attraction she'd felt curling inside her was out of the question. It didn't matter that she found him appealing, or respected his skills as a father or admired his loyalty to his family. And she couldn't give a zip that he loved running as much as she did.

Nothing in this world could make it okay to give in to this attraction to Seth Taylor. Her grandfather's beliefs precluded it. More than that, though, the hurt in Philip's eyes whenever she mentioned Seth in a positive light, or even the good things about the school, made these feelings she had for Seth absolutely taboo.

She glanced out at the snow, which had indeed let up. She needed to go, get home and forget all about spending a few cozy hours in this man's house.

Seth returned just as Joey came down the stairs. He was dressed in heavy clothing and headed for the closet. "We're going sledding out back, Dad." He pulled on a heavy parka, gloves and a hat. "The kids should be here any minute."

Headlights shone on the front of the house.

"Dad? Okay?"

"Sure. Just be careful. The pond isn't quite frozen yet. Stay away from it."

"I will. I'll turn all the outside lights on, too." Joey faced Lacey. "Nice to meet you. Thanks for your help."

"Anytime."

After Joey left, Lacey stood up and said, "I'm leaving, too."

"You are?"

"Yes, I think I'd better."

After a long and meaningful pause, he nodded. "Maybe you should."

As Seth followed her to the front door, they heard the kids greet each other outside and then it got quiet as the group made their way to the back.

Lacey bent down, fumbled for her boots and tugged them on. When she straightened, Seth was holding her coat open for her. She avoided his eyes and turned her back to him. She slid her arms into the sleeves; she was so close to him that she could smell his woodsy cologne again. *Please, God,* she prayed. *Let me get out of here before I do something stupid.*

She yanked the parka around her and heard Seth say, "Your hair's caught. Let me fix it."

Warm smooth fingers slid inside her collar and lifted her hair. Her neck felt cool, bare of its natural covering. When he didn't release her hair, Lacey held her breath.

Then she felt it. Just the light brush of lips, butterfly-soft and kitten-smooth on her nape. Then nothing. Then his mouth found her neck, just below her ear. "Lacey…" His voice was a harsh whisper.

She knew she should pull away. Instead, she sank back against him.

His hands gripped her arms. He kissed her neck, then hesitated before he sucked gently on her skin. Her body tingled with the caress, and she bit her lip to keep from saying anything. But a moan escaped from deep inside.

"Turn around, Lace."

She shook her head.

"Please."

Swallowing hard, she begged for strength, for deliverance from the rush of feeling for this man who held her so tenderly.

It didn't come. Slowly, she pivoted to him.

His face was ravaged with need, with sadness, with the same knowledge she possessed—that this was wrong, so, so wrong.

But his eyes stayed locked with hers as he slid his hands inside her coat…beneath her sweater… under her T-shirt to her rib cage. He caressed her now-burning skin. She gasped and leaned into him. Tilting her chin, she stared at his mouth, craving to feel it on hers.

He lowered his head.

She thought his kiss would be gentle and tender, like everything else he did. But it wasn't. His mouth covered hers hungrily as he crushed her to him. His lips pressed into hers, claiming them as his own. He widened his stance and pulled her even closer. She stood on tiptoe so she could meet him more fully. His hands slid to her back and up over her bra.

She fit him perfectly, Seth thought as his need for her raged out of control; he was powerless to stop it. She made his senses swim—the feel of her silky skin against his hands, the smell of a subtle, sexy perfume on her neck, the sweet, sweet taste of her mouth. His tongue traced the soft fullness of her lips, demanded entry and then explored her fully. He let his hands roam freely over her back, down to her soft full bottom. The intimate touch sent shock waves through his body.

After exquisite moments of kissing her—and on the verge of succumbing to the intense passion spiraling within him—he let her mouth go but held her close and buried his face in her neck again.

It was only then that she pulled away. And, God help him, he knew why. She'd remembered who they were, what they meant to each other.

He stepped back. The color had drained from her cheeks. Slowly she raised her hand and touched her lips. It was the horror in her eyes that wounded him the most.

"We...I...oh, God, we can't do this, Seth."

He swallowed hard, ready to protest the unthinkable. Except that she was right.

It would kill her grandfather.

She didn't have to say the words. They both knew the truth.

Which was why he stepped farther back, saying softly, "I know."

Which was why he let her tear herself out of his arms, fling open the door and rush into the night.

CHAPTER SEVEN

Lacey stood on the roof of Barker Island Prison, the strong arms of her own, personal superhero surrounding her.

"We'll be inside in a minute, Ace," he said, nuzzling her. He kissed her neck softly, then hesitated before he sucked gently on her skin; she closed her eyes to savor the woodsy smell of his cologne.

Then he took her hand in his, strode to the edge of the roof and jumped a few feet to the ledge below. She went with him. His slate blue eyes were serious as he said, "We'll have him out in no time. I made a mistake and now I'm correcting it."

Her brother was going to be free, all because of this man, who now placed his hands on the steel bars and yanked them apart. In no time, they were inside.

It took her a minute to adjust to the dimness. They were in Kevin's cell. It was barren and smelled faintly of disinfectant. Across the room, her brother slept on the narrow bunk.

Lacey walked over and shook his shoulder gently. Kevin hated to be awakened abruptly. "Kev, it's me." She brushed her hand over his baby-soft hair. "Come on, we're getting you out of here."

His beautiful brown eyes opened slowly, focusing on her. Then he smiled. "I knew you'd come, Lacey. I knew you'd fix this, too."

She took his hand and helped him up from the bunk. They turned toward their savior.

But instead, Seth Taylor stood there, dressed in a navy blue suit, with the superhero jersey underneath.

"I...I don't understand," Lacey said.

Kevin threw off her arm. "What the hell is he doing here?" He turned accusing eyes on Lacey. "Lace, why'd you bring him? He put me in here."

Lacey stared at Seth. "I...I..."

"How could you do this to me...? I don't ever want to see you again, Lacey. Don't come back..."

"No...no, Kevin, please...Kevin..."

Her brother stepped backward into the darkness and began to disappear.

"Kevin..."

"Lace," Seth said. "Turn around..."

She shook her head, her back to Seth.

"Please..."

Still she stared into the darkness, where Kevin had been. "Kevin," she whimpered. "Kevin..."

LACEY AWOKE bathed in sweat, sitting up in her bed, shaking. She gasped for breath and looked around the room. Instead of the grim walls and bare facilities of Barker Island Prison, she was in her own bedroom, decorated exactly as it was when she left home years ago. She scanned the room again, just to be sure. The four-poster bed and matching bureaus were in place, her beloved Impressionist prints hung on the cream-colored walls, her desk nestled in the corner.

She sat back into the pillows. It had all been a dream. *Thank God.* She glanced at the clock: 5:00 a.m. Wearily she rubbed her eyes to stop the nightmare's images, but then she remembered last evening.

Raising her hand to her mouth, she recalled in vivid detail the solid pressure of Seth's lips on hers. How his tongue had caressed hers. She whimpered in the darkness and sank into the mattress, drawing the covers up tightly. She felt like a little girl again, cowering in her bed. How many times had her grandfather come to chase away the demons?

That's it, she told herself, think about Grandpa.

But she couldn't completely forget last night. She could feel Seth's hands sliding into her coat, under her sweater, beneath the T-shirt. They were big and warm and she'd wanted them all over her. She wanted Seth's touch right now. He'd tug off her UCLA nightshirt, run his hands across her bare skin, then his mouth, then...

''No,'' she moaned and whipped off the covers.

The chill of the early-morning air brought goose bumps to her arms. It sobered her. Quickly, running from the fantasy, she sprang out of bed and hurried into the bathroom. Then she found her robe and slippers and strode downstairs. Grandpa was still away so she didn't have to worry about waking him.

She'd feel better, more in control, after she had coffee. It was still dark out, she realized when she reached the living room. Distracted, she went over to turn on a small lamp beside the telephone.

The red light on the answering machine blinked. She hadn't checked for messages last night. She'd been so upset when she'd returned from Seth's, she'd raced into the house, upstairs, and into bed without thinking someone might need her.

She pressed the button. "Hi, honey, it's Grandpa. I wondered if you were all right. I tried the paper, too. I hope you've had a nice evening. Leonard and I are playing chess and reminiscing about old times." There was a pause. "I love you, Lacey. Take care of yourself."

Lacey closed her eyes to stifle the guilt. Philip sounded wary, and his voice shook. Their confrontation over Seth had been hard for him, and it hurt Lacey to know she'd caused him pain. What would Philip think if he knew she'd been at Seth's, in his arms, kissing him?

The second message started. "Lace, it's me, Kevin. Where the hell are you? I thought we agreed I'd call at seven on Friday." Another sin she'd committed. She'd forgotten that when he couldn't get her on the phone last week, they'd made this arrangement. "Geez, I hope you're not mad at me because I wouldn't see you. I...I'm sorry about that. It was stupid. Will you come up here Wednesday? I'll see you then."

The last message took her by surprise. "Hi, Lacey. This is Linc McKenna. I, um, wondered if you'd like to go out tomorrow night. The new theater in town is showing all those movies.'' Hesitation, then his deep voice came back. "I'd…like to get to know you better, and thought…um, boy, I hate these machines. Call me. My number is…''

Linc McKenna seemed pretty interested in getting to know you, Seth had told her.

Furious with her inability to get Seth out of her mind, she stood. She had to forget him, forget the kiss, forget how right his arms felt around her.

She *would.* She glanced at the clock. It was too early to call Linc back, but she'd do it as soon as she could. She'd go out with Linc McKenna, maybe let him kiss her.

Staring at the answering machine, she vowed she'd do whatever it took to forget about last night. And what it felt like to be in Seth's arms. For her grandfather's sake. For Kevin's. For them all.

MOVIETOWN, the new theater complex, was crowded with high-school students, kids home from college and adults in a holiday mood. It was the talk of the town with its stadium seating, eight screens and fast-food restaurants inside the building.

Lacey preceded Linc into the huge foyer, determined to enjoy herself. The traditional smell of popcorn pervaded the area and the sound of people bustling to their seats or getting refreshments was familiar.

"Hungry?'' Linc asked as he took her elbow.

"I wouldn't mind some chocolate,'' she said. *Chocolate would help.*

"What kind?"

"Doesn't matter. Just so long as it's chocolate."

He grinned at her. "Wait here, I'll be right back."

Lacey leaned against a glittery silver post watching him thread his way through the crowd. Linc was a nice man, interesting and attractive if you liked dark hair, dark eyes and the body of a weight lifter. Lacey struggled not to let herself speculate on a long, lean runner's body. She turned to stare at a poster of Andy Garcia.

"Lacey?"

She startled at Seth's voice.

"What a coincidence." This was from Joey.

Numbly, Lacey turned, her body braced as if for attack. "Hello, Joey," she managed to say. She faced Seth. "Hi."

His eyes looked sad. They roamed her face... hungrily.

"Which movie are you seeing?" Joey asked.

Tearing her gaze away from Seth, Lacey had to think, movie, which movie? "Oh, the George Clooney film."

"Us, too."

Seth still hadn't said more than her name. But he looked her up and down, noting her tailored khaki pants and the soft maroon turtleneck under her coat. The coat he'd slipped his hands into.

Linc returned, laden with boxes of candy. "Oh, hi guys."

"Hi. Mr. McKenna," Joey said enthusiastically, extending his hand. "Nice to see you again."

"You too, Joe. How's school?"

"Terrific." He glanced at the candy. "Looks like you're hungry."

Linc smiled at Lacey. "I bought a lot because I didn't know which kind you liked."

Woodenly she smiled back; out of the corner of her eye, she saw Seth's jaw tighten.

"Well, I'd ask you guys to sit with us," Linc said good-naturedly, sliding his arm round her, "but I finally got Lacey to myself and I don't want to share her."

Seth stared hard at Linc's hand caressing her shoulder.

Joey laughed.

Seth didn't. Instead, he turned his piercing blue eyes on Lacey. Now they were snapping with anger. "Enjoy the show." His words were clipped, curt.

Lacey only nodded.

Seth tried to calm himself all the way to his seat. Once there, he tried not to look for Lacey and Linc, but he devoured the sight of her when the two came into the theater. Thank God they sat behind him and he didn't have to watch McKenna touch her all night.

Seth could still summon the feel of her under *his* hands, *his* lips. He could still smell her, taste her...

He'd had a rough twenty-four hours. After Lacey left, he'd gotten in his car and followed her at a distance to make sure she made the trip safely.

She did.

Then when he'd returned home, he'd prowled the house, upset and angry and more frustrated than he'd been in his whole life. Turning in early had been a mistake. He'd torn the covers off the bed thinking about her.

He hadn't slept long enough to dream, thank God. But he'd gone running at the school this morning, hoping she'd be there. She wasn't.

"Dad? Don't you think so?"

Preoccupied, he'd missed his son's question. "What?"

"That Mr. McKenna and Ms. Cartwright make a cute couple?"

Seth swallowed his first reaction, which was a word Seth had taught Joey never to use. "Sure, I guess."

"He's a neat guy. All the kids think he's the best guidance counselor in the school. Does he still coach the track team?"

"Yes." Seth had forgotten that tidbit.

"The girls were always drooling over him. Some of them went out for track just because…"

The lights dimmed.

"Shh," Seth said abruptly.

He was grateful when the previews began so he wouldn't have to hear any more McKenna accolades. He sat through two coming attractions, staring blindly at the screen. But when the third preview came on, he paid attention. And felt his gut twist. A new superhero movie was due out this summer. On the screen, a blond woman—strongly resembling Lacey—embraced the hero.

In his peripheral vision, Seth saw someone hurrying down the stairs, going out into the lobby. Lacey. He watched her for all of twenty seconds, then leaned over and said to his son, "I'll be right back. I'm going to the men's room."

He caught up with her just as she reached the door to the ladies' room. He grabbed her arm before she could go inside. "Wait, Lacey..."

She whirled, then jerked her arm. "Let me go."

"I can't."

"Hey, Mr. Taylor," someone called from behind him.

Releasing Lacey, Seth turned to find that three Bayview Heights students had come up to him. "Oh, hi, Jack, Suzy, Patty." He made some small talk, trying desperately to think of a way to get Lacey alone.

There was a corridor to his right. As soon as the kids left, he practically dragged her down it. A deserted nook gave him hope that he might be able to talk to her privately.

She didn't say anything, just leaned against the wall and closed her eyes.

Remembering how McKenna had touched her, Seth felt jealousy stab through him once again. "Twenty-four hours ago, you came apart in my arms," he told her, unable to stifle the fury and hurt he felt. "How could you go out with some other man tonight?"

Opening her eyes, she stared at him with such anguish that he cursed his knee-jerk reaction. She raised her hand to his mouth and brushed her fingers across it. "It's *because* I came apart in your arms, Seth."

At her touch, and her words, his heart trip-hammered in his chest. He said recklessly, "Maybe there's a way...maybe we can..."

Staring at him with the bleakest eyes he'd ever seen, she drew back her hand. "No, there's no way. Please, Seth, don't do this." Her lips trembled. "There is *no* way."

He swallowed hard, knowing he had to make this easier for her somehow. She was hurting badly, and he needed to make the pain stop. So he drew back, too, and took a deep breath. "You're right. I've got to accept that." He glanced up at the ceiling, then back to her. "But I can't bear the thought of you with...of him... Just promise me you won't let him touch you. Not tonight, at least. I'll go crazy thinking of—" his gaze dropped to her lips "—you, with him..."

She shook her head, sending golden waves around her face, onto her shoulders. "No, I won't promise you anything. We can't make promises like that. This connection between us has to stop."

She tried to sidle around him. When he grasped her arm, she said, "Let me go, Seth. For good."

The desperation in her voice halted his protest. He stepped back. "You're right. I'm sorry. I'll let you go."

As she walked away, he vowed to himself, *I'll do it, too, even if it kills me. I can't cause her—that family—any more pain. I just can't.*

SETH FELT he had a handle on things until he stood in the doorway of the Franklin Street Day Care toddler room on Monday afternoon and saw Lacey with Josh. The boy had just fallen off the jungle gym.

Lacey knelt down and dragged Josh onto her lap, cooing to him. Dressed in a soft grass green sweater and skirt, with a flowered scarf, she looked feminine and fragile again.

"Shh, sweetheart, it's okay. Just a little scrape." Slowly, she rubbed Josh's arm.

"Lacey's great with him, isn't she?" Mary Jarrett had come up next to Seth.

Jamming his hands into his pockets, Seth nodded to the day-care director. "Yeah."

"Do you know her very well?"

"Well enough. Why?"

Mary motioned Seth out into the corridor. Lacey and Josh were still in his line of vision.

"She's been here three times since last Monday."

Surprised, Seth faced Mary. "Really? Why?"

"Well, a few days after you were here together, she came back on business for the paper—or so she said. She wants to do an article on us for the *Herald*."

"That would be good, wouldn't it?"

"Yeah, sure. But I think she really came to see Josh. She asked if it would be all right if she spent some time with him, then when she left, she asked if she could come back."

Seth smiled at the pair he and Mary were watching. Josh grabbed Lacey's scarf and draped it over her head like a veil. The boy babbled, "Ace, Ace..." She laughed aloud as she peeked out from under the scarf. The sound went straight to Seth's groin. "Isn't it all right if she visits him?" he asked.

"I'm not sure."

"What do you mean?"

"Josh is here temporarily. His grandmother has custody of him. Apparently his mother died in a car crash out in Oklahoma, and the father is unknown. The baby was shipped back here because there were no other relatives."

"The poor kid."

"It gets worse. Mrs. Cornwall is seventy, and she recently fell and hurt her hip. Now she can't take care of Josh by herself, which is why he's in day care. The county's providing some help at night. As soon as they find someone to take him, he's going into foster care."

Seth frowned, studying Lacey. She stood gracefully, picked up Josh and headed for the paint table. "I'm afraid that happens all too often these days," he said. "I deal with foster-care agencies all the time."

"Well, then you know chances are he won't stay in Bayview Heights. There just isn't much good foster care here."

He turned to Mary. "And?"

"I don't want Ms. Cartwright or Josh to get too attached, Seth. It's not good for either of them."

His eyes narrowed, Seth watched Lacey guide Josh's hands as he dipped them in finger paint. She seemed unconcerned about the expensive outfit she wore, though she'd taken the time to fit Josh into a smock.

"I see your point, Mary." *It's not good to get too attached to someone you can't have.* He took a deep breath. "I'll talk to her."

"LET'S WRAP THINGS UP before we leave." His suit coat off, his tie loosened, his white shirt accenting the breadth of his shoulders, Seth looked exhausted, but so sexy, Lacey felt her reaction to him straight to her toes—and other parts of her body.

"Tonight we reached consensus on these plans." He pointed to the chalkboard. "First, the community committee will investigate getting speakers for special assemblies on aggression and stress. They'll also get some recommendations for youth-services workshops to be given at the high school on an ongoing basis. Finally, they'll determine what programs are available to parents who have trouble controlling their own aggression. The faculty committee will explore how to approach the staff about being more visible in problem areas of the school until we can get additional monitors and security. They'll also look at developing curriculum for all classes on anger control, problem solving and conflict resolution."

Bosco sat forward, scowling. "I didn't agree to the last point, so you don't have consensus. I won't teach any of those things in biology class."

Lacey could see Seth's temper rise. When had she come to know that the slight tensing of his jaw and a telltale flush on his neck meant he was very angry?

She faced the teacher. "I thought we were talking about what we've decided to *investigate,* Mr. Bosco," she said calmly. "It was my impression the faculty would determine as a group which options are viable. We're going to get more information on these ideas and *approach* the faculty."

"It wasn't a concensus." Bosco's face flushed and his tone was whiny.

''We're quibbling over words,'' Mitch said. ''Let's finish up here.''

Seth turned back to the board. ''The student subcommittee will work out a plan for setting up anger control groups, Helping Hands groups and a student court to go along with our current peer mediation program.'' He looked at the school psychologist, Barbara Sherman, and Linc McKenna. ''You two will work with us on that.'' Lacey detected no trace of the animosity he seemed to feel toward Linc two nights ago.

''That about wraps it up,'' Seth said. ''We'll meet once more in subcommittees to solidify these plans, present them to the whole task force and then formulate a report right on schedule—just in time for Christmas.'' He scanned the room. ''Any questions?''

When there were none, he smiled. ''Thanks for all the work you've done. I think we've really got something here. See you all two weeks from now. I'd like to meet with my committee and Barbara and Linc for a minute.''

Everyone else filed out and Lacey glimpsed Monica Matthews trying to catch Seth's eye. She didn't. Instead, he focused on the group gathered before him. Lacey noticed Nick sidle in close to Darcy. The girl stepped away from him immediately.

''Can everybody meet here next Monday night at seven to flesh out our recommendations?'' Seth asked them.

The two other adults and the kids nodded. He looked to Lacey. ''Fine.''

''All right, see you then.''

"Can I use your phone, Mr. T.?" Darcy asked. "I've got to call for a ride."

Nick said, "I'll drop you off, Darcy."

The young girl whirled on him. Lacey braced herself, thinking Darcy would give the boy a setdown that he didn't deserve. Instead she gave him a wide-eyed look and said, "For real?"

"I don't bite," Nick joked.

"Yeah, that's not what all the girls say."

"Been talkin' about me, McCormick?"

"Not on your life, Leonardi. But, yeah, I'll take the ride."

As the teenagers trailed out, Lacey stared after them. "What was that all about?"

Seth laughed. "East meets west, I think."

Linc McKenna said, "I'll walk you out, Lacey."

"I'd like to talk to Lacey for a minute," Seth interjected smoothly.

Lacey quelled the urge to close her eyes and sigh. God, she was tired, and not up for a confrontation with Seth.

Liar. You'd like nothing more than a few minutes alone with him. You've been cataloging everything about him tonight, right down to the color of his socks.

"You can walk me out, Linc," Barbara said, breaking the tension. "I want to talk to you anyway."

When Linc and Barbara left, Lacey sank onto a chair.

"Want some coffee?" Seth asked. "You don't look like you've got enough energy to drive home."

Lacey blew out a frustrated breath. "I'm

whipped. But coffee would be a mistake. I haven't been sleeping well since we—" Lacey broke off, realizing what she'd admitted.

Dropping down next to her, Seth stretched out in the chair. His head back, he rubbed the bridge of his nose then looked at her. "Me, neither." Mirrored in his eyes Lacey saw all the conflict and doubt she felt.

And the loneliness.

"Joey's gone back to school?"

If possible his eyes got bleaker. "Yeah."

"He called me Sunday."

"I know. I'm sorry, Lace. I didn't know what to tell him. I'm sure you don't want him at the paper for a month over his school break, but I couldn't come up with an excuse to give him."

"I'm going to hire him," she said simply.

"Why? I thought you wouldn't want him around because…"

"It won't matter. I can't stop thinking about you anyway. Having him at the paper isn't going to make that worse."

"I meant—" He stopped midsentence. "You can't stop thinking about me?"

Lacey wanted to cry at the pleased look on his face. "I shouldn't have said that. Admissions like that won't help us." She sat up straighter. "What did you want to talk to me about?"

At first, his gaze narrowed on her and she feared he wasn't going to let her slip go. Then he said, "Josh."

"Josh? From the day care?"

Seth nodded. "Mary told me you've been visiting him frequently."

"Is that a problem?"

"Only because I don't want to see you get hurt."

She bit her lip to keep from telling him it was too late. "I don't understand."

Seth told her about Josh's situation.

"Poor little thing." She frowned. "Point taken, though. He shouldn't get too attached to me, especially if he'll be leaving soon."

"You, too."

"What do you mean?"

"How long are you going to stay in Bayview Heights?"

"I don't know, Seth. I'm not sure I can stay here...now." It hit her with stunning force as she said the words aloud. She was attracted to this man. She didn't love him. Yet. But in just a few short weeks she'd come to like and respect him enough to know there was danger here. Perhaps the kindest thing she could do for them all—especially her grandfather—was to leave Bayview Heights before anything irrevocable happened.

Seth leaned toward her and reached out. She thought he was going to touch her, but he drew back his hand before it made contact. "I know what you mean." He waited long seconds before he added, "If it makes any difference, I have an interview this Friday for a job in Albany."

Lacey felt her stomach knot painfully. Was he giving up everything he loved because of *her?* Then she remembered Cassie's comment at The Spaghetti House. *Seth's been in a funk lately. I think it's a*

midlife crisis, teacher burnout combination.
"You're thinking about leaving Bayview?"

"Yes. There's a job open at State Ed."

She stared at him.

"So, if your leaving Bayview has anything to do with me...what I mean is, you don't have to give up your family because I'm here. I might be gone."

"How soon?"

"Could be as early as the first of the year."

"I see." Seth. Leaving Bayview. The rest of Cassie's words came back. *I want to do something special for him, something to show all the good he's done at the high school.* Lacey forced herself to meet his eyes. "Well, for what it's worth, I think leaving the high school would be a crime. You've done wonderful things at Bayview, Seth. They need you here."

His chiseled jaw dropped. "I can't believe I'm hearing this. From you."

"Believe it. These last few weeks I've seen your influence on the kids. Maybe you made a mistake with Kevin, maybe you didn't." She waved her hand around the room. "And judging from this committee, I can tell how hard it is to run this place. To juggle everybody's needs. You do a good job."

Without warning, he stood, and this time when he reached for her, he didn't stop himself. He drew her out of the chair. And God help her, she couldn't resist. He pulled her into a tender hug that brought the threat of tears.

"Do you know how much it means to me to hear you say that?" he whispered hoarsely in her ear, his arms encircling her.

Briefly, she let herself sink into him, burrow into his chest, smell him, feel his muscles tense against her. Then she stepped away, and out of his arms. "It's all true. If nothing else, I want you to know that."

Before she changed her mind and threw herself back into his strong, safe embrace, she turned and fled the office.

LACEY WATCHED Cassie playfully slap Johnny Battaglia's hand away. "Don't open that, kiddo. The mother-to-be gets to unwrap *all* the presents."

Sitting on the floor next to her, Johnny pouted as he handed over a brightly wrapped package. But his dark eyes were shining with warmth. "Geez, I can't even do one? You've already opened at least a thousand."

His exaggeration was well founded. The huge living room of Zoe Caufield's condo was packed with the friends, students, colleagues and relatives of Cassie and Mitch Lansing for a mixed-gender baby shower. Lacey swallowed hard, thinking of how nice a life her friend had made for herself.

Cassie wore a long denim shirt, maternity jeans and black boots. Her hair hung loosely around her face—which glowed. She looked a lot more rested than she had yesterday afternoon at the *Herald*.

When Cassie had entered the office, Lacey was immediately alarmed...

"Cass, what's the matter?"

"I came to go through the microfilm of the old newspapers."

"You look upset."

Dragging a hand through her hair, Cassie sank onto a chair. Lacey was astounded to see tears in her friend's eyes. She sat down and took Cassie's hand. "Honey, what is it?"

Swiping impatiently at her face, Cassie said, "Nothing. I told you before, I cry at the drop of a hat these days. All pregnant women do."

"Still, it's so unlike you. Something must have brought it on."

"It's stupid."

"Tell me."

"Mitch and I had a fight."

Lacey bit her tongue to keep from laughing. The old Cassie would have flown into a rage at him instead of being reduced to tears. "About what?"

"He doesn't want me to do this search for Seth's students. He says it's ridiculous to spend so much time and energy hunting down old newspapers to find something that may or may not have been printed about Seth and the people he helped." She sniffled.

"Maybe he's right." Lacey sat back, uncomfortable. She had all the information Cassie needed in the computer that hummed behind her.

"Maybe. But I don't care. I need to do something. Seth finally told me he *is* thinking about leaving Bayview. I can't let him go without taking a shot at keeping him here." She closed her eyes. "But Mitch yelled at me. He's really mad."

"He *yelled* at you?"

Cassie gave her a weak grin. "Well, he raised his voice some."

Lacey laughed.

Cassie sniffled again. "I don't know what to do."

Lacey had shrugged at the fates, turned to her computer, copied the private investigator's file about Seth's accomplishments onto a disk and swore Cassie to secrecy about where she'd gotten the information, except for Mitch, of course...

Now, watching Cassie lean into her husband and whisper something in his ear, Lacey was glad she'd given her friend the disk. Forcibly she quelled the sharp pang of guilt she felt. What she'd done was clearly a betrayal of her grandfather's trust. But she'd done it for Cassie. Lacey's gaze strayed across the room. And for the man who sat next to Darcy McCormick smiling broadly as Cassie opened gifts.

Seth was contemplating leaving Bayview Heights High School because he'd lost sight of the good he'd done there. Well, at least she could give him tangible proof of what he'd accomplished. If she couldn't give him anything else.

She looked back at Cassie. A lump formed in Lacey's throat as Cassie held up a tiny white cotton undershirt. It was so small, so delicate, and elicited such a big swell of wistfulness in Lacey that she had to move. Spying an enclosed porch off the back of the house, she slipped out of the room. Cassie was just about done with presents, anyway.

Minutes later, Lacey was staring at the bay, when she heard the sliding doors swish open behind her. Turning, she saw Mitch standing just inside the room, his hands stuck in his tan wool slacks, his forest green sweater making him appear even bigger and more intimidating than ever.

"Are you all right?" His voice was gentle.

"Of course."

"Can I talk to you a minute?"

"Sure."

He walked closer and instead of saying anything, stared out at the bay. Finally, he looked at her. "Cassie told me about the disk."

"I said she could. But no one else is to know, Mitch."

"I won't say anything. First, thanks for giving it to Cass. I couldn't stop her from wearing herself out over this."

Lacey saw a flash of pain in his eyes. What would it be like to have a man care about you so much that he'd hurt over a silly little fight?

"But I've got to say it doesn't sit right with me that your grandfather had Seth investigated."

She swallowed hard. "It doesn't sit right with me, either, Mitch. But it's not against the law."

"I was talking as Seth's friend, not as a cop."

"I'm glad he has good friends like you."

Mitch cocked his head and studied her. "Lacey, Seth's a good man. He cares deeply about people."

"I know." She cleared the emotion from her throat. "You don't have to convince me of that."

Slowly he nodded. "I see." Lacey was very afraid that he did. He added, "Is there anything I can do?"

She shook her head, willing herself not to cry at his kindness. The door opened again. Seth stepped onto the porch carrying a sweater in his hand. His forehead creased as he glanced from Mitch to Lacey. "Zoe saw you come out here. She sent me with this. It's cold."

Mitch looked at Lacey, then turned, clapped Seth on the back and left.

"Did I interrupt something?"

"No."

She was lying, he could tell by the way she wouldn't look at him. He crossed the room to her. "Here." Reaching out, he circled her shoulders with Zoe's sweater. It covered the silk jewel-necked blouse she wore. Tugging the wool around her, he closed the top button under her chin. His fingers grazed her throat and his palms rested on her chest. He knew he should remove his hands—the touch was intimate—but instead, he flattened them out and caressed her. When he felt her sharp intake of breath, he leaned over and kissed her forehead.

For his own sake, and hers, he stepped back.

He examined her face for a few seconds, then angled his head into the living room. "Coming to this shower was hard for you, wasn't it?"

"How did you know?"

"I haven't been able to take my eyes off you."

Her look was so sad he wanted to hold her against his heart and tell her everything would be all right.

"Seth—"

"And, from the few hints you've dropped, and watching you with Josh, I can tell how much you want kids."

She just nodded.

"You'll have a family someday, Lace." The knowledge that it would be with some other man ripped him apart. "Really. You've got so much to give…"

She turned her back on him. "Please, Seth, don't."

Placing his hands on her shoulders, he kissed the top of her head. "All right. I'll go in now. Don't stay out here too long. It's cold, even with the sweater."

Pivoting, he made himself leave the porch. He knew if he looked back and she was crying, no force on earth could keep him from her.

CHAPTER EIGHT

"ADAMS PRIVATE INVESTIGATION."

"Mr. Adams, this is Philip Cartwright."

"Mr. Cartwright. I was just about to call you." Herb Adams, the private investigator Philip had hired two years ago to get something on Taylor, had a deceptively mellow voice. He was as ruthless as they came.

"Have you found something?"

"Not yet. It's taken me a few days to review the facts. I'd shelved this case after your heart attack."

"Understandable."

"I think the best tactic now is to go back for the details of Taylor's college days and his early years of teaching. As a matter of fact, next week I'm taking a trip to Binghamton where he grew up, to find out more about what he did before he came to Bayview Heights."

"You never delved into that period much."

"No, you had the heart attack before I could. Then we tabled everything."

"Well, as I said last week, I'm ready to go ahead again."

"Fine."

"I want to bury Taylor, Mr. Adams."

"I understand. If there's any dirt on him, I'll find it. I'll be in touch."

Philip clicked off the phone and dropped onto the chair in his den.

Scowling, he tapped his fingers on Wednesday's edition of the paper. This week's School Page editorial was a sin. It detailed how each Christmas the students at the high school, in addition to supporting needy families, did a good deed for a member of the school itself. Once, they'd given a new wardrobe to a student whose family had lost everything in a fire. Another time, they'd provided plane tickets for a soldier—the brother of a Bayview Heights student—to come home to see his ailing father. Last year, they'd bought theater tickets to *Phantom of the Opera* for a custodian.

Leaning back into his worn chair, Philip admitted these *were* admirable things the students accomplished. But Lacey's column was making Taylor look good. Philip couldn't let this continue. Lacey shouldn't focus only on positive things. She needed to balance her pieces with what the *Herald* had become known for—hard-hitting, controversial editorials.

Before he could stop them, Celia's comments came back to him. "Face it, Philip. You're hurt that Lacey won't go along with you on this."

He'd denied it then, but after Celia had left, he'd been forced by his own sense of honesty to recognize the truth. He *was* hurt. How could Lacey side with his enemy? *Their* enemy. Her defense of Taylor and his school was the worst kind of defection.

The thought hit him out of nowhere. *Something's going on between Taylor and Lacey.*

"No!" Philip said aloud and slapped his hand on the desk. She'd never do that. She'd never turn against her family like that. She'd never betray him. This was the girl he'd raised and loved more than anything else in the world.

And as he'd done all those years, he'd take care of her now—even when she didn't think she needed it, even when she disagreed with him. He'd do what was best for her, as he always had. Picking up the paper, he knew just where to start.

He found her at the kitchen counter, a large bowl in one hand as she stirred with the other. Her face was smeared with chocolate. "Hi, honey." He sniffed. "Smells good."

"I was dying for some brownies." She smiled over at him. "Keep me company."

Philip harrumphed as he plunked down at the island counter. "You should be going out on a Friday night, not baking with an old man."

She glanced at him and smiled again. Underlying the gesture was a weariness too old for someone her age. "Kevin's calling. I wanted to be around for that."

"I'm worried about him."

"Me, too. He seemed so edgy Wednesday when I drove up there. I wonder what's going on."

Philip stared at her. "Prison's tough on a man, Lacey."

"I know."

"I wanted to talk to you about something."

As she scooped lumpy batter into a pan, she asked, "What?"

"Remember we discussed my getting back to the paper?"

"You could do some things, Grandpa, without *over*doing it."

"Well, I have an idea."

"Great." Wiping her hands on a towel, Lacey crossed to the oven, put the brownies in, then came to sit at the counter with him. "Where would you like to start?"

"With next week's School Page editorial."

Her look was blank. "What do you mean?"

"I'd like to write next week's editorial."

The color leeched from her face. The fluorescent light hummed overhead.

"Well?" he asked. "What do you think?"

Reaching out, she laid her hand over his. "Why do you want to do this, Grandpa?"

He didn't even consider lying. "I've made no secret of the fact that I'm not happy with your stance on school issues lately. I think I'm entitled to balance it with the other side."

"Why? I don't understand."

"Lacey, for some reason, you're not seeing things clearly. The high school has to be kept in line so more things like what happened to Kevin don't go on there."

"Good things are going on there."

"So are bad things. I'm wondering why you don't see that anymore."

She jutted out her chin. "I see that. I've just chosen to focus on the Christmas activities because it's the holiday and I think everyone wants good news now.''

Though he knew he was playing dirty, Philip used his ace. "You've watered down the paper." It was the ultimate insult to a newspaper reporter.

"What?"

"You've shied away from tackling real issues."

"I have not."

"I think you have." After a long silence, he asked, "Why? Is something going on I don't know about?"

"Like what?"

"Is there some reason you don't want the school to look bad?"

"No."

"You're sure?"

"Yes."

"Good, then I'm going to tackle a *real* issue for next week and get us back on track."

"And if I don't agree?"

Just then the phone rang. "Think long and hard, Lacey, about disagreeing. Especially while you're talking to your brother—" he angled his head to the phone "—who's going through unimaginable horrors in that hellhole." Philip got up to answer the call. Just before he picked up the receiver, he said, "Because of that school you're so enthralled with these days."

HER FEET POUNDING the hardwood floors of the Bayview Heights track only intensified Lacey's headache. The dull thud at her temples seemed to have taken up permanent residence. She'd done thirty laps and she knew she should stop, but she needed the outlet and couldn't make herself quit. She'd barely slept the night before after hearing Kevin's voice quake on the phone. "I'm scared, Lace. Don't tell Grandpa, but things have gotten worse in the last couple of days."

It seemed the opposing factions of Barker inmates were more at odds than usual. Somehow, Kevin had been caught in the middle. Because of his position in the laundry, he'd told her. Lacey guessed his temper and belligerent attitude hadn't helped, but he didn't admit that.

She ran faster as she thought about her grandfather.

Philip suspected that Lacey had feelings for Seth. She could see it in his eyes. And she knew nothing short of her caving in on the editorial would convince him otherwise. The problem was he was right. She had a whole range of feelings for Seth Taylor that she shouldn't have. Although she was valiantly resisting them, it was like putting out brushfires. She'd get herself under control and something would happen to ignite her feelings—her desire— all over again. Like his insight about wanting a baby. No one else—not even her best friend, Dani— had guessed how Lacey felt.

Dani—who'd called last night after Kevin with news...

"Lace, listen. Michaels is *leaving*. You've wanted his column for years. I'll bet you Scooper would jump at the chance to get you back..."

Suddenly exhausted, Lacey dropped to the track and buried her face in her hands. Her eyes were gritty and her lower back ached. She was so tired she couldn't think straight. Maybe she should go back to California. Maybe if she got far enough away from Seth, she'd stop remembering what his touch felt like on her shoulder, her arm, against her chest. She'd stop thinking about his lips brushing her hair, how seductive it was when he said, "Lace..." in a harsh whisper.

"You didn't get hurt again, did you?"

Lacey threw back her head and peered up into the very eyes she'd been trying to forget.

"No. I collapsed."

He dropped down next to her. "Rough night?"

She nodded, avoiding his gaze.

"What happened?" When she didn't answer, he added, "Or shouldn't I ask?"

"Meaning?"

"Were you with McKenna?"

Oh, God, how wrong could he be. "No. It's other things."

She braced her arms behind her back and stretched out her legs to ease the fatigue-induced cramping in her calf. "Things I don't want to talk about."

After a pause, he said, "All right."

"How was Albany?" she asked, hoping to change the subject. It felt good just to talk to him.

"Fine. They want me to come back for a second interview."

"Oh, great. I thought you might have stayed up there longer for some fun."

"Fun? What's that?"

They laughed.

His eyes twinkled. "No leaves to jump in this time of year."

"But you could have gone ice-skating."

"I might have, if you'd been with me."

The intimacy implied in the statement stalled the conversation. Finally Lacey said, "Well, I'd better go. I've got work to do today."

"It's Saturday."

I know, but if I don't keep my mind busy I'll go crazy. "Hey, news in the big city doesn't stop for the weekend," she joked.

Seth's grin made her nerve endings stand at attention. In that instant, all she wanted out of life was to keep that smile on his face. "Can't argue with you on that, Ace."

She stood and he rose, too. "What are *you* doing today?" she asked.

"Some work here, after my run. The Kris Kringle and soup kitchen activities get off the ground on Tuesday and I haven't had a chance to review their plans. Then I thought I'd do some Christmas shopping."

"Well, shopping sounds like fun. Enjoy it."

She was halfway across the gym when he called after her. "Lace." She stopped and pivoted to treat herself to one last look at him. "Try to have some fun today, too."

SHE WOULDN'T THOUGH, Seth knew as he began his laps around the track. She wouldn't have any fun today. He couldn't believe how utterly exhausted she looked. More than likely, worrying had interrupted her sleep. He'd bet his Phi Delta Kappa pin that her grandfather was giving her grief over the tack she'd taken with the school in her editorials. Rounding the curve, he wished like hell he could make things easier for her.

Who was he kidding? Everything he did made it harder for her. Worse, he'd developed feelings for her. Strong, deep feelings *in addition to* a very potent physical attraction. Thursday night, at the baby shower, he'd had to touch her. Right now, he felt a physical ache and an emotional longing just to be near her. He ran faster.

Three hours later, he was no better off. He'd done a hard five miles and taken a scalding shower, but it hadn't helped. He'd spent the last ninety minutes going over Alex's report on the rest of the Christmas projects. He checked the clock. Eleven-thirty. Maybe he'd drive into town and get some pizza for lunch. Then he could shop for Joey's Christmas presents. It might be fun.

Fun! Damn!

When he reached the pizza parlor ten minutes later, Monica Matthews also approached the door. "Well, what a coincidence." She leaned over and kissed his cheek. Seth was startled. He'd dated Monica a couple of times, and although she'd made it clear she wanted to take their relationship further, he'd backed off.

"Here for lunch, handsome?"

"Yes."

"Me, too." She grabbed his hand and dragged him into the restaurant. "Let's share."

Inside, they scanned the small interior. Booths were filled and the place was crowded with shoppers. The smell of spicy Italian sauce warmed him. "See, we can save on space," Monica joked.

What the hell? Seth thought.

Fifteen minutes later, they were sharing a large pizza with everything on it. Monica was good company, and very distracting, which was what Seth needed.

He was laughing aloud when Lacey walked in. She made it to the take-out counter before she spotted him. She started to smile, until she noticed Monica. For as long as he lived, Seth would never forget the look on her face. Shock. Disapproval. Jealousy. And, God help him, a part of him reveled in it.

After she paid for her pizza, Lacey stopped at their table.

"Hi, Seth, Monica."

"Lacey." Seth couldn't quell the huskiness in his own voice.

She'd changed into jeans that gave her pinup-girl legs a worthy showcase. Underneath her suede coat she wore the same sweater she'd had on the night he'd kissed her at his house. He took a long drink of soda and tried not to drool.

She made small talk with Monica for a minute.

"Still working?" Seth asked.

"Yes." She smiled, but the strain around her mouth and eyes remained. From the tension in her expression, he'd bet she had a headache.

"On Saturday?" Monica's question was rhetorical. "Really, dear, you should have some fun."

Her gaze flew to Seth.

"What'd I tell you?" he asked.

Instead of answering, Lacey shook her head. "Well, I'd better go. Nice to see you."

And she was gone.

Seth extricated himself from Monica as soon as he could. With Herculean effort, he resisted detouring to the *Herald* to explain how he'd come to be with Monica. "Not Lacey's business," he told himself. Twice, though, as he went from shop to shop, he noted that the lights were still on in the newspaper office. By four o'clock, he decided he'd head home. He'd make one stop at the shoe store and pick up the new running shoes he'd ordered and some boots Joey had been eyeing for months. Then he'd go home—dreading the emptiness he'd find there.

It was inside the store that he saw them. Pristine white leather with shiny aluminum blades. Skates worthy of Hans Brinker. Decorated with a bright red bow, they were displayed on the wall next to the window. Ignoring them, he crossed to the counter to get his sneakers and Joey's boots. While the clerk ducked into the storeroom, Seth wandered over to the skates again. From that vantage point, he could see the *Herald* well enough to know she was still there.

The skates beckoned.

She beckoned.

God, he'd thought he had more willpower than this.

LACEY TURNED OFF the computer she'd been glued to for almost two hours. She'd been trying to block out the disconcerting image of sultry Monica Matthews fawning over Seth in the pizza parlor.

"Looks like he found some *fun*," she said sarcastically. Her voice echoed through the empty office.

Then she buried her face in her hands for the second time that day. The bell over the front door tinkled, and she knew she should check it out. But she didn't want to. And she was tired of doing things she didn't want to do. So she stayed where she was, hoping whoever was out there would go away.

She sensed the cold first, then looked up. Standing in front of her was Seth Taylor—gorgeous in a battered bomber jacket with a festive plaid scarf around his neck. He wore indecently tight jeans and a navy crewneck sweater. His hair was mussed and his eyes sparkled. In his hands he held a beautiful pair of white figure skates tied up with a red bow. Before she could say anything, he reached down and dragged her out of the chair. "Come on, let's go."

"Go?" she managed to say. "Where?"

"Out to the pond at my house. I put up lights around it a few years ago." He pressed the skates into her hands. "We're going to have some fun. I'm not letting you work one more minute today."

"I'm not done yet."

"Yes," he said implacably, "you are."

She smiled. Then she sank back into the chair, hugging the skates to her. "These are beautiful, Seth. I can't believe you bought them. How did you know my size?"

"From that day at the track when you hurt your foot. I held a lot of feet when I was a track coach. I guessed you were about a seven."

"Six and a half."

"No problem. I'll lend you some thick socks."

"Seth, I appreciate the gesture, but I can't go with you."

Leaning over, his face still red from the cold, and his cheek so close she could see a little nick from where he'd shaved this morning, he braced his hands on the arms of the chair. "Come on. I promise I won't touch you." His eyes dropped to her lips. "Or do anything else." He straightened and sighed heavily. "Look, one of us is probably leaving Bayview anyway, so this...this feeling...between us can't go anywhere. We won't hurt your grandfather by being together for a few hours. I promise." He took a breath and Lacey knew she was not going to be able to resist him. "Please." He held out his hand. "Come with me, Lace. Just once more—let's have some fun together."

Mesmerized—and more than a little seduced—Lacey stood and put her hand in his. "All right," she said. "Just once more."

LACEY STUCK her foot in a skate and smiled at the fit. From the bench, she caught a glimpse of Seth, who had donned his own skates and now watched her put on hers. At five o'clock, it was already getting dark, but she could see him clearly in the light from around the frozen pond.

"Want some help?" he asked, his eyes smiling.

"No, I've got it." She tightened the laces and tied a knot at the top.

He stood and executed a quick turn. "Ah, it feels good to have these on again."

"That's right, you played club hockey in college."

Seth stopped his pivot and looked at her. "How did you know that?"

Lacey's heart rate speeded up. "Didn't you tell me?"

"No."

"Maybe Joey did. Or Cassie."

Seth shrugged. "Probably. But yes, I did play. And Joey and I hit a few pucks every winter when the pond freezes." He surveyed the rink. "That is, we used to until he left for school."

Lacey noted the sadness that suffused his face. "It must be hard to lose your son to adulthood."

Seth stared at her. "You'll get a chance to find out."

Finished with the skates, Lacey stood up on them. "Hey, this is supposed to be fun. No depressing talk."

"I agree." He inclined his head to the ice. "Think you still remember how to do this?"

"Are you kidding? Tara Lipinsky, watch out."

Lacey dug her toes into the ice, took four steps on tiptoe, then let the blade flatten. Seth stood on the edge of the ice watching her.

Her scarf sailed out behind her. As she skated to the end of the rink, the cold wind bit her face. She could see fat puffs of breath come from her mouth. A light snow had started to fall and she stuck out her tongue; the flakes melted on it. The taste and texture reminded her of all the times her mother had taken her skating. After Jenny Cartwright died, Philip tried to re-create the experience for Lacey.

Though it hadn't been the same, she'd appreciated his effort. She could still see him stumbling behind her in his newly bought skates.

Philip had done everything he could to make up for the death of her parents.

And this is how you repay him?

Banishing the guilt-ridden thought, she looked for Seth. He'd begun to skate, too, and caught up with her. "You're pretty good, there." He fell into an easy rhythm alongside her. His cheeks ruddy, his nose a little red, he looked healthy and happy.

"I love this." They traversed the ice together. "You're not bad," she said idly.

"Not bad?" he answered with mock insult. *"Not bad?"* He turned and skated backward, effecting the change in direction without a hitch. Facing her squarely, he said, "Looks like you need a demonstration. Stay here."

Stopping, Lacey watched as he dug his toes into the ice to get a strong start. He skated quickly down the pond, then came back. As he whizzed by her, he turned around and skated backwards, fast and graceful.

"Good, but not too complicated. A judge would probably score you five point five."

He scowled, then skated the length of the ice again. On his way back he veered off to the side, circled around and completed three short turns in a row.

"Very graceful," she said. "Maybe a five point eight."

He scowled again. "You're a hard woman."

She watched as he skated off, fascinated with this

lighthearted side of him. Returning to her, he focused on a mound of snow that was piled at the edge of the rink. When he reached it, he bent his knees, ready to leap into the air. Unfortunately, his foot caught on the edge and he went sprawling on the ice.

Lacey could see from where she was that he wasn't hurt. After he landed, he sat up, an indignant expression on his face. He was about ten feet away, but she saw his eyes narrow on her. "Are you laughing at me?"

She giggled.

"You're laughing because I fell?" He came to his knees.

She giggled harder.

"That's it, woman," he said, standing up. Ominously he began to skate toward her.

She caught on and maneuvered herself backward. He skated faster. As he came toward her, she spun around and headed the other way.

About twenty feet of pond was in front of her. She picked up speed, but could hear his skates grating on the ice behind her, closing in. When she reached the end of the pond, she knew he'd catch her if she circled around. So instead, she went off the rink and into the few inches of snow that covered the grass around it.

After four steps she was tackled from behind. She fell ungracefully into the snow. His deep laughter resonated in the still, cold air and so did hers. Both of them flipped to their backs and stared up into the inky sky. When their laughter finally subsided, Seth peered over at her.

He'd never seen a lovelier sight. Her woolen hat scrunched her hair down, but some flaxen strands peeked out from underneath. He longed to touch them. Her eyes sparkled and a few snowflakes had gathered on her lashes. He longed to brush them away. Her cheeks were pink and almost iridescent, her lips full. He longed to taste them more than he wanted anything else in the world.

But he'd promised.

Get up, he told himself.

He was just finding the willpower when she said, "Seth."

There was no mistaking the breathlessness of the word—or the invitation in it. He anchored himself on one elbow and leaned over—still not touching her—to brace his arm on the other side of her. Staring down at her, he said, "I promised."

The amber of her eyes deepened. "I don't care."

"Yes, sweetheart, you do."

She shook her head. Raising her right hand to her mouth, she bit the top of her glove, tugged it off and let it fall to the ground. Slowly—so slowly he thought he might die—she lifted her bare hand to his mouth. She outlined it with her fingertips, tracing a sensuous path that short-circuited his sanity. All the while she watched him with a sober, sure gaze. "Kiss me. I want to feel your mouth on mine again."

The knight in shining armor surfaced from within him; he shook his head.

"Cover me with your body," she whispered achingly. "Just once, I want to feel your weight on me."

That request dissolved his restraint. Seth rarely broke a promise, but even divine intervention couldn't keep him from obeying her plea. Angling over her, he aligned their bodies from hip to toe. When his middle met hers, she arched into him.

Even through layers of thermal underwear and jeans, he could feel her curves meet him in exquisite harmony. The sensation was so precious he closed his eyes to savor it. His legs entangled with hers, their skates cumbersome as they clanged together. His arms braced on either side of her to take some of his weight, he let his chest sink into hers. Heat rippled through him, contrasting vividly with the near-zero weather. Somehow this simple clothed intimacy seemed a raw act of possession.

Greedily, he stared at her, searching her face. He studied the small mole to the right of her mouth, the little upturn of her nose, how delicately her eyebrows arched. Her lips parted at his slow and sensual perusal. She raised her hand to his neck and slipped it inside his collar. He shivered. She exerted a slight pressure. "If you don't kiss me now, I'll die."

He lowered his head—trying to be gentle, trying to go slowly. Somewhere in his mind, he thought that if this was all he was ever going to have of her, he had to revel in it. But when her lips met his, his body took over. He sank into her, losing himself in the sweet sensation of her mouth, of her tongue meeting his with almost savage intensity.

She bit his lower lip and he jolted hard against her. She moaned again and yanked him closer. At one point, her lips broke away from his and she gave him tiny kisses down his jaw, on his nose, on the part of his neck she could reach. They weren't gentle kisses, though. When he felt tremors go through her, he dragged his mouth back to hers in a hot tide of desire. He craved her hungry, needy kisses that weren't enough. Could never be enough. In a last coherent moment, he swore silently at their intrusive clothing.

When he let her go, she looked up at him and said again, "Seth."

He stared at her. How far could he break his promise to her?

She decided. "Take me up to the house. Build a fire."

He struggled for nobility. "Lace, do you know what you're—"

She put her bare hand on his mouth and it was freezing cold on his hot, tender lips. "I know what I'm saying."

Honor battled with desire.

Honor lost.

Slowly, he eased from her and stood. He drew her up and grasped her hand. Wordlessly, they crossed to the bench. She sat down; he knelt before her. His fingers trembled—not from the cold—as he unlaced her skates and fitted her boots back on her. He made quick work of his own. Still, they hadn't spoken.

Rising, Seth tied each pair of skates together and slung both sets over his shoulder. He took her hand in his again and they trudged up the incline. At the top of the hill, Seth saw a large figure come around the back of the house. He gripped Lacey's hand. A few more feet, and Mitch Lansing stepped into the light.

When they reached him, Mitch said, "Thank God I found you."

"What's wrong?" Seth asked. "It's not Cassie, is it?"

"No." He looked at Lacey. "I'm here in an official capacity, Lacey. To see you."

Lacey could feel her heartbeat accelerate. "Is it Grandpa?"

"No." Mitch's face was somber. "It's your brother, Kevin."

CHAPTER NINE

LACEY'S KNEES BUCKLED and she sagged against Seth.

"What happened?" Seth asked as he let go of her hand and encircled her shoulders with his arm.

"Kevin was hurt in a fight in prison. He's conscious and he's in satisfactory condition. I have sketchy information on the altercation."

The wind picked up and whipped Lacey's scarf around her face. She shivered.

Seth drew her closer. "Let's go inside for the details. You're freezing out here."

Leaning heavily on Seth, with Mitch behind them, Lacey trudged to the back door and into an entryway on the first floor. In minutes, they were in the kitchen. Lacey stood immobilized, gripping the large butcher-block table. "He's okay? You're sure?"

"Yes." Mitch shrugged out of his coat.

Seth reached over and loosened her scarf and a few buttons on her jacket. "Get this off and sit down."

When they were all seated, Lacey asked immediately, "How did he get hurt? What's his injury?"

"The infirmary director said he'd been slashed with a razor blade."

She flinched. "Is it bad?"

"Well, it's worse than it should be." Mitch caught Seth's eye and something telegraphed between them. Seth reached out for her hand and held it. "It's a new kind of weapon, Lacey," Mitch told her. Again he glanced at Seth, then back to her. "Are you sure you want to hear the details?"

"Yes!" He still looked unsure. "Mitch, please, I have to know the extent of what happened."

"He was hurt with a homemade weapon. It's made by splitting a razor blade in two, heating up the end of a toothbrush and inserting the blades into the soft plastic, both halves facing out the same way. When the plastic cools, you have a double-edged weapon that makes two slashes. Deep ones that can't be stitched because the wounds are so close together."

"Why would anyone make a weapon like that?" He hesitated.

"Tell me, Mitch."

"It leaves an ugly scar."

Lacey covered her mouth with her hand.

"Where did they slash him?" Seth asked.

"On the arm. He lost a lot of blood, but he's in stable condition."

Lacey willed back the tears. "Does Grandpa know?"

"No. Barker infirmary officials called me when they couldn't reach you."

"Why didn't they call Philip?" Seth asked.

Mitch looked at Seth again, but returned his gaze to Lacey. "Apparently, Kevin was coherent enough to tell them to track you down and not your grandfather. When he told medical personnel about Philip's heart condition, they were sympathetic.'' Mitch stared at her before he finished. ''A few weeks ago, I did some checking on your brother, Lacey. I know a couple of people at Barker from my years in New York City. So, when they couldn't reach you, they called me.''

''How'd you know where to find her?''

Mitch shrugged, uncomfortable. ''Cassie and I were in town today and saw you leave the paper together.'' His face reddened. ''I guessed you'd be here after I had Cassie call Philip's house and he said you weren't there.''

''I've got to see Kevin.''

Mitch nodded. ''Cassie knew you'd say that. I talked to the warden. They'll let you see him to-night.''

''Where's my purse?'' Lacey asked Seth. ''I need my car keys.''

Mitch said, ''I'll drive you up.''

''And leave Cassie alone for hours?'' Lacey shook her head. ''No, she's only a month away from delivery. It's a two-hour drive each way. I'd never forgive myself if something happened while you were with me. Thanks anyway, Mitch.'' Lacey stood and impulsively gave him a hug. ''And thanks for doing all this for me.'' When he still scowled, she said, ''I'll be fine.''

Seth stood, too. ''Yes, you *will* be fine. Because I'll go with you. We'll take my Blazer. It does better in the snow than your Honda.''

Briefly, Lacey thought about objecting. She'd done everything on her own for years. And God knew there was reason for Seth, of all people, not to accompany her. But staring into his troubled blue eyes, looking at the concerned expression on his face, she knew there was no one else she'd rather be with. "I'd like you to drive up with me, Seth. It would mean a lot."

"Good, because I wouldn't have it any other way." He turned to Mitch. "Thanks for pulling these strings, buddy. I owe you one."

Mitch studied Seth for a moment—a quizzical look on his face. But he let the personal remark go. "Just call us after you've seen Kevin. No matter what time it is."

"All right."

After Mitch left, Seth drew Lacey into his arms and his lips grazed her hair. "Are you all right?"

She nodded, but cuddled close to him for a minute.

"You don't have to hold back with me, Lace."

"I know. It's just that I've got to keep it together until I see Kevin."

Reaching for her coat, he said, "Then let's go."

AT NINE O'CLOCK, Kevin saw Lacey come into the ward. She was blurry because he was lookin' at her through one eye that only opened halfway; the other was swollen shut. He lay on a narrow bed that had a lumpy mattress. The lights were too dim and the whole ward smelled like piss. He tracked Lacey as she crossed to him after the fag orderly pointed his way.

She smiled down at him, but her eyes were worried. Kevin had lost count of the number of times he'd put that look there. "Hi, honey," she said softly. "You all right?"

"It hurts like hell." His words were slurred by his fat lip. "Those bastards," he added, letting out a string of obscenities. "They cut me up bad."

The color drained out of Lacey's face. Dimly, Kevin realized he should go easy on his sister, but it was hard because of the freakin' pain. Besides, Lacey had always been strong. She could handle anything.

Slowly she sat down next to the bed, eased off her coat then took his hand. It felt good, even though his knuckles were scraped. "How did this happen, Kev?"

"It wasn't my fault."

Doubt flickered over Lacey's face and it made him mad. "You don't believe me, just like Taylor didn't believe me about Bosco." Lacey didn't answer. "All right. I did hit Bosco. But I didn't do anything wrong today. I been workin' in the laundry. These two jerks, Brazil and Black Eyes, been fightin' over who's gonna be the main importer." At Lacey's blank look, he said, "Just stuff like cigarettes and food." *And razor blades and a shitload of weed.*

"Anyway, they made all the laundry guys choose sides. I went with Black Eyes 'cause he's got more bro in his corner." Kevin closed his eyes, remembering the terror of being trapped when he went to the storeroom to get towels. "I was afraid, Lace," he told his sister. But he remembered knowing he could never show the fear. *"You hurt me and Black Eyes is gonna come after you,"* he'd warned the two

guys who'd pounced on him. No need to tell Lacey
about that little display of power. It hadn't worked,
anyway.

"I'm so sorry, honey."

Kevin felt his insides twist at her hurt tone.
"Grandpa know?"

"No. I'll tell him when I get home. I just wanted
to see for myself that you were all right."

Kevin yawned and his eyes grew heavy. They'd
shot him up with something just before Lacey arrived and it must be kickin' in. "Tell him I'm all
right." He looked up at her. "You gonna be okay
to drive back?"

"I'll be fine," she told him. "Don't worry about
me."

"Yeah," he said, his eyes closing. He wouldn't
worry about Lacey. She could take care of herself.

LACEY MADE IT out to the foyer area before she
burst into tears. And Seth was there to hold her
when the flood finally broke loose. Turning his back
to Cramden, who watched them with the leering
eyes, Seth hugged her to him. "It's all right, love.
Go ahead and cry."

And she did. Lacey wept from the pain of seeing
Kevin hurt in a place like this and from real fear for
her brother. He could have been killed with that vi-
cious weapon. She was also drained from the tension
of the two-hour drive up, and the anxiety of wondering what effect this whole incident would have
on her grandfather's health.

So she held on tight to Seth, who'd been a rock

through the interminable car ride, and whose body gave her strength just by its nearness.

After she settled down, she drew back and peered up at him with watery eyes. "Sorry."

He took out a handkerchief and dried her cheeks. "Don't apologize, sweetheart."

She looked around the waiting area of Hope Hall. The infirmary was only slightly less dismal than the other prison buildings. There were still bars on the windows and a bored guard at the desk. She brought her gaze back to Seth. "This isn't your problem, Seth."

His face told her exactly what he was thinking. *Isn't it?*

In that instant, Lacey realized she truly didn't blame Seth for what had happened to Kevin. Her brother had admitted hitting Bosco. Kevin's cocky attitude, his supposition that he could do anything he wanted with impunity had landed him in Barker Island and probably gotten him into trouble inside the place. Kevin hadn't been able to control his behavior—even with medical help. His situation was tragic, but it was definitely not Seth's fault. Lacey glanced over her shoulder at the guard. "Let's call Cassie and Mitch from the cell phone in the car. Then I want to talk to you."

Ten minutes later, they settled into Seth's Blazer. The car warmed up as Lacey called the Lansings, for the second time that evening, to fill them in on Kevin's condition. Earlier, on the drive up, she'd phoned to alert them that she was going to call Philip and tell him she was sharing a late supper with them. That way, she could say she'd been at their house when she'd been notified about Kevin, and that Mitch had driven her up.

She could never tell Philip the truth—that Seth Taylor had accompanied her to Barker Island.

Now, looking at the man toward whom Philip had directed all his anger, she said, "I need to tell you something."

He grasped the steering wheel as if bracing himself for a blow.

"I don't blame you for Kevin's being injured, or for the fact that he's in prison."

He held her gaze for a minute, then stared past her. "Thank you for that. But I'm not sure you shouldn't."

Prying one of his hands from the steering wheel, she held his warm palm between the two of hers. "It's time to stop blaming yourself. Now. Kevin told me what he did to worsen his situation. It's the same thing he's done his whole life." Lacey drew a deep breath. "Seth, Kevin told me tonight that he *did* attack Bosco all those years ago."

"What?"

"He admitted it. So you see, it reinforces what I'm trying to tell you. Kevin does exactly what he wants without thinking. He carelessly makes people angry, then rubs their faces in it." She sighed heavily and looked out at the prison jutting into the sky before her. "You know, I'm not sure it's possible to change him. This place is only making it worse, but all the best psychiatrists in the world couldn't keep him out of here."

"Lace…"

Her eyes filled. "I'm not sure he's ever going to

change, Seth. No one's been able to do it. All those years ago, you couldn't either. It wasn't your fault.''

"Maybe. But I wish I could have helped your brother. And I hate seeing you go through this.''

"Holding me right now would help.'' She couldn't still the quavering of her own voice.

Gently he drew her into his arms. He was so solid, so warm and so safe. Just hours ago, swept away by passion, she'd wanted to burrow into his chest and touch him as a woman touches a man. Now, she took comfort from him that had nothing to do with sexual attraction, with his physical appeal. And this reaction was even more potent than the first.

EIGHTEEN HOURS LATER, Lacey drove back from Barker Island Prison once again—this time with Philip alongside her. He sat as still as death in the front of the Honda, his head thrown back on the seat, his color alarmingly pale.

Outside, the snow fell in big fat flakes, so she kept the windshield wipers on; they beat a soothing rhythm as she covered the miles to Bayview Heights. She'd turned off the radio when it began playing the melancholy notes of "I'll Be Home for Christmas.''

"Are you all right, Grandpa?''

He grunted, then ran a hand over his face. "He's hurting bad.'' Philip's strong vibrant voice was hushed with sorrow.

"I know.''

"How can they have done this to my boy?''

For a minute, Lacey wanted to tell him that "his boy'' had more than likely provoked the inmates with his cocky attitude. She didn't say it, of course, and was ashamed of her unkind thoughts.

"There's no rhyme nor reason in a place like that. Don't waste your energy trying to figure it out."

He was silent, staring into the blackness of a winter Sunday night. Then he said, "Who did you come up here with last night?"

Lacey swallowed hard. She'd stuck to her story when she'd gotten home at midnight and went through the hellish experience of telling Philip that Kevin had been wounded. She knew he'd been so upset he barely heard the details.

"I told you last night, Mitch Lansing drove me up."

From the corner of her eye, Lacey could see Philip scrutinizing her. Keeping her hands on the steering wheel, she willed her body not to tense. Lying had never come easily to her. After a long silence, Philip said, "The guard—the one Kevin hates—told Kevin he saw you falling all over some guy in the waiting area of the infirmary."

Taking in a breath, Lacey said, "I...um...was crying."

And Seth held me, and calmed me and—did the impossible—made me feel better.

"Isn't this Lansing guy married to your friend Cassie?"

"Yes, and they're expecting a baby. It was just platonic comfort, Grandpa."

"Cramden said it looked like you two were ready to—" Philip broke off. "Well, I don't need to repeat the words, you get the picture."

"Cramden was wrong, I guess."

Philip didn't ask any more questions but Lacey was afraid she hadn't convinced him. The deceit gnawed at her, but what was the alternative? To confess, *I was with your worst enemy, Grandpa. No telling what would have happened if Mitch hadn't interrupted us at Seth's house earlier. And later, when we got back from the prison, his goodbye kiss—which he meant only to give solace—was more passionate and arousing than anything I've ever felt in my life.*

Thankfully there was no conversation for the rest of the trip, and she and Philip arrived home by eight o'clock.

Philip headed straight for the den, and Lacey was glad she didn't have to talk with him. Grabbing a pound bag of M&M's from the cupboard, she trudged upstairs and ran a bath while she devoured the candy.

The hot water soothed away some of the tension. Relaxing in the water, letting down her guard, she couldn't stop her mind from replaying all that had transpired between her and Seth at the pond yesterday afternoon.

After her bath, Lacey felt marginally better. An hour later, as she sat reading in a stuffed chair by the window, there was a knock on her bedroom door.

When she asked him in, Philip crossed to her. Now, instead of being pale, his face was unnaturally flushed. One vein in his neck stood out more than the others. Suddenly the house felt cold and she could hear the wind bang a tree limb against her window.

"What's wrong?" Lacey asked.

He handed her a sheet of paper. She looked down at it and her stomach lurched. "What's this?"

"You know what it is."

"I thought maybe you'd…"

"Given up on it?" he finished for her. "No. Tonight, after seeing Kevin in there, I wrote it." He peered down at her, so much the vibrant, robust man who had raised her that for a minute she forgot his ill health and disability. "And I feel even more adamant about it being this week's School Page editorial."

She said nothing.

"I don't have good feelings about things, Lacey. First you start defending that school, that man. Then, I don't know where you are most of the time. Who you're with." He swallowed hard. "Mostly, I'm afraid you're not telling me the truth." He batted the editorial with his other hand. "Print this in Wednesday's edition. Prove to me I'm imagining things, that I'm wrong in my suspicions. I need that from you now."

Lacey forced herself to face him. This was the man who had given up much of his adult life to raise her and her brother. In that instant, she realized she had no choice.

There's always a choice, she'd once told Seth. But staring at her beloved grandfather, she realized that wasn't true. She reached for the paper he held. Family always came first. She had to print the editorial—or admit that she was falling in love with Seth Taylor.

And that would surely kill the man in front of her.

"OH, LOOK, it's a Tonka truck." Seth watched Lacey finger the bright yellow vehicle lovingly.
"Kevin used to have this one." Checking the aisle
to make sure the students they'd come with were in
some other part of the toy store, Seth raised his hand
and squeezed her neck gently.

She looked so sad today, he wanted to whisk her
away to his house, build a fire and hold and comfort
her. *Who are you kidding, Taylor? You want her in
your bed in a way you can't ever remember wanting
a woman.*

That was true. Since she'd left him Saturday
night, he'd chided himself for the nonstop lust that
had been plaguing him. But coupled with that was
a yearning just to be with her, just to help her
through the pain of Kevin's injury. Right now, he'd
settle for comforting her because he couldn't bear to
watch her suffer. He knew in that instant that he'd
do anything to stop it.

Even give her up?

Even that.

"Seth?"

He smiled down at the dump truck she held. "It's
a great toy. Joey had one, too." He checked the
price tag. "How much do we have left?"

"About fifty dollars."

They'd divided up the day-care money to buy
gifts for each of the ten children at the Franklin
Street facility; the students had solicited decorations
and food for the party next week from local businesses so the school money could all be spent on
toys. Right now, Hope, Hannah, Nick and Darcy

were combing the store for bargains for nine of the kids. Lacey and Seth wanted to shop for Josh.

Seth had called her at the *Herald* first thing this morning to see how she was and had reminded her of this shopping trip. She'd seemed hesitant at first and he'd been afraid she was going to back out. But she'd come along when he told her they'd be picking out toys for Josh. She'd been edgy though, and distant. Damn, there'd been no opportunity to talk to her privately.

"Go for it," he said.

She smiled at him.

"That's good to see."

"What?"

He ran his thumb over her bottom lip. "That smile."

"The only thing that makes me forget about Kevin and Grandpa is Josh." She lowered her gaze. "I went to see Josh again."

"You need a respite, Lace. Take it from Josh."

"I shouldn't. He's already too attached to me. Mary says he looks for me every day."

So do I.

She bit her lip, then whispered, "I wish he were mine."

Before Seth could respond, the four teenagers turned the corner. Hope and Hannah wheeled one cart and Darcy and Nick another. They laughed aloud and pointed to something they'd selected. Unhappy at the interruption, Seth nonetheless turned to the cheerful group.

"Hi, guys," Darcy said. "Look what we got."

Seth watched patiently as they showed off their

choices. All the while he stole surreptitious glances at Lacey. She was trying to concentrate but he could tell her interest was feigned. She was really hurting today. "We're not done yet," he told the kids once they'd finished their demonstration.

"Well, we're gonna check out now," Nick said. "Wanna meet us over at Pepper's for hot chocolate and doughnuts?" The diner owner had agreed to provide the refreshments all week for the students who were shopping and wrapping presents for the Good Deeds Project.

Darcy scowled. "I'm not going to Pepper's."

"Why not?" Hannah asked.

"I don't belong there."

Nick said, "Come on, Darce, it'll be fun."

When she looked up into Nick's eyes, Seth thought, *Uh-oh.*

"I can drive you home after," the boy suggested hopefully.

Darcy sighed, as if, in spite of herself, she was getting sucked in. Seth recognized the sentiment. "All right." She glanced at Lacey. "Will you come, too, Ms. Cartwright?"

Lacey smiled more genuinely at her. "For a little while. We'll be done in about a half hour."

After the kids left, Seth faced Lacey. "Darcy likes you."

"I know. She's stopped by the paper several times just to talk. I think it's because I'm friends with Cassie." Lacey stared after the teenagers. "She also likes Nick."

"I could tell." Seth scowled. "I didn't mean it to go quite that far."

"Sometimes you can't help what you feel." Lacey's eyes held such misery, Seth gripped the handle of the cart to keep from touching her. "But that doesn't mean it's right. I don't want her to get hurt."

"Lace, I..."

She turned away. "Let's finish up here."

Seth let it go. For the next thirty minutes, they picked out presents for Josh. It was almost a sacred ritual to Lacey. She pondered over a Nerf basketball, considering its size and durability, analyzed an action figure for its safety and scrupulously read the directions for a board game. Superimposed over her study of the toys, he kept seeing her with Josh, cooing over him, cuddling him, closing her eyes as she rocked him.

I wish he were mine.

The thought stayed with Seth.

After they checked out, they headed for Pepper's. Seth hoped he'd get to talk to her there, or afterward. It was almost five and there was a task force subcommittee meeting tonight. Maybe he could take her somewhere to eat before the session.

Lacey had refused to ride to the toy store with him, joining him there instead. But he followed her car over to Pepper's and held her arm on the icy sidewalk that led from the street to the diner. All around them, Christmas winked and twinkled in the decorations that the town had put up this weekend. Street lamps were fringed with holly, signs had big red bows on them and holiday lights sparkled everywhere.

When he reached for the front door of the diner, it opened from inside. Through the doorway came

Philip Cartwright with board member Leonard Small behind him. Philip was pulling on his gloves as he confronted his granddaughter—and his worst enemy.

His face went chalk white.

His eyes widened.

His hands fisted.

He glared at Lacey, then looked at Seth with hatred so strong it made Seth step back and catch his breath. Then, without a word, Philip cut between them and headed down the street.

CHAPTER TEN

Are schools social-service organizations? Should taxpayers bear the responsibility of providing psychological help for students? These questions become relevant in light of a task force, a "safety" task force, that's been meeting at the high school the last few weeks. Principal Seth Taylor has charged the committee with the task of helping to make the school safer. Why can't the administration conduct a safe school by themselves? We pay them huge sums of money to do their jobs—the cost of three principals is exorbitant. Now they want *more* money to bring in workshops on stress and aggression management, to set up "student courts"—all examples of their newfangled approach to discipline. It's time they went back to proper, ongoing discipline where the kids don't have the opportunity to act out. It's time they stopped foisting their problems on the community.

What do you think?

FOR A MINUTE, Seth couldn't breathe. A few months ago, when he was running outside, he'd stumbled over an exposed tree root and had the wind knocked out of him. The sensation was the same now. He drew in deep, painful breaths and blinked. He couldn't believe it. This must be some mistake. Lacey *wouldn't* do this to him.

More slowly, he read the editorial again. And again. By the time he finished, a lump the size of a fist had lodged in his throat. Thank God it was six o'clock at night and everyone in the school, except the custodians, had gone home. He'd been out of the building all day at district meetings and hadn't had a chance to see Wednesday's *Herald*. Foolishly, he'd been looking forward to reading what Lacey had decided to print this week. He'd never expected to be sucker punched.

Sinking into his chair, he shook his head. How could she do this—to him and all those people on the committee who'd trusted her? His defense of her to Monica and the others made him cringe in light of this unfair action.

Struggling to think rationally, he closed his eyes. All right, she'd been understandably upset Monday when they'd run into Philip at Pepper's. She'd gone home after a short stop inside the diner to see Darcy and the rest of the kids, and she'd missed the task force meeting that night. Seth had tried to call her all day Tuesday but she'd been out of the office and had not returned his calls. Today, he'd been committed to meetings.

Had she planned this all along? Getting in good with the high school just to sabotage it? No, he wouldn't believe that. He could still see her standing up to Jerry Bosco. And she'd searched the Internet for ideas for the student subcommittee. It didn't make sense. Why, *why* had she done it?

He glanced at the phone. He could call her and ask her. But some self-protective instinct warned him not to. Had he been taken in so easily by a pair of guileless light brown eyes and a soft sweet mouth? Had she seduced him into letting down his guard? No, he couldn't call her; he needed to think about this—long and hard.

Abruptly he stood and tossed the editorial into the trash. He strode out of the office and down the hall to the track, which, thankfully, was empty. After changing, he ran five grinding miles—trying to out-distance the cold anguish seeping into him. Then he went home. He didn't answer any phone calls, but prowled the semidark house in an effort to make some sense of what had happened.

By Thursday morning, he was forced to deal with the fallout.

At 7:30 a.m., the kids appeared at his office door.

Darcy McCormick, who he'd once seen stare down four girls from a gang that was messing with her, had tears in her eyes. "Why'd she do this, Mr. T.?"

Nick put his arm around Darcy and she stepped closer to him. "Yeah, why?" the boy asked.

"I don't know," Seth answered simply.

"You talk to her?"

"Not yet."

"Why?"

I don't trust myself.

His attention was diverted by Zoe Caufield, who

appeared at the door. After the teenagers left, she asked Seth, "Are you all right?"

Seth said, "Hey, they pay me the big bucks to be all right."

"I don't understand it."

He shook his head. *Maybe I just got too close.* "I don't, either."

"Cassie's at that conference until tomorrow. Mitch went to Albany with her."

"Thank God. I couldn't deal with her yet."

"Can I do anything?"

"I don't think so, Zoe. But thanks."

As Zoe left, his secretary came in. "Seth, you have a call from Family Services."

He wanted to put his fist through the wall to release the suffocating sensation inside him. "Take a message, will you? I can't deal with *that* right now."

Minutes later, Sue looked back in. "Your friend George said he's couriering the forms tomorrow. Whatever that means."

"I know what it means."

Zombie-like, Seth got through that day. Somehow he summoned the professional side of himself and took care of business. He staunchly refused to give in to the gnawing pain that had taken up residence in his heart. He still didn't call Lacey. Too much was at stake now and he couldn't afford to be fooled again, if that's what had happened. He'd think it out first, then act.

It wasn't until the next day that he realized he wasn't doing a very good job of dealing with his feelings. First, he snapped at Sue. "Aren't those memos for the board ready yet?"

She'd looked at him with pity in her eyes. "No, I'll finish them now. I didn't know there was any hurry."

He'd stormed out of the office without apologizing. Jerry Bosco caught him before he went ten feet. "I was just coming to see you. I want you to know I've filed a grievance for harassment and wrongful supervision." A few days before, Seth had told Bosco he wanted to see weekly lesson plans that reflected some of the new teaching methods they'd been trying to get him to implement.

Seth stared at the man before him. "File away, Jerry."

Bosco drew in a deep breath. "Well, at least someone is doing something about what's happening around here." He held up Wednesday's edition of the *Herald.* "Looks like you aren't going to get away with this one," he said pompously.

Resisting the urge to tell Bosco to go to hell—the union would love to have that on him—Seth walked away.

It was hours later, when he stopped three girls and asked to see their hall passes—then raised his voice to explain school policy—that he realized he was losing it. He backtracked to his office and told Sue to cancel his afternoon appointments. He couldn't stay here any longer.

On the way out, he met the courier with a letter from Family Services. Wonderful timing, Seth muttered to himself as he headed for his car.

IT WAS EASIER if she just didn't let herself feel. Lacey sank back against her office chair at four o'clock on Friday afternoon and tried to stay numb. But the images of the week finally caught up with her and brought with them a primitive grief. She could still see her grandfather's hurt face after the encounter at Pepper's. She'd hurried home as soon as she could get away...

He sat in a rocker, wrapped in a throw blanket she'd given him last Christmas. The living room was dark and only the moonlight slivering through the windows allowed her to see him. She turned on a light...and wished she hadn't.

His skin was pasty. His eyes were red-rimmed. His face was bracketed with lines of stress.

She crossed to him. "Grandpa, are you sick?"

He stared up at her a minute, looking old and bereft. "I was right, wasn't I?"

When she was younger, and had a problem, she often came to him, knelt down and put her head on his knee. Without analyzing it, she dropped to the floor and rested her head where she had so many times before. After a moment, his hand came up and smoothed down her hair. "You were partially right," she said.

"What does that mean?"

"I...like and respect Seth. If things were different, I could care more." She looked up at him. "It hasn't gone that far."

"Thank God." She closed her eyes and he continued the soothing action. "You have to stop seeing him. Even professionally."

She shuddered at the acute sense of loss that shot through her. "I know."

"I'd do anything for you, Lacey, anything but that."

"I know, Grandpa."

"Maybe you should go back to California…"

Lacey remembered the utter desolation she'd felt. But she hadn't answered him. Tears had clogged her throat and made talking impossible. She'd been so fearful she was going to lose *everyone* she loved.

Then there'd been Darcy. The young girl had come to the paper Thursday morning…

"Darcy, aren't you supposed to be in school?"

Darcy had shaken the snow off her combat boots and unzipped her leather jacket. "Yeah." The teenager just stared at her with accusing eyes. "Why'd you do it, Ms. Cartwright?"

Lacey swallowed back the emotion that threatened. More than anything in the world, she wanted to tell Darcy the truth. But she knew if she did, the girl would go straight to Seth. And if Seth knew that she hadn't written the editorial, he'd find a way to keep seeing her. Lacey had tried everything she could think of to stay away from him and he kept seducing her back with his tender concern and gentle manner. No, it had to be done this way.

So she faced Darcy and said simply, "Sometimes we have to do things that are hard for others to understand."

"That's adult bullshit."

Lacey watched her, saying nothing more.

"You aren't gonna explain this to me, are you?"

Solemnly Lacey shook her head.

"Then, in my book, you're just another phony."

"I'm sorry you feel that way."

"Yeah, me too…"

Now, holding on to her fragile control, Lacey booted up her computer. She sent for her E-mail and found several messages from Seth, all written before the *Herald* hit the stands on Wednesday. "I know you're hurting, Lace," one note read. "I can help. Don't shut me out."

He wouldn't feel that way now. He'd never feel that way again. He'd never call her Lace again. He'd never kiss her hair, or look deeply into her eyes and say without words what he felt.

How was she going to live without that, now she'd had a taste of it?

She slapped her hand on the desk so hard that her palm stung. *No,* she told herself vehemently. *You've only known him eight weeks. You can't possibly feel that strongly about him.*

"I love him," she said aloud. "Oh, God, no, I love him."

And, realizing the scope of what she'd given up, she put her head down on the desk but refused to let the tears come. She had to be strong.

A long time later, she heard from behind her, "Lacey."

Her head snapped up. Seth. When she turned to him, her heart rammed against her chest. His face was ravaged. There was a glazed despair in his eyes. "I just have one question."

She nodded.

"Why?"

Digging her fingernails into her palms, she battled

back her wretchedness. "The paper needed to be more hard-hitting. It was getting watered down, and I needed to resurrect the controversial stance it had taken before I took over."

His eyes narrowed on her. "Those don't sound like your words."

Lacey panicked. Oh, God, he couldn't know the truth. He *had* to believe this. He *had* to think she'd betrayed him. She could see in his eyes that he was ready to make excuses for her. If he even as much as suspected that Philip had written the editorial, she'd cave in and tell him the truth. Then he'd say there was a way to deal with the situation with her grandfather. He'd tell her they could work it out. And she knew, if he did that, she wasn't strong enough to let him go. So she angled her chin. "They *are* my words."

A muscle in his neck knotted. "Did you plan this all along?"

"I told you I'd report the goings-on fairly."

"You can't mean you think that editorial is fair."

No, it's an abomination. "That editorial presents another side." She arched an eyebrow and tried not to choke on the words. "I've given the school a lot of good press. Even in this issue. Surely you can't object to a differing view."

"How can you say this to me?" He crossed closer to her, and for a minute she drank in the sight of him in the long tweed coat, navy scarf and leather gloves. Towering over her, he asked harshly, "Don't we mean anything to each other?"

She averted her gaze by swiveling her seat and

facing the computer. "I told you weeks ago, that was impossible."

The chair whipped around and she was yanked out of it. He grasped her wrist roughly. "Look at me when you're stomping on my heart, Lacey."

She almost gave in then. It was only her grandfather's face, just as haggard and just as anguished as Seth's, that kept her from throwing herself at him. Instead, she glanced pointedly at his hand gripping her wrist. "You're hurting me."

His eyes widened. He let go of her and stepped back. "Well, I guess we're even then."

He gave her a long, studied look then handed her a FedEx envelope. "This was going to be a Christmas present. But I don't expect to see you again. Stay out of my school and away from my students. And me. You've done enough damage."

With that, he turned and left.

Gripping the envelope he'd given her, Lacey sank into her chair. She took in deep breaths and tried to steady herself. But her eyes blurred and her hands trembled. Ultimately, she became aware of the letter she held. She tore open the seal.

Inside were official forms from Family Services.

For foster care.

To be given by Lacey Cartwright.

For Joshua Cornwall.

There was a note from the director of foster care stapled on the front.

Seth,
Thanks for recommending Ms. Cartwright. Instead of just sending over the forms, I've taken

the liberty of partially filling them out. The papers could be signed by Mrs. Cornwall very
soon and take effect any time. We desperately
need people for foster care and we're hoping
our efforts to expedite the process will be added
incentive for your friend to agree to take the
boy.

There was a smiley face after the message that
was signed ''George.''

It was all too much. Sobs erupted out of her and
racked her body. Seth had given her a chance at
having a child—the one thing she wanted more than
anything in life. And he'd followed through with it
even though she'd hurt him badly. How could he be
so unselfish after what she'd done to him? She loved
him so much. She put her head down again and wept
long and hard, soaking the precious papers.

''Well,'' she heard behind her. ''This doesn't
look like the manipulative bitch that everyone in
school is griping about.'' Cassie's voice was gruff.
But through her haze of pain, even Lacey could tell
it was undercut with sympathy.

Slowly she faced her friend.

Cassie walked toward her. She squatted awk-
wardly in front of Lacey, gripping the chair arms to
steady herself. ''All right, let's have it. And don't
give me any of the garbage you've been giving everybody else, Lacey. I know you. I know this isn't
what it seems.''

''It's…it's…'' She saw before her her grandfather's pale face, etched with misery. Superimposed

over that, she saw Seth's tortured expression. How could she possibly choose?

"It's what, honey? Tell me." Cassie's coaxing voice penetrated Lacey's agony. "Lace, tell me the truth, I can help."

THERE WERE STARS in the sky; Seth remembered how he'd loved to come out here to look at them on these crisp winter evenings. He and Joey used to make wishes on them. Like now, there'd be a bite in the air and he could see his breath, but both of them would bundle up and they'd stay out a long time sharing wishes. What would he wish for tonight?

He stopped staring at the sky and began to skate. Up and down. Up and down. He skated faster, aware that this wasn't the best choice of activity tonight; it held too many memories of what he'd lost. He'd tried staying in the house. He'd built a fire and poured a scotch, hoping the liquor would soothe him. But the flames only reminded him of the burnished honey color of Lacey's hair; the liquor only intensified the burning ache he felt for her. The entire living room echoed with memories of the night she'd brought Joey home—and Seth had kissed her for the first time.

At his wit's end, he'd thought about calling Joey just to talk, but didn't want to worry his son, who would know from the sound of Seth's voice that something was wrong. The boy was astute and insightful. He was going to make a good newspaperman.

Newspaper. Damn it. Everything led back to her.

He skated to the end of the pond and stared long and hard at where he'd lain with Lacey just last week. He balled his hands into fists, trying not to remember what it felt like to touch her.

Apparently it didn't mean as much to her as it had to him. She'd betrayed him without a qualm.

Not true.

The personal cost of her treachery had been clearly etched on her face today. She'd been paler than the snow that fell around him; underneath her bloodshot eyes were mauve smudges.

Swearing, he skated the perimeter of the ice fast and furious, searching for a way to dull the misery he felt. Eventually he lost count of the laps he'd done, but his breathing was coming in heavy pants and he was sweating.

He decided to go inside, and had just removed his skates and donned his boots when he saw a figure making its way down the hill. Again, he was reminded of Lacey on the night Mitch had come here to get her. Curious, he watched the person descend. It only took a few yards before he realized it was her. He'd recognize that graceful sway of hips anywhere. She stepped into the light, a few feet from the rink. His heart thrummed in his chest.

Still, he stood where he was, watching her.

She stopped when she must have realized he'd seen her. His body tensed. She started walking. When she got about three feet away, she stopped again. He stuffed his hands in his parka to keep from reaching for her. He bit his tongue to keep from talking.

She wore no hat and her hair flared around her

face. Her jacket was partially unbuttoned and her hands were bare. Her eyes were huge, her shoulders stiff. Yet there was something different about her, something...lighter than when he'd seen her hours before.

But he didn't ask. He didn't speak.

Raising her chin, she looked at him squarely. "I didn't write the editorial. My grandfather did. I didn't give him the information. Leonard Small got it from our committee report. I didn't want to print it, wasn't going to until Kevin got hurt. Then Philip gave me an ultimatum. He'd guessed my feelings for you. He said I had to choose. I chose him." Her voice cracked on the last words and something inside of Seth pulled tight, ready to snap.

Once again he held himself in check.

She took a gulp of air. "I chose him because he gave up so much to raise me and Kevin, and I can never repay him for that."

"And now?" Seth asked, holding his breath, his hands curling into fists inside his pockets.

"Cassie came to the paper after you left. She helped me to see I don't owe Philip the rest of my life. That he raised us because that was *his* choice. She convinced me *I* have a choice in this."

"What are you saying?"

"I'm saying that I love my grandfather. But..." She drew in a deep breath, and Seth held his. He needed to hear it all, and she needed to say it.

"But I love you, too, Seth."

He swallowed hard and wanted to fall to his knees and thank God for this gift.

Lacey rattled on, picking up speed. "We have to

find a way to work this out with him. Because I won't give you up.'' When Seth didn't immediately respond, she bit her lip. "That is…" She stuttered. "That is if *you* want to." Again, he was silent. After a long pause, she whispered raggedly, "Seth, say something."

Cocking his head, sure now that she wasn't going to steal back her declaration, he said, "I love you, too." She closed her eyes briefly. "And yes, I want to work this out. We'll find a way." He looked her up and down. "Now come here."

Lacey didn't hesitate. She threw herself into his arms. He caught her and held on so tight he knew he must be hurting her but couldn't stop himself. He whispered in her ear, "Tell me again."

"I love you."

"I can't believe this." After one more encompassing hug, he set her away from him, stooped down and slid an arm under her knees and one around her back. When she was securely against his chest, he started up the hill.

He barely felt her weight—she could have weighed a ton and it wouldn't have mattered. He felt as strong as any superhero, and he never intended to let her go.

DIMLY, Lacey was aware of their climb up the hill. She clung to him, wrapping her arms around his neck and burying her face in the crook between his jaw and shoulder. He carried her into the house. When they got inside the back hallway, she slid down his body, never losing contact. She flung her arms around him and brought his head down. And then she kissed him, devoured him; he kissed her back hungrily.

He buried his face in her neck and took love bites on the sensitive skin there. Each one jolted her closer to him. Drawing back, she pulled at his scarf, then yanked open his jacket, desperate to touch his skin. She swore when she found a sweater and shirt to get through. He released a husky, incoherent sound as she practically ripped off his clothing and tossed each piece to the floor.

He did the same to her clothes. Lacey gasped at the exquisite sensation of bare skin meeting bare skin and she ran her hands over his chest. His body bucked.

He allowed her caresses for a minute then scooped her up again. She protested with a moan and found his mouth. "Lace, not here," he said, grabbing a breath in between kisses.

She nodded, saying, "Hurry," and searched for his lips again. Quickly he strode through the hallway, past the kitchen to the living room.

She caught sight of the fire he must have started earlier. He set her down in front of it, bent over, unlaced her boots and yanked them off. He kicked off his own.

Lacey reached for his jeans. The snap stuck; she swore again and his grip tightened in response to her urgency. She ran her hands around to his back and inside his waistband, her fingers digging into his buttocks, her breasts crushing against his chest. He groaned long and loud and she managed to re-capture his lips in a bruising kiss.

Then she felt her own slacks loosen. He dragged

them down along with her panties. She jolted when his teeth scraped her stomach. When he came upright, he shucked his jeans and grabbed her. She'd never seen him so out of control.

Together they fell onto the plush rug. He raised her arms over her head and covered her body with his. She arched against him.

"Lace..."

"Seth..."

They could manage no more words. Seth let himself sink into the sight and smell and feel of her; he devoured her mouth. When he moved off her to touch her in more places, she rose onto her side and pushed him to his back. She molded her body to his.

He wanted to see her, to take her breasts into his mouth, but there wasn't time, there wasn't the sanity, to do it.

She looked down at him, her hair a tangle around her face, her eyes glazed with passion, her breathing erratic. Possessively she took his mouth, bit his shoulder, his chest, then reached down and grasped his full, hard length in her hand. He practically ricocheted off the floor. Somehow he was over her again. His hands roughly explored her smooth belly, her rounded hips, between her parted legs. He plunged his fingers into her and groaned at how warm and wet she was. He wanted to see pleasure etch itself on her face, but she gripped his wrist. "No," she said, her voice hoarse. "Together."

"All right. Now."

He thrust inside her. Deep, almost touching her womb. Again. And again.

It took only three strokes and she splintered

around him. Her quick and violent response overwhelmed his control. Holding on to her as tightly as she held on to him, he exploded inside her with a stunning force that slammed through his entire body.

Afterward, Lacey's heart raced in her chest as she sank back onto the rug. Now it felt scratchy and rough. "I can hardly breathe."

Seth also fell back to the floor. "Me, neither."

His hand rested lightly on her hip, his fingers brushed her slick skin. She shivered.

He sat up and dragged pillows along with a lush blanket from the couch. Soon they were settled back comfortably on the floor, the downy cover tucked around them. Though there were several, they shared a single pillow. Lacey's face rested near his cheek and the light rasp of his beard prickled her sensitive skin.

Stroking her shoulder, he stared at the fire. She ran her hand through the whorls of dark blond hair that covered his chest. His heart still drummed wildly. "What are you thinking?" he asked after a long silence.

She grinned into his chest. "That for such a gentle man, you were pretty…tempestuous."

His chuckle reverberated through his rib cage. "Well, lady, for such a gentle woman, you were just as out of control."

Again she grinned. "There are scratches on your back. I've never behaved that way in my life."

"I'm glad to hear it." He hugged her closer and brushed his lips across the top of her head. "You've got bruises on your hip. I've never been that way either, Lace."

She'd needed to know that.

His arm tightened around her and one hand came up to cup her head. "We didn't use anything, sweetheart."

For a minute, she didn't follow him. Then she said, "Oh, God, I've never done that either."

"I'm sorry. It's unforgivable to be so careless."

"I know. I'm sorry, too."

After a moment, he said somberly, "We've got to talk."

She inched closer, entangling her legs with his. "Only if we can do it like this."

Holding her tightly, his fingers stroked her bare arm, raising goose bumps. The gentleness was back. "Why didn't you tell me right away that Philip wrote the editorial?"

She kissed his breastbone, then raised onto an elbow so she could look at him directly. The earlier sadness shadowed his face. "I believed not telling you was the only way to keep us apart. At that time, I was convinced there was no chance for us."

"Never keep anything like that from me again." Reaching up, he locked his hand on her neck. "We'll find a way to work it out with your grandfather."

Dragging her down, he buried his face in her breasts. He nuzzled her, then suckled her nipples, lingering over each one. Lacey felt a response rush through her, and her lower body squirmed against his. When he raised his head, his eyes were serious. "Tonight, I'll take you home. We'll talk to Philip together, right away. No more lies, no more deceit. His heart's strong enough, isn't it?"

"I think so. Maybe we could suggest some counseling. For all three of us together."

"I'll do anything to keep you." Seth caressed her. "I can't believe you're with me." He felt his eyes mist but he finished anyway, "Two hours ago I wanted to die I hurt so much."

"I'm sorry." Her eyes glistened.

"You did, too. I could tell from your face."

"I wasn't sure I'd get through the night."

"It's all changed now, Lace. We can do anything together."

"I couldn't believe you did that with Josh. That you could be so unselfish after you thought I'd used you."

"I wanted him to have you even if I couldn't."

"Oh, Seth."

He put his fingers on her mouth. "Shh, we'll talk about Josh later. Right now, I want you again."

She smiled, then eased to her side. When Seth started to rise to go get protection, she pushed him to his back and took advantage of the position to trail her hand down his body and grasp him again. He was already half aroused.

"Wait a second, sweetheart," he said. "I'll go to the bathroom to get…oh, Lace…don't…wait." He sucked in a breath. "Ohhhh…"

"You're not going anywhere."

"We need…"

"Not for this." With excruciating slowness, she kissed her way down his chest, past his waist, past his abdomen. Her tongue made small circles on his skin and he felt her hair brush his stomach. He remembered the night he picked leaves out of that thick mane, fantasizing about having it spread across his chest. "Lie back and let me love you," she whispered.

Seth did, thinking briefly he'd never be able to deny her anything now.

Then he didn't think at all.

LACEY SNUGGLED CLOSE to Seth in the front seat of his Blazer, still steeped in the sensations of their lovemaking. She sighed contentedly.

"Feel good?" he asked, squeezing her knee and tugging her leg closer. He hadn't stopped touching her all night.

"I feel great."

His laugh was throaty. "Me, too."

She knew they were both thinking the same thing. How explosive they'd been together.

"I don't feel forty-six," he joked.

"Not used to three times?" she teased.

"Hardly."

"Me, neither."

Lacey shivered just remembering what it had been like between them. The second time, she'd touched and caressed him with her hands and mouth. Afterward, he'd sent her spiraling the same way. Then, later, they'd found a need for those condoms. Lacey's skin still sizzled with the intense physical pleasure he'd brought her. Along with it came an emotional satisfaction so great she was flooded with her love for this man. She wanted to drown in it.

Only thoughts of her grandfather diluted the true joy she felt for the first time in her life. Not wanting to spoil the night, she hadn't told Seth some things he'd need to know when they faced Philip. As they neared her street, she asked, "Can you pull over a minute? I want to talk before we get home."

Giving her a quick sideways glance, Seth swerved the Blazer to the side of the road. Once he parked he raised his arm, rested it on the seat back and threaded his fingers through the hair at her nape. "What is it?"

Lacey's heartbeat speeded up. It felt like such a betrayal of Philip, but she had to protect Seth.

"Sweetheart, tell me," he said. "Nothing can change things between us now."

"I hope so." She stared at the intense blue eyes and creased forehead that she'd come to love so much, so quickly. "My grandfather had you investigated, Seth. A private investigator gathered a whole file on you."

"What?"

"I'm only telling you this because I want you to understand the scope of what we're up against. Philip will do anything to hurt you." She felt the tears behind her eyelids. "He's a wonderful man, but he's got this bizarre vendetta against you that clouds his thinking. He'll try to keep me away from you. And it scares me."

Seth pulled her into his arms and rested his chin on her head. "It's okay. I'm just shocked at how far he'd go to get back at me." After a moment, she felt his body stiffen. "What kinds of things did he find out?"

A tremor went through her, some foreboding that made her grip his neck tighter. He seemed to sense it and held her close. "Not one single bad thing."

He relaxed.

"Seth. Is there—"

He interrupted her. "Lace, we'll work this out, I promise. Nothing he can do would make me give you up."

Lacey believed Seth, and that scared her even more. She couldn't bear the thought that Philip would hurt him because of her. Struggling to calm her fears, she recalled the information on the disks. There was nothing in the private investigator's report that could be used against Seth, she told herself. So it would be all right.

She hugged him back. "I won't give you up, either."

Releasing her, Seth kissed the tip of her nose. "I love you. If you love me, we'll be able to weather this." He stared at her. "Believe me."

"All right."

Lacey clung to her optimism up until they turned onto her street.

Until she saw two black-and-white police cars and an ambulance in front of the sprawling two-story home where she'd grown up.

"Oh no."

Seth gripped her hand as he pulled to the side of the road in front of her house. Flinging open the door once the car had stopped, Lacey raced across the snow-covered grass. She almost lost her footing on the icy driveway, but Seth was there to keep her upright. She made it to the porch, with him behind her, in seconds. The front door opened just as she reached for the handle. Mitch Lansing stood in the doorway, grim-faced, sober.

''Mitch, what's happened?''

He looked at her, then nodded to Seth and stepped aside. She felt Seth's arm go around her as he drew her into the house and closed the door. Together, they faced Mitch.

''I'm sorry, Lacey,'' Mitch said. ''Kevin's dead.''

CHAPTER ELEVEN

"DEAD?" Staring blindly at Mitch, Lacey sagged against Seth.

"I'm sorry, Lacey."

"Kevin? *My* Kevin?"

Mitch nodded. Seth's arms drew her back against him. A deep, gnawing pain started in her gut and slowly spread through her. To contain it, she circled her arms around her waist.

Hearing noise in the living room, her gaze flew to the source. "Grandpa." She took a quick glance at the door. "The ambulance. What—"

"It's precautionary," Mitch told them. "Doc Meyers and Philip are old friends. I called the doctor before I came with the news."

Lacey told herself to be calm. She had to take care of her grandfather. She couldn't think about her baby brother...dead...in prison. It seemed impossible, felt horribly unreal.

"I want to see her," Lacey heard just before Philip appeared in the doorway.

She had a minute to register his alarmingly white skin and shocked eyes. Then she was in his arms. "Oh, Grandpa."

He held her close. "My boy, Lacey...my boy..."

Lacey made soothing circles on his back. "I can't believe it."

"I..." Philip's voice cracked and she could feel him shake. Willing back her own tears, she held on to him as he cried for the child he'd raised.

After a minute, Philip stiffened. She felt his hands grip her arms and set her away. He was staring at the doorway, fists at his sides. "You bastard," he snapped. "You killed my boy." Lacey whirled just in time to see him lunge for Seth.

The force of Philip's momentum drove Seth back into the wall. He knocked his head against a picture. It crashed to the floor. Philip drew back his arm and landed a solid punch on Seth's face before anyone could react. Then Mitch was on Philip, dragging him off Seth, who'd never even raised his hands to protect himself.

Immobilized, Lacey's world spun as she watched her grandfather attack the man she loved. "Oh no." Lacey covered her mouth with her hands. She felt an arm go around her. Cassie was next to her.

"Let go of me," Philip shouted, wrenching his arms, trying to escape Mitch's hold. Two uniformed policemen ran into the hall and posted themselves on either side of Mitch, ready to assist him. Doc Meyers came into the foyer, too. He crossed to Seth, examined his jaw and the back of his head and asked a few questions. After Seth's response, the doctor faced her grandfather. "Philip, calm down."

"Get him out of my house." The words were loud and full of hate. Philip's face had gone beet red, and a vein bulged in his neck. He turned to Lacey. His eyes pierced her with an unrelenting wrath. "You were with him…that bastard…when your brother was killed."

Lacey swallowed her pain. "Grandpa, I…"

Suddenly, Philip swayed back into Mitch, who still held his arms.

The doctor leaped forward. "Is there pain?" Philip shook his head. "Dizziness?"

"Some. But I'm all right. It doesn't feel like the last time."

Doc Meyers felt the pulse in Philip's neck and checked his eyes. "Nonetheless, we're not taking chances. The ambulance is here, we're going to the hospital."

"No."

Finally able to move, Lacey stepped forward and touched Philip's shoulder. "Please go, Grandpa. I'll ride with you. Please," she said, battling back the terror. "I don't want anything to happen to you." *To you, too,* she'd been about to say.

Philip stared at her for a moment, then hooked his arm around her neck and drew her close. Always, *always* in a crisis, this man had pulled through for her. "I'm all right, girl. Nothing's going to happen to me."

"Do as the doctor says. Please."

Reluctantly, he nodded.

Doc Meyers led the way, with Philip close behind him. Lacey only had time for a quick look at Seth, who had straightened up from the wall. His face was ravaged and a bruise was already forming on the side of his mouth. He watched her with an unreadable expression, then nodded for her to go. She'd never felt more torn in her life.

From behind her, Cassie said, "I'm going with them, Mitch." Together, Lacey and her friend followed the doctor to the ambulance.

"HERE, Captain." One of the cops handed Mitch an ice pack.

Mitch took it and crossed to Seth. Seth looked at him blankly.

"Your mouth's bruised," Mitch told him. "It'll swell."

Seth shook his head, his gaze straying to the door where Lacey had exited. "I've got to go with her."

"I'll take you to the hospital. You need to put this on your face first."

Swallowing hard, Seth placed the ice pack on his mouth. The sting surprised him. "How did Kevin die?"

"I'll fill you in on the way. Do you want something before we leave? Something to drink?"

"No, I want to get to Lacey."

Mitch scowled. "Philip can't see you there."

Seth shook his head to clear it. "Of course not. I'll stay in the waiting area. Hell, I'll stand outside in the snow all night if I have to. I've got to see her…"

"She's going to need a lot of help with this one, buddy." After giving Seth an assessing once-over, Mitch grasped his shoulder. "All right, let's go."

The roads to Bayview Heights Hospital had turned slick, and a light snow fell all around them. As they drove through the streets, Seth adjusted the ice pack and said, "Tell me about Kevin. Don't spare any details. I have to know the whole story."

"The official report is that Kevin died from contusions received in a fall down a steep stairwell. He'd been released from the infirmary on Sunday, but his transfer hadn't come through yet. So they kept him in another wing."

"Transfer?"

"In medium-security prisons, after an altercation like the one Kevin had with the razor blade, the inmate is most often transferred to another facility for his own safety."

"Did Lacey know about this?"

"I don't think so." Mitch scanned the intersection he'd come to and glided through it. "In any case, the warden said they were worried about Kevin's involvement with two inmates—guys called Black Eyes and Brazil."

Seth raked a hand through his hair. "The names sound like they came from a grade-B movie."

"The whole thing does. Anyway, they isolated Kevin."

"Then how did this happen?"

Mitch cleared his throat. "Kevin left the protective wing. He was in an off-limits section of the prison, a dangerous one."

"I don't understand."

Mitch blew out a heavy breath. "Kevin was in on some kind of trafficking of illegal substances. The authorities think he was looking for his cohorts."

"Oh, Lord, why would he do that?"

Carefully Mitch turned into the hospital parking lot. He shut off the engine and faced Seth. "Kevin's had a history of making bad decisions. Unfortunately, this time it got him killed."

"Lacey will be devastated when she finds out how it happened."

"She has to know."

Seth nodded. "Yes, she does." He looked at the three-story hospital, looming before them. "But that doesn't change how much it'll hurt her."

LACEY CLASPED Philip's hand as the monitor blipped its repetitive rhythm. He was calm now, resting, but he wasn't asleep.

"Do you remember his first two-wheeler?" Philip's voice was sandpapery.

Oh, God, she couldn't do this. "Yes. It was red. When he refused to let you put on the training wheels, you spent hours behind that thing, holding the fender upright so he wouldn't fall."

"I was afraid he'd get hurt."

Lacey said nothing, the reality of what had happened sinking in by degrees. Kevin was dead. The little boy on the big red bicycle was dead.

"And he hated haircuts. I had to sit in the barber's chair with him on my lap. Remember that, Lacey?"

She smiled at the vision of Kevin, a beautiful child with thick blond curls. Like Josh. The bittersweet memory tightened the cramps in her stomach. "I remember."

Philip raised his hand and scrubbed it over his face. She could see the sheen of tears from his eyes, the moisture wetting his cheeks. "I loved him."

"I did, too." Lacey prayed the sedative the doctor had given Philip would take effect soon. With supreme effort, she quelled the emotions pushing to get out, but she wasn't sure how much more of this she could take.

Her grandfather turned to her with bruised eyes. "All I have left is you, honey." He looked old and weary. Lacey could remember how, after her father's funeral, Philip had let both her and Kevin sleep in his bed that night while he watched over them from a chair. Tonight, she had to be the strong one. She had to get him through *this* death.

"I'm here, Grandpa. I'm here for you."

His lids drooped. When he took her hand, his was limp. "Promise?"

"I promise."

"I wouldn't want to live now, without you."

Lacey bit her lip so hard she was surprised she didn't taste blood. "You'll never have to do that."

He closed his eyes on a satisfied sigh. She sat there clutching his hand, lost in memories of Kevin, of her mother, of her father. Everyone she loved was gone, except Philip.

And Seth.

She wouldn't think about Seth now. About losing Seth, too.

She couldn't.

So she held on tight to her grandfather's hand and closed her eyes until she sensed someone standing before her. She looked up into Doc Meyers's kind old eyes.

"Come on, young lady," he grumbled, pulling her to her feet. "You've had a shock and you need some rest." He nodded at her grandfather. "Philip's resting comfortably. He'll sleep through the night and we'll watch him."

Slowly, she stood. She bent over Philip and kissed him on the forehead. "I love you, Grandpa," she whispered, then followed the doctor out of the room.

SETH'S HEART hammered in his chest as Lacey entered the lounge area, walking behind the doctor. The older man spoke softly to her, squeezed her hand then went back down the hall. Seth stood where he was, waiting to see what she needed from him.

After only a moment's hesitation, she flew across the room into his arms. He caught her, drew her close and locked his hand on her neck. He hadn't realized how afraid he'd been that she'd blame him for Kevin's death.

Her tears finally came. Sobs. Aching, wrenching sobs. They wracked her whole body. It had been almost two hours since she'd learned of Kevin's death. Seth couldn't believe she'd been able to keep her emotions bottled up this long.

His own eyes misted. He said nothing. He caught a glimpse of Cassie weeping quietly in Mitch's arms on the couch across the waiting room. Mitch was granite-faced and held on to his wife.

Several minutes later, Lacey quieted. When she pulled back from him, he took out his handkerchief and wiped her face. Then he framed it with his hands. "I'm so sorry," he said simply.

Her eyes darkened. She reached up and ran her fingertips over his swollen jaw. He winced involuntarily, belying his attempt at reassurance. "It's okay."

She shook her head, then turned to the Lansings. "You shouldn't have stayed."

"Don't be silly," Cassie told her as she got up, crossed to Lacey and pulled her into a sisterly embrace. "I'm sorry, Lace."

Mitch stood behind Cassie. "Me, too." Then he said, "Is there anything we can do?"

Lacey smiled weakly. "No, thanks. Now, take your wife home, will you? She needs rest."

Mitch nodded, then to Seth he said, "Here are your keys." While they'd waited, Mitch had had his guys fetch Seth's car.

Cassie hugged Lacey again, then Cassie crossed to Seth, hugged him too and whispered, "This is *not* your fault."

"Thanks," he said gruffly. During the hours they'd waited, Mitch and Cassie had staunchly asserted that Seth was not to blame for Kevin's death. He'd tried to banish the nagging doubt that Lacey might not feel the same.

After the Lansings left, he led her to the couch and sat down with her. She went willingly into his embrace and burrowed into him. Slowly he stroked her arm. "You need rest, sweetheart."

"After you tell me about Kevin. I want to know everything."

With a heavy sigh, Seth recounted the grim story. Telling her what had actually transpired was one of the hardest thing he'd ever had to do in his life. He had to stop several times when she started to cry. All through it, he cradled her against him.

When he finished the account, he said, "We need to go."

She nodded into his chest.

He started to rise, but she drew him back down. "Wait." When he sat again, the look she gave him made him want to weep. "Grandpa was terribly wrong, Seth. You aren't to blame for Kevin's death."

He sucked in a breath. "We don't need to discuss this."

"Yes, we do. *You* need to know that now."

He nodded, unable to speak for the emotions roiling inside him. Gratefully he closed his eyes.

"Okay," she said, composing herself. "Take me home. And stay with me. Please."

"I'll do anything you ask, love."

THE SLIPPERY ROADS made the driving slow, but didn't deter Seth from his errand. Today was Wednesday, and this was the most positive, pleasant thing he'd done since Friday night when they'd discovered Kevin had been killed. As the traffic inched along, Seth's mind wandered to the events of the last few days.

When he'd driven Lacey home from the hospital, she'd clung to him like a lifeline. At her house, she resisted sleep, so he made her change into a comfortable sweat suit, settled down on the couch with her in his arms, and, as he'd hoped, she'd fallen asleep. He remembered thinking she'd need the rest to deal with the horror of the upcoming days. Seth had dozed, too, soothing her through the nightmares that awakened her twice.

It was the last time he'd touched her, though she'd called him late every night, after her grandfather had

gone to bed. The first time was to tell him she'd
survived bringing Philip home from the hospital.
The second night, she'd needed to talk about what
had happened that day. Her voice was raw and he
knew she'd been crying. Though he hurt for her, he
was glad she was letting go with him, at least...

"It was awful," she'd told him hoarsely. "We
had to pick out a casket. It's oak, lined with red
velvet." Her voice broke when she said, "Kevin
always loved bright colors."

"Oh, Lace, I wish I could help."

"I wish you could hold me right now."

"I'm there inside your heart, honey, even though
I can't be with you."

She sniffled. "If you were really that superhero,
you could fly over to my window and see me."

He'd chuckled, glad she could forget for a minute
the grinding grief inside her.

Starting on Monday, he'd had business to take
care of. First there were the kids.

"Ms. Cartwright's not coming?" Darcy had
asked when they met that afternoon to wrap presents
for the party coming up at the day-care center on
Saturday. The smiling Santa Claus paper mocked his
mood, but Seth struggled not to spoil the activity for
the kids.

"No, Darce, she's not coming."

When he'd told the young girl about Lacey's
brother, Darcy had been horrified. The way Nick had
comforted her was the only thing that had brought
a smile to Seth's lips in days.

He wasn't smiling at the task force meeting,
though. By Monday evening, most of the town had

heard about Lacey's brother. But Monica Matthews was still on the warpath about last week's *Herald*. God, Seth remembered thinking, had the editorial only come out five days before? It seemed like a lifetime ago.

"I'm sorry about Kevin Cartwright," Monica had begun, "but we have to deal with Lacey writing that editorial. She's off this committee, I assume."

Seth checked his temper. "Since there's only one meeting after this, and I doubt Lacey will have the energy to attend, that's a moot point. However, we need to clarify some things." He turned a blistering gaze on Leonard Small. "Don't you think we should do that, Leonard?"

The older man had squirmed, turned red, but finally confessed, "Ms. Cartwright did not divulge the workings of this committee." He lifted his chin. "I did. The information is not confidential, after all, and as the board's representative, I found it well within my rights to make public the proposals we're considering."

He sounded so pompous Seth wanted to lash out at him. But it was Linc McKenna who'd pounced. "And to whom did you *divulge* this information, Mr. Small."

"Philip Cartwright."

Linc said, "I knew Lacey wouldn't turn on us. She didn't write the editorial, did she, Seth?"

"No," Seth told the committee, "she didn't."

Afterward, late Monday night—the night before the funeral—he waited anxiously for Lacey to call. At eleven o'clock she did. "I just needed to hear your voice," she'd told him.

The funeral service had been on Tuesday. Seth had agonized over whether he should attend, acutely aware that if Philip saw him, he might create a scene. Seth's presence could upset the old man so badly, Philip might have another heart attack. In the end, though, Seth simply couldn't stay away. He'd gone to the church, stood in the anteroom behind a large pillar and watched Lacey grieve for her brother. The church wasn't big, and though there were more people in the pews than he'd expected, it wasn't filled to capacity.

Lacey wore a dark blue suit trimmed in green. Her flaxen hair was pulled into a knot at her neck. Her face was pale and her eyes were hollow. He remembered wanting to go to her, to hold her. Instead, he stood on the outside, watching Darcy and Nick, Cassie and Mitch, Linc McKenna and others comfort her. And standing there in the anteroom, Seth experienced his own sense of overwhelming grief, accompanied by an insidious fear. Was he going to be excluded permanently from Lacey's life?

She'd called him late last night but he managed to keep his fears to himself.

"I needed to talk to you," she'd told him.

"I needed to talk to you, too."

"I wanted you there…today."

"I was there, honey." He told her what he'd done without confessing his own sense of loss.

"Oh, Seth, I feel so bad that you had to hide like that."

Once again he'd marveled at this wonderful woman's sense of selflessness. "I was fine," he lied. "Except watching you suffer kills me, Lace."

"Seth…" He could tell she was struggling not to break down. "I'm going to the paper late tomorrow afternoon. Celia's taking Grandpa out for a drive. She's been a godsend, getting him to rest, getting his mind off…things."

Seth's heartbeat accelerated. "Would it be all right if I stopped over at the paper?"

"I want you to…"

Which was where he was heading right now. After a little detour, he thought, smiling to himself and pulling over to the curb on Franklin Street.

OUT OF THE HOUSE, in the newspaper office again, Lacey could finally breathe. The numbness of the last four days was wearing off, and she'd had to do something normal, something that didn't deal with loss and grief. She'd come to the *Herald* at five. After hugs and consolation from her employees, she was blessedly alone.

She walked into the office and to her desk. Knife-sharp pain lanced through her when she glimpsed the picture of Kevin and her on the wall behind the desk. It had been taken the Christmas before he'd gone to prison. They sat by the tree, surrounded by colorfully wrapped presents. Slowly she traced his upturned nose, his smiling mouth, his chin that was just like hers. Then she removed the photo from the wall and placed it in the drawer, unable to bear looking at him and remembering Christmases past. The thought of the holiday—just ten days away—without Kevin, was unbearable.

She sank into her chair.

Waiting.

She didn't lie to herself; she had come here partly to get out of the house, but mostly she'd come to see Seth. She'd missed him so much, she cried herself to sleep every night wanting his arms around her, wanting him to take away some of this horrible pain.

When she heard the bell over the door tinkle, she hurried to the outer office.

And what she saw took her breath away.

Seth was standing—big and beautiful—in the doorway, dressed in his tweed coat, scarf around his neck, his gloved hands holding a squirming, red-faced baby boy. Josh.

Stunned, she watched Josh's eyes sparkle when he saw her. "Ace...Ace," he babbled, reaching out his snowsuited little arms to her.

Immobilized, she stood there while Seth crossed the room, his eyes gleaming. Gently he handed the baby over. She took Josh into her arms, burying her face in his bulkily clothed body. She closed her eyes savoring the smell of baby powder and shampoo. Happily Josh tugged at her hair, batted her head and repeated, "Ace...Ace..."

Finally, when she was in control, she opened her eyes and looked at Seth. His smile warmed every inch of her that had been chilled for days. "How did you know to do this?"

He reached out and smoothed down her hair. "I just knew."

"How did you get him?"

"Mrs. Cornwall signed a release. Since you're considering foster care—they're counting on that, Lace—it was easy."

"I love you," she said.

"I love—"

But his declaration was cut off by the sound of the bell over the door again. Both Lacey and Seth turned to the entry. The baby cuddled into her and stuck his fingers in his mouth when he saw the stranger standing in the doorway.

Tall, lanky and disturbingly lean, the man surveyed the office with a practiced glance. His eyes landed on Lacey and the baby, remaining cool. When they took in Seth, they widened, almost imperceptibly. "I was looking for Philip Cartwright."

"He's not here," Lacey said. "May I help you?"

"Ah, no." The man gripped the envelope he held. "I was just passing through Bayview Heights. I'll catch up with him another time."

Seth crossed to the visitor. "Would you like to leave that for Philip?" he asked, pointing to the envelope.

Casually, too casually, the stranger stuffed the envelope inside his coat and shook his head. "No, thank you. Sorry to interrupt." As quickly as he'd come, the man was gone.

Lacey watched Seth. His back was stiff, his hands curled into fists. "Seth," she asked, snuggling Josh closer. "What is it?"

He pivoted, his face carefully blank.

"Tell me."

"The envelope he carried?"

"Yes."

"The return address read Adams Private Investigation."

CHAPTER TWELVE

"I'VE FOUND SOMETHING." Herb Adams looked smug and self-satisfied as he stood before Philip in the den.

Philip leaned back into his leather chair and released a heavy breath. It was a week since Kevin's death, and this was the first time he'd felt the constricting band of emotion around his chest loosen. "Sit down."

The tall, stoic man took a seat, his posture straight, his eyes alert. With precise motions, he withdrew his report from an envelope. "Do you want to read it, or should I summarize?"

"Both. Tell me first."

"Seth Taylor didn't start out teaching at Bayview Heights High School."

Philip arched an eyebrow. "Really?"

"He spent a year in a small rural district just outside of Binghamton."

"Why didn't we know that?"

"He kept it a secret." Adams produced another set of papers. "Remember how you had that board member get a copy of Taylor's original application to Bayview Heights School District?"

Philip nodded.

"Taylor left the space blank where it requested former teaching experience."

Philip steepled his hands. "Unethical, for sure. Is it illegal, too?"

Adams gave him a silky smile. "That depends. It's a gray area. In any case, it's definitely damaging to his reputation. That's what we're after, isn't it? To destroy his reputation?"

Nodding, Philip asked, "What did he do?"

"I'll tell you in a minute. Look at his application first."

Philip took the forms and scanned them. His trained reporter's eye caught the private investigator's point right away. Not only had Taylor failed to indicate his first job in the space provided for previous teaching experience, he'd put an asterisk in the blank and at the bottom had written a matching asterisk followed by: traveled extensively in Europe—Paris, Florence, Vienna, London.

Philip laughed for the first time in days. "He lied on his application."

"Withholding information can be construed as lying. Regarding the travel, he *did* tour all those places. Summers. Vacations. But he deliberately misled the school district into thinking he'd taken the year off after college to do it." Adams stared hard at Philip. "To cover up what he'd done."

Every muscle in Philip's body tensed. "Tell me."

"Apparently Taylor was denied a second-year contract at Carson City High School because of an incident with a student."

Philip braced himself. "A sexual incident?"

"No."

"What?"

"There was a troubled student, a boy named Tim Johnson, in one of his English classes. Taylor took the kid under his wing. He arranged for counseling, bailed him out of minor scrapes, intervened on several occasions with the administration. In one particular circumstance, the boy actually had a legal hearing. Taylor testified on his behalf. He specified only good things about Johnson's progress. Even indicated he'd be willing to work with the kid, the probation people, etcetera, if they'd give the boy another chance."

"That was…" For a minute, Philip felt admiration for the twenty-one-year-old teacher Taylor had been. Then he remembered Adams's call two days ago, telling Philip he'd run into Lacey and Taylor together in the newspaper office. Philip gripped the edge of the desk. "So he tried to help a kid. That's more than he did for Kevin." Philip's voice broke. He took several moments to compose himself. "Do we have anything to destroy the man?"

"How about the fact that he lied for the kid?"

"Lied?"

"Yes. The district was considering kicking Johnson out of school on the grounds that he was a threat to others. Taylor was asked on the stand if he had any knowledge of the boy's violent tendencies. Taylor said no. Later, it came out that the boy had shown up twice at Taylor's apartment, in bad shape after a fight, and once Taylor had dragged him out of an altercation in town."

"So Taylor lied."

"Yes."

Philip thought of the disk with reports of those kids who'd turned out well because of Taylor's intervention, despite their past mistakes. His heartbeat accelerated. "Make my day. Tell me *this* kid let him down."

"Big-time. Johnson raped a girl at school two weeks after Taylor got him off. She was also badly beaten up."

Stunned, Philip sank back on his chair. "My God."

Adams shifted in his seat, crossing his ankle over his knee. "Some hotshot lawyer argued that the school district shirked their responsibility by not getting Johnson the help he needed. The attorney said that Taylor, as a representative of the school, knew the kid needed help and didn't get him the right kind. Needless to say, nobody looked favorably on Taylor after that. Even if the district hadn't decided not to renew his contract, he probably would have left. The town resented the hell out of him, blamed him." He grinned. "It got pretty messy."

"Why wasn't any legal action taken against Taylor?"

"Taylor's attorney contended that a lot of students got into fights, so Johnson's actions weren't that out of the ordinary. He also showed that Taylor had set up several counseling sessions for the boy, which Johnson skipped. The lawyer did a pretty good job of showing Taylor in a good light, and by then the district was in such an uproar, they decided to let Taylor go. The girl's parents, who wanted it over too, settled for that."

"No wonder he didn't put his teaching experience in Carson City on his application."

"You can bury him with this, Mr. Cartwright. He lied for the kid, then lied again on his application. Make this public and he's ruined."

Philip said, "I was right. The man shouldn't be working with kids. He's got to be stopped."

LACEY DREADED coming home. At six o'clock on Friday night, she let herself in the house with the same clutch in her heart that she'd had since she'd run into Philip's private investigator on Wednesday. Not only was she walking on eggs, fearful that he'd told Philip she'd been with Seth and wondering why Philip hadn't confronted her, but she was worried about Seth and what the investigator might have found.

By tacit agreement, they'd not discussed the private investigator. Instead, they'd played with the baby for a few hours, then taken him home to Mrs. Cornwall. They'd spent a little time with the older woman…

"My boy loves you, Miss Cartwright," she'd said. "Are you goin' to give him foster care?" The old woman rubbed her injured hip, her eyes muddy with pain. "I'd feel better knowin' he wasn't with strangers."

Lacey had hugged Josh, who sat on her lap. "Yes, I'm going to apply for it. Seth is sure I'll get him."

"He needs you," Mrs. Cornwall told her.

Lacey had brushed her lips across Josh's silky head. "I need him, too."

Once they were back in his car, Seth held Lacey for the first time since the night Kevin died.

"I've missed you so much," she'd said, her words muffled by his coat.

"I've missed you, too."

She looked up at him. "I meant what I said, Seth. I don't blame you for Kevin's death."

His face was taut, his eyes wary. "Tell me how you feel again." He grasped her shoulders. "I need to hear it."

"I love you. I'll always love you."

He'd returned the sentiment, over and over again. Then he nodded to Mrs. Cornwall's house. "Josh could be ours, Lace. Permanently."

Lacey sucked in her breath. "What are you saying?"

He smiled and her heart stuttered. "I want to marry you. I know this has happened fast, but I don't care. I want you to be mine for the rest of our lives." He hugged her to him, resting his chin on her head. "And Josh, too."

When he raised his hand to brush her cheek, she took it in hers, kissed it gently. "I want that, too. I want to be your wife."

His heavily expelled breath told her he hadn't been sure of how she felt. It made her ache for him. She continued kissing him, tiny little pecks on each knuckle, the outside of his hand, his fingernails. "We'll have to go slowly, of course. Because of Grandpa." She scowled. "It could take a long time for him to accept us, after Kevin's death." Even saying her brother's name caused the pain to surface.

"I'll wait however long it takes," he said. "I won't make you choose between us, Lacey, but I won't let you go, either. When things settle down, when he's stronger, we'll find a way to work it out."

Before she'd left Seth, she'd mentioned the private investigator. Seth had hugged her again, told her not to worry, nothing could hurt him, but there'd been a tension in his face, and a catch in his voice that had made her anxious…

That anxiety was still with her as she closed the door behind her. She stopped in the dimly lit foyer, shed her coat, gloves and boots and walked in stocking feet into the living room.

The house was eerily quiet. No television or radio playing Christmas stories or songs that made her miss Kevin more. The decorated Christmas tree stood in the corner, but the festive little bulbs had remained off since Kevin's death.

Philip's light was on in the den. A good sign, she thought. Mostly, he just sat in his recliner and stared into space. Lacey headed toward the room.

Her grandfather slouched behind his desk, his eyes closed, his hands crossed over his stomach. There were papers spread across his desk. Only a small reading lamp illuminated the dusky atmosphere. A tingling sense of foreboding skittered through Lacey. Because of it, she came fully into the den instead of leaving Philip to doze. She crossed to the desk and stood on the other side of it.

Upside down, she could see that the papers scattered across the surface were from Adams Private Investigation. Lacey's stomach knotted painfully.

"He's not a good man." Philip's voice penetrated the fear that enveloped her.

Her gaze locked on her grandfather's face. "Yes, he is."

Rousing, Philip straightened in his chair. "Sit down, honey."

She sat, her legs suddenly so weak she had no choice.

Philip picked up the papers. "He taught somewhere else before he came to Bayview Heights. Did he tell you that?"

Woodenly she shook her head. He hadn't. Why?

As if reading her mind, Philip continued, "I know why. He made a mess of things his first year of teaching. He took some troublemaker under his wing. Got him off the hook with the law, I understand. Then the kid went out and raped a girl."

Lacey swallowed hard. "Oh, God. Poor Seth. That must have killed him."

Philip slapped the papers down on the desk. "What about the girl?"

"I'm sorry for her, too. And her family. But the boy's actions weren't Seth's fault." She raised her chin. "Just like Kevin's weren't, Grandpa." She leaned over and reached out for his hand. He didn't give it to her. "You're too biased to see that Seth isn't to blame in either case."

"Aren't you upset about this at all?"

"Of course I am. I hurt for everyone involved. But it's still not Seth's fault." She softened her voice. "Grandpa, he was so young. Almost a kid himself. He made a mistake."

Her grandfather flung back the chair and stood.

"He made an even bigger one by lying—first on the stand about the kid's violent behavior, then to the school district here that he'd had no previous teaching experience."

Lacey sat up straighter.

"That surprises you, doesn't it? Well, not me. He's a con man and a menace to young people."

Slowly Lacey shook her head. "No, Grandpa, he's not."

Philip stared at her for a long time. She didn't flinch or release his gaze. Finally he sat back down. "I'm going to make this public, Lacey. I'm going to run a full exposé and hopefully it will end in Taylor's dismissal from Bayview Heights High School. I wanted to discredit him in your eyes, and thought this would do it. But even if his reprehensible actions don't turn you against him, I'm going public. I'll smear his reputation so badly, he'll have no choice but to leave Bayview Heights."

A chilling cold seeped into every pore of Lacey's skin. It raced through her body, making her shiver. She banded her arms around her stomach as the realization sunk in.

She'd been a fool to think her grandfather could accept Seth. She stared at the man she'd loved for all her life. And she was grateful for one fact: she didn't have to choose between him and Seth.

Philip had just taken that choice from her.

She stood, her hands tight around her waist. "No, you won't do that, Grandpa. I won't let you."

Fear—clear and potent—suffused his face.

"I want you to destroy those documents. Get the

originals from the private investigator you hired and destroy those, too. I won't let you hurt Seth.''

With the intuition of the star newspaper reporter he'd been, Philip asked, ''And if I don't?''

''If you don't, I'll go back to California and never see you again. I love you more than I can say, but I love Seth, too, and I'll do anything to keep you from hurting him.''

Philip's body sagged. His face was a mirror of the night he'd found out Kevin was dead. Gently she circled the desk and put her arm around his shoulder. ''But if you stop this vendetta against him, and leave him alone, I'll stay here, Grandpa. I'll run the newspaper and stay with you.'' She waited a meaningful moment, then said achingly, ''We've lost Kevin, let's not lose each other, too.''

Philip stared up at her with eyes so old it made her throat clog. ''You'll have to give Taylor up, Lacey.''

Her grandfather's face blurred, and Lacey grasped the back of his chair. ''I will. I won't see him or have any contact with him at all.''

''You'd do that for me?''

She leaned over and kissed his forehead. ''I'd do it for you both.''

SOMETHING WAS WRONG with Lacey. Something more than Kevin's death. Seth studied her from across the room Saturday morning at the Franklin Street Day Care, as the much-awaited children's Christmas party got under way. They'd made special arrangements to have all the kids in attendance today to culminate weeks of preparation.

"Isn't this cool, Mr. T.?" Nick came up beside him, his hand linked to a small boy who gnawed on a Rice Krispies treat. The child had wrapped a red ribbon around Nick's neck. The sight of the big football player tending to the little boy reaffirmed once again how positive the entire Christmas Good Deeds Project was. Seth had done something right. He'd been thinking about all the things he'd done right here in Bayview Heights, especially since he expected to hear from Albany about the State Ed. job at the end of the week.

"Mr. T.?"

"Oh, sorry. It's a great party, Nick. You did a good job with this committee."

"Nah, we all did it." His eyes strayed across the room and stayed there. "Darce is great with kids, isn't she?"

"Yeah."

"Who would've thought?" Seth smiled at the adolescent chagrin on Nick's face. "I'm going to ask her to the Winter Ball."

"Sounds like a good idea to me," Seth told him.

"Yeah, well, not to my buddies. Nobody can believe I'm interested in her for anything but—" He broke off, his face reddening, and made a project out of bending over to wipe the little boy's mouth.

"You are, though, aren't you, Nick? Interested in her as a person," Seth said smoothly. "I can tell."

"Yeah." Nick crossed his arms over his chest and continued to stare at Darcy. "But the odds are against us."

"You can beat the odds," Seth said, staring at Lacey across the room. She sat on the floor with

Josh and a little girl as they both ate doughnuts and Lacey played mop-up.

"Maybe." The toddler Nick was in charge of darted away. "Oops, see you later." Nick raced after the boy.

Seth mulled over his own words, using them to comfort himself as he watched the woman he loved. Two days ago, Lacey had agreed to marry him. He'd talked to her every night, but hadn't seen her since. Last night, he'd almost gone over to her house when he heard the absolute despair in her voice.

Seth understood grief. He knew you went in and out of it; some days were better than others. Nights were the worst. He wished he could have held her last night. She obviously hadn't slept. Though she looked great in her bright red sweater—that hugged her curves nicely, he noticed—and jeans, her face was too pale. He hadn't seen her up close yet, so after perusing her at a distance, he sauntered over to where she sat.

He dropped onto the floor next to the two toddlers and across from Lacey. "Hi."

Before she could answer, Josh looked up and grinned at him. "Se…Se," he babbled.

Lacey watched them. The brief flare of anguish in her eyes alarmed him. But she covered it with a smile. "Hi."

"Enjoying yourself?"

She nodded.

"You okay?"

She wouldn't look at him; she just nodded again. With strained precision—as if she was thinking about her every move—she smoothed a hand down

Josh's hair. The boy grinned up at her and mushed part of the doughnut he was eating into her mouth. She laughed and Seth's stomach relaxed.

"Can I see you for a few minutes after the party?" he asked her.

"Sure." Still she kept her eyes on Josh.

He was just about to call her on her evasion, when he heard Nick say, "All right, guys. Guess who's here?"

Everyone in the place turned toward Nick.

"Santa Claus!" the children squealed in delight and scrambled to their feet.

"Stay where you are now, and Santa will sit in the middle," Nick told them.

Lacey grasped Josh, and Seth pulled the other child onto his lap. Over the little girl's head, he caught Lacey's gaze. His said, *This can be us. Forever.*

Her eyes glistened but she gave him a weak smile.

The children tore into the presents Santa distributed. Lacey held her breath with each package Josh opened. Her eyes sparkled when he kept touching the Tonka truck she'd so lovingly purchased.

Inside Josh's stash was a small gift. Lacey frowned when Josh picked it up. "What's this?" she asked. "We didn't buy anything this small and soft."

Seth smiled. "I got it for Josh. It's a special present."

Before she could comment, Josh had ripped it open. Lacey chuckled when she saw the bright blue and red colors of a pair of superhero pajamas. Josh grinned and stood up. "On," he said to Lacey, shoving the pajamas—complete with a bright red cape—at her.

She took the outfit with trembling fingers and held up the top while Josh poked his head and hands through it; then she fastened on the cape. Flinging his arms to the side, Josh said, "Rmmmmmmm…" and took off across the room, with the little girl following.

Lacey finally met Seth's eyes. She still held the pajama bottoms. "These are adorable."

Reaching over, Seth flicked a tiny piece of doughnut off her chin. "Hey, we've got to start the kid off right, Ace."

"I hope he grows up to be just like you." She said the words so somberly Seth was momentarily silenced.

"Lace…"

Before he could finish, Josh was back, diving into Lacey's arms. She caught him to her and buried her face in his hair.

Just before she did, Seth thought he saw tears in her eyes.

As LACEY EXITED the day care, she saw Seth's car parked by the curb and halted momentarily. She made a show of searching her purse to delay going to him.

You have to handle this right, Lacey.

If only she wasn't so tired. Her temples throbbed and her eyes were gritty. Her lower back ached. After her discussion with Philip last night, she'd lain awake, second-guessing her decision, crying into the covers and even getting angry at the fates. She'd punched her pillows so hard her hand hurt today.

Now she had to begin the process that would wrench Seth out of her life...

"I have two conditions," she'd told Philip.

"All right. What are they?"

"That you let me do this my way. Tell Seth and handle the break in my own way."

Philip's jaw had clenched but he'd nodded his assent.

"And that I go ahead with a foster-care arrangement I'd been planning."

Then she'd told Philip all about Josh, including Seth's part in the process.

To her surprise, Philip had been delighted. "It'll be wonderful to have a baby around here again," he'd said. "I'll help."

Now, as Lacey picked her way down the icy path toward Seth's car, she tried to hold on to the joy of having Josh come to live with her.

I wanted him to have you, even if I couldn't. Seth's words tormented her all the way to the Blazer.

When she opened the door and slid in, she was greeted by a blast of heat, a sharp contrast to the frigid weather outside.

Without a word, Seth locked his hand on her neck and drew her close for a thorough kiss. "There, that's better." He brushed his thumb under her eye. "Rough night?"

She nodded.

"Can I do anything?"

She managed a weak smile. She wanted to say,

"Yes. You make me feel better just by being with me." Oh, God, how was she going to survive without him?

"Honey?"

"No, thanks." She glanced at the day care. "Our party was a success."

He nodded.

"I love the pajamas."

"Maybe I'll order a pair in my size."

She laughed, then, as he'd meant her to. "I'd like to see that."

His fingers grasped her neck again. "You can see anything you like, anytime," he joked.

She tried to participate in the mirth, but the knowledge that she'd never see him naked again, never kiss his chest again, never feel him full and firm inside her made her throat close up.

Seth's eyes narrowed. "Lace, honey, I'm not pressuring you for anything. I know that grief can dampen the libido. I was trying to cheer you up."

Oh, God, how wrong could he be? She'd like nothing better than to make love with him now, to lose herself in the sensations of his body against hers, to forget this awful aching grief for a few hours.

"I know that's what you were doing." She cleared her throat. "What did you want to talk about?"

His hesitation told her she hadn't quite convinced him. Finally he said, "I want to see you. To spend more than a few stolen moments together."

"You're busy tonight, aren't you?" she said, casually setting into works the first part of her plan.

He rolled his eyes. "Yeah, Cassie's having a dinner at Lambert's for me. To celebrate my twenty-fifth year at the high school."

Bravely Lacey smiled. She knew that once tonight was over, she'd have to tell him goodbye. She'd told Philip she wouldn't do it before Cassie's party and spoil the event for Seth.

But she could do it after.

"I wish you could be there," he told her.

I will be, along with a lot of others you don't expect.

"Me, too. Cassie's keeping it more intimate." She took a deep breath. "How about afterward?"

"Oh, honey, Joey's flying in this afternoon." He checked his watch. "I have to pick him up at the airport in an hour. We won't have any privacy at my house."

She stiffened. She'd planned to tell him tonight, and for her own sanity she needed to get it over with. "Let's meet somewhere. Just for an hour. Then you can go home to Joey."

If he was puzzled by the unusual request, he hid his feelings well.

"All right. Where?"

"How about the Marriott Hotel about ten miles outside of Bayview on the way to New York."

"In the bar?"

"No, I'll get a room." *We'll need the privacy.* In her heart, she knew Seth wouldn't take what she had to say to him easily.

He didn't respond immediately, then his arms enclosed her. "You're on, sweetheart," he said into her ear, though she caught the anxiety underlying the lightness.

Just wait, she thought ruefully. *Just wait.*

CHAPTER THIRTEEN

"DAD, are you okay?" Joey's voice penetrated the daze Seth had fallen into as he drove to Lambert's Party House at six o'clock that night.

"Sure. Why?"

"You've been quiet since you picked me up at the airport."

Seth glanced at his son. God, it was good to have Joey home. He chided himself for not enjoying it more.

"Sorry. I'm a little preoccupied, I guess. Did I tell you how great it is to see you?"

Joey grinned. "Yeah, you did." He reached over and gently punched Seth's arm. "It's good to be home. I'm really looking forward to Christmas."

"Me, too." Seth drove down a lane, searching for a space to park. "I wonder what else is going on here? The lot's packed."

"Must be some party."

"I still don't know why Cassie's having a get-together here for only ten or twelve people."

"What did she say?"

"That they've added on some smaller rooms and the chef was a former student at Bayview. She wanted to give him business."

"Sounds like Cassie."

"Yeah, but I hate being the center of attention."

"Dad, twenty-five years in education is something to celebrate."

Nodding, Seth thought about the phone call he'd received before he left tonight. From Mike Thomas—offering him the State Ed. job. How ironic. "I know it's a big deal," he told his son now, but he still didn't like the idea of a party. However, Mitch had asked him to humor Cassie, and Seth had agreed. He supposed he could handle a small celebration with a few close friends. Seth only wished Lacey could be here, but he knew that if Philip found out she'd attended, it would make things even worse.

As he and Joey made their way inside, Seth sidestepped the slush and looked up at the sky. He hoped the weather didn't get too bad for Lacey to drive out to the hotel later. He needed to talk to her; he was anxious to find out what she was thinking, feeling. Something was definitely wrong. Oh, hell, maybe it was just grief over Kevin. He quelled the notion that it had something to do with him.

When Joey pulled open the glass door to the party house, they ran into Mitch coming out of the rest room.

"Hello," Mitch said easily. "Perfect timing." He shook Joey's hand. "Hi, Joey."

"Hi."

"We're in through here." Mitch nodded toward a large room.

Before Seth could comment, Mitch opened the door and stood aside. Seth threw him a puzzled look but went in ahead of him.

And froze.

"Surprise!"

Inside, the room was filled to capacity, with people standing around individual tables set for dinner.

Seth didn't move. For a split second he didn't understand.

Then he saw his mother, two sisters and their families. Then Carolyn Spearman, Alex Ransom, Zoe Caufield and several other teachers. Board members, including Leonard Small. The superintendent of schools.

And when Cassie left her seat and headed toward them, he caught sight of Lacey standing and clapping, too.

Briefly he closed his eyes when he realized what Cassie had done.

"Congratulations, Seth," Cassie said, reaching out and giving him a hug.

When he pulled back, he glared at her. Before he could say anything, she slid her arm around Mitch's waist and leaned into her husband. "Ah, honey, you'd better tell him not to yell at me." She rubbed her protruding belly. "I'm pregnant and shouldn't be upset."

Mitch chuckled. "He's not going to yell at anyone. He's going to be gracious and enjoy his party. Aren't you, buddy?"

"Of course I am," Seth said, his glare encompassing Mitch.

He saw Joey slink away to his family's table.

"Come on and visit your guests for a while," Cassie suggested. "Dinner's in half an hour."

Seth spent the time hugging his mother, two sisters and their husbands, a nephew and two nieces. Then he went from table to table, greeting half of Bayview Heights. He took the ribbing good-naturedly, answered several times that, no, he'd had no clue this was in the works, and joked that it worried him that his staff could keep this shindig a secret for so long.

He worked his way back to Cassie's table—where Lacey sat. She wore a multicolored velvet jacket with sparkling gold threads woven through it. Her hair fell loosely around her shoulders. Her eyes were sad.

"You, too, Brutus?" he joked.

She stood and gave him a quick hug. "Me, too."

"I'm glad you came."

She smiled. "I wouldn't have missed it."

When Cassie and Mitch turned to a waiter, he leaned over and whispered, "Are we still on for afterward?"

She nodded. "If you can get away—with your family here."

"I think I can. The girls flew in today and my mom drove down from Binghamton. They'll probably be exhausted by then."

"All right. You'll be a while getting out of here. I'll go on ahead and leave an envelope with a key at the desk."

Drawing back, he gave her a searing look. "I can't wait."

She squeezed his arm. "Enjoy this, Seth. You deserve it." Her voice cracked on the last word and he wondered why.

The dinner passed in a blur. He visited with his

family and the people who stopped by his table. He learned that Cassie had been planning this for months, that his sisters had lied about not being able to come for Christmas and that the party house hadn't built any new rooms.

Seth was filled with a sense of well-being. The only dark spot in the evening was Lacey. He could see her clearly at the next table with the Lansings. Although she chatted with everyone, her smile was brittle and she pushed her filet mignon around the plate, barely eating any. She sipped wine but her hand gripped the glass a little too tightly. He kept reminding himself that Kevin's death was still uppermost in her mind.

Abruptly he was roused from his reflection by the screech of a microphone turning on. He swiveled toward the noise and saw his son standing next to Johnny Battaglia on a small raised dais. Each held a mike. Behind them was a large-screen TV. Seth frowned and his gaze flew to Cassie. Glancing over at him, she shrugged and nodded for him to pay attention to the boys.

"Welcome, everybody," Johnny said with an ease that surprised Seth. Garbed in dressy black pants and a black silk shirt, he looked confident and poised. "In case some of you don't remember me…you know, like you, Mr. Ransom, or you, Ms. Spearman—" the audience laughed "—I'm that kid who was always in trouble at school. And this is Joe Taylor, my foil—got that, Mr. Taylor, foil, a good literary term."

Joey's deep voice came over the mike. He wore

a navy suit, with a white shirt and red tie. "I'm the angel, he's the devil."

"I'm the bad seed, he's the good one."

Again the crowd laughed, including Seth. The guys traded a few more barbs, then sobered.

Joey said, "We've got a short video clip to show you before we go on. It'll help explain the program we have planned."

Johnny broke in. "This was Ms. Lansing's idea. You know how those English teachers love symbolism."

There were chuckles around the room as the video began.

Seth watched with interest as he heard the strains of Christmas music. Jimmy Stewart's *It's a Wonderful Life* came on the screen. He listened to the kids tell George Bailey's story as they fast-forwarded into the movie. They paused at the scene where Bailey hovers over the bridge, crashing waters beneath him.

"George Bailey's about to commit suicide here, and he's rescued by a somewhat tarnished angel," Joey told them.

Johnny joked, "Like me, maybe?"

"Nope, *I'm* the angel."

"Anyway, this is the scene we want you to see."

George Bailey sat in the guard's office and the angel, Clarence, told him he'd come to save George's life. When Bailey said his life wasn't worth saving, that it would be better if he'd never been born, the angel replied, "You just don't know what you've done."

Then the screen flicked off. Seth held his breath, suspicion coupling with warmth inside him.

"Don't worry, my dad's not suicidal," Joey said. "But for a while now, he's been questioning exactly how much good he's done at Bayview Heights High School."

Johnny added, "And we don't have the ability to transform the world to show him how life would've been if he'd never come to Bayview. But we've got something almost as good."

"So sit back and enjoy the program. You, too, Dad."

The stage darkened and a spotlight focused on Johnny. "I asked to go first. I'm a premed student at Columbia University. I just got my grades for first semester and they were a perfect 4.0. Seth Taylor played a major role in this accomplishment. He started an At-Risk Program that a lot of people opposed. He hired the best teachers—" Johnny glanced over to Cassie's table "—and gave us his support. Without that, I would never have gotten this far. I'd never be the successful doctor I'm going to be, or led the life I'm going to lead. That's what you've done for me, Mr. T."

The audience clapped. Seth felt his throat tighten.

Johnny added, "Now, Mr. T., don't come up here during the program and hug me or anybody else." He assumed a tough-guy posture. "Wouldn't want to ruin my image." He smiled at Seth. "Just sit there and relax." He angled his head to the right. "And listen to our next speaker."

Seth vaguely recognized the tall lanky man who

approached the mike. "Hi, Mr. T. Remember me?" The voice did it. Seth nodded.

"I'm John Henderson," the former student told the group. "I was class valedictorian in 1985. I used to wear those big horn-rimmed glasses and a brush cut—before it was in style."

And he'd been expected to go into his father's law firm, Seth remembered. Which he hadn't wanted to do.

"Mr. Taylor gave me some good advice my senior year. He told me I could do anything I wanted in life. I didn't have to live up to everybody else's expectations. Just my own. Now, I could've been a hotshot lawyer, and some of you might think that I wasted my life. But I didn't. I switched majors and took creative writing. I'm doing what I love." He held up a hardcover book. "I wrote this," he said proudly. "And my agent sold it within two months. Doubleday Book Club just picked it up as an alternate choice." There was a hush over the audience, although some people knew John had become a writer. The man opened the cover. "I'd like to read you the dedication. 'To Seth Taylor, who showed me that I could do anything I wanted.'" He stared out at the audience. "That's what you've done for me, Mr. T."

Amidst enthusiastic applause, Seth closed his eyes. He scrubbed his hands over his face. When he looked up, a tiny old woman made her way to the mike.

"Hello," she said in a quavering voice. "I'm Florence Bellamy." She peered out over wire-rimmed glasses at the audience. "I had many of you for typing years ago." Several people in the crowd clapped as they recognized the teacher. Seth swallowed hard as she told her story of how he'd helped her cope with being almost sixty and trying to keep up with teenagers. She couldn't retire because she hadn't been teaching long enough to draw a pension that would support her and her husband, who was ill. "At first I thought those newfangled teaching ideas were bunk. And that Seth Taylor was too young, at thirty-five, to be a principal. But he taught me how to deal with young people effectively. I ended my career at sixty-five happier than I'd ever been in my life. Thank you, young man," she said poignantly.

Though they'd told him to stay seated, he couldn't do it. He threw back his chair and strode to the front. He gave Mrs. Bellamy a big hug and escorted her from the stage.

By the time he was in his chair again, a man Seth had never seen before was at the podium. "I'm Jack Carrington. You don't know me, Mr. Taylor, but I married Judy Larson." Seth remembered vividly the shy young girl who'd been abused by her uncle. When Seth had found out about it, he'd gone to the authorities and gotten her help. "Judy died four years ago in a car accident. She'd been employed as a social worker in a youth shelter in New York City. She talked about you all the time. She said she wanted to help kids like you helped her. And she did. Scores of girls passed through Gentlehands, and Judy was there to give them what *you* gave *her*— understanding and hope." The man's voice broke on the last words. "She would've wanted me to come here tonight and tell you this, Mr. T."

Tears filled Seth's eyes. He tried hard to suppress them, and succeeded by locking his fingers tightly together. He sat through more students—a soldier decorated in Desert Storm, a boy who'd been on the verge of suicide, a popular cheerleader who'd been heavily into drugs. Seth remembered working with them all.

Then Cassie got to the podium. She carried papers in her hand. "We also received many letters from those we contacted who couldn't be here tonight. We'll give them to you later, Mr. T. But I'd like to end the program by reading this one. It's very meaningful to me and I think you'll see why."

Seth shifted in his seat. Already overcome with emotion, he wasn't sure he could handle more. His sister reached over and took his hand. He squeezed it and held on. Cassie read:

Dear Mr. T.,

I'm not sure you'll even remember me, but I was in your tenth-grade English class twenty-five years ago. My name was Sally Sorensen. I got pregnant at the end of my sophomore year and was going to have an abortion. I told you about it. You didn't lecture me. You didn't tell me what to do. You just talked about values, about caring and making the right choices. And I listened. I didn't have that abortion. I dropped out of school, remember? I had a baby boy.

Eventually, I met and married a wonderful man, went back to school and got my high-school diploma. I didn't do much after that, but I had my baby because of you.

I couldn't come to your celebration tonight because my son—James Seth Stanton—is graduating from Harvard Medical School today, the day of your party. Yes, it's early. He's been ahead in grades all through school. Remember how I couldn't tell a noun from a verb? Well not him. He's graduating magna cum laude and plans to study with the best researchers in Europe. Who knows, maybe someday he'll discover a cure for cancer or win a Nobel Prize in medicine.

And I almost didn't have him. This boy might change the world, Mr. T., because of you.

Thank you from the bottom of my heart.

Sally

By the time Cassie finished reading, she was sniffling. So were his mother and sisters. Seth put his head in his hands and dug his fingertips into his eyelids.

Dimly he was aware that everyone was standing and clapping. Then Joey touched his arm. "Dad, you've got to go up there."

At first Seth was shocked that he was expected to be coherent. So many emotions swirled inside him. Then he looked up and his gaze sought Lacey. She was on her feet, too, applauding. She angled her head to the podium, telling him to go there.

He did. He wound his way around several tables, patting people on the back as he passed them. When he reached the front, he took the mike from Johnny, who stepped back, and said, "None of that hugging stuff." But Seth embraced him anyway.

Facing the audience, Seth cleared his throat. "A friend of mine once told me he envied teachers because the good that they do has a domino effect. When he said that, I half listened. I was in a pretty bad funk then, wondering what good I'd done at Bayview Heights." He smiled at the crowd. "Well, thanks to all of you, I know that my buddy was right. Those of you who came up here today, or wrote letters, say I touched your lives. I won't forget that again, I promise. And I want you all to know that you've touched mine, too. Thank you for reminding me of that."

Amidst cheers and applause, Seth made his way back to his seat. By the time he reached the Lansings' table, Lacey was gone.

LACEY STARED out the window of her room at the Marriott Hotel, watching the puffs of snow drift to the ledge. Her own reflection was mirrored in the glass. Her shoulders were stiff, her face drawn tight.

Relax, girl, or you'll never convince him. If he sees you hurt and crying, he'll never agree to what you have to do.

So she summoned the earlier images of him: his eyes glistening with unshed tears at all the stories told about him, his dazzling smile as he addressed the crowd, the huskiness in his voice when he thanked them.

Juxtaposed to that she heard her grandfather's

strained accusation, *He's a con man and a menace to young people.*

Lacey swallowed the lump in her throat. Now, more than ever, she couldn't let her grandfather ruin him. Not after what she'd witnessed tonight. All those lives he'd affected…he had to continue as principal of Bayview Heights High School.

The only thing she wasn't sure of was how she was going to stand by and watch him go on with his life, day after day, year after year. He was such an attractive man, he'd surely marry someone else. Would his wife have the baby Lacey longed to give him? Could Lacey bear to watch that?

"Stop it!" she told herself. She'd cope with that if she had to. She'd do anything to protect the man she loved.

After all, she'd coped with all kinds of loss. Her mother. Then her father. Most recently, Kevin. The acute pain caused by his death settled heavily in her soul.

Her reflections were interrupted by a noise at the door. A key. Then Seth was there, standing before her, looking so happy she wanted to weep.

"Hi," he said as he entered the room.

"Hi."

He held up a bottle of champagne and two glasses. "To celebrate."

"Where did you get it?"

"We had a toast, and since you weren't there, I brought you some." Setting down the bottle and glasses, he strode to her and hauled her into his arms. His kiss was long and thorough and had her clinging to him. When he was done, he drew back.

His eyes were still glowing. Brushing a lock of hair off her cheek, he asked, "Why did you leave?"

"You needed time with your friends and family. I didn't want to intrude."

Drawing her close again, he brushed his lips against her hair. "You should have been next to me tonight. I never want to go through anything good or bad again without you by my side."

She struggled not to stiffen.

"Lace? What is it?"

"Nothing. Did you get a chance to visit with your family?"

"Yeah. I went back to the house with them for a while. By ten-thirty, everybody was more than ready for bed."

"Good. Let's have some champagne."

He hesitated but turned to the bottle. As he went through the uncorking process, he babbled. "I can't believe Cassie pulled this off without my knowing."

"She was so excited."

"I'm shocked Mitch let her do it. He said she had help locating the people who attended."

Lacey shifted. Just then Seth looked up to hand her a glass. "What?"

She shook her head and took the wine. "Nothing. Let's toast."

"Not until you tell me what you were thinking when you got that guilty look on your face."

As good as any way to begin. "Okay, I'll tell you. But a toast first. To Seth Taylor, the best educator in the world."

He grinned. "How could I have ever considered leaving the high school?"

They clinked glasses. The champagne was tart and its bubbles tickled her nose.

"Now, tell me what part you played in this," he said.

Her throat closed up. Oh, God, how could she do this? "I gave Cassie the names of those people who spoke tonight."

He stilled. "I don't understand."

"They were in that file my grandfather had on you from the private investigator."

"What?"

"Adams dug up only good things about your career, Seth." She hesitated then added, "Until last week."

Seth's eyes widened. He sighed heavily and then took a sip of champagne. Then another. Finally he said, "He found out about Carson City."

"Yes."

"You know the whole story."

"Yes. I know the facts, and I also read between the lines."

"Meaning?"

"Meaning Tim Johnson's actions were no more your fault than my brother's were."

Seth reached over and ran a hand down her cheek. "What did I ever do to deserve you?"

Turning her face into his palm, she kissed it lightly. "All those wonderful things they talked about tonight."

"Lace, I made a terrible mistake with Johnson." Seth's voice was raw with remembrance. "It still haunts me. I've spent twenty-five years trying to make up for it. It's one of the reasons I've been so vehement about helping new teachers. And why I'm tough on violent students." He waited a minute. "Like Kevin."

"I understand... You were twenty-one years old. What's more, your crime was believing in a kid."

"I used bad judgment."

"At twenty-one most of us use bad judgment. Frequently. You were only a few years older than Joey. That's pretty young, Seth."

"I..." His eyes clouded with pain. "The girl was never the same after the rape."

Setting down her glass, Lacey went to him and wrapped her arms around his neck. "I'm so sorry."

He held on to her with one hand. His champagne glass—to toast all his accomplishments—teetered in the other. Lacey didn't miss the irony. After a moment, he said, "Thanks."

Slowly she drew back. "Seth, Philip's private investigator unearthed this information last week."

"So that's what the guy was doing at the *Herald*'s office."

"Yes."

"And Philip told you about this hoping to discredit me in your eyes."

She smiled. "It didn't work." Her smile faded. "But that was only part of the reason he got this on you."

"Why else?"

"He planned to ruin your reputation with it. Make it public along with the fact that you omitted your year at Carson City on your application to teach at Bayview."

"How did he know that?"

"He got a copy of your application."

Seth paced to the other side of the room. "My God, he must really want to hurt me."

"He does. But I'm not going to let him."

Seth whipped around. "What does *that* mean?"

She raised her chin. "I'm not going to see you after tonight. In return, Philip won't make this information public."

"No! That's blackmail. I won't allow it."

"Actually," she said, "I blackmailed him."

"I don't understand."

"Philip didn't set the terms. He was going to go ahead and reveal the story, thinking to destroy you. I put the terms to him."

"You're kidding."

"No. I told him I'd leave town—and him—forever if he made the story public. If he killed it, I'd stay here, but call it quits with you."

A flush climbed up Seth's neck. "The hell you will."

"There's no other way."

"We decided we could be together and work this out with Philip."

"We decided we could be together *if* Philip would accept you."

"And?"

"Don't you see that this threat to expose your past shows he'll never accept you?"

Thunderclouds passed over Seth's face. "All right, so he never accepts me. We'll be together without his blessing."

"Then he'll make the information public and destroy your reputation."

"I don't care."

"Well, I do. Think ahead a little. We suffer through a scandal, you lose your job here. You may or may not get another job in education. Depending on how far Philip goes with this, it could follow you anywhere. You'd be miserable."

"Not if I had you," he said, coming to stand before her.

"That won't be enough."

"Lacey, I—"

She held up her palm. "No, let me finish. If we get married, what do you think will happen to my grandfather?"

"He'll die a lonely old man. Like he deserves."

Lacey gasped.

"I'm sorry. I shouldn't have said that."

Regrouping, Lacey went on, "Seth, Philip gave up his career as one of the country's top journalists for me. He doesn't deserve to die alone. Besides, a scandal and losing me could lead to his having another heart attack. One he might not recover from. Do you honestly believe you and I could live happily together knowing we'd killed my grandfather to do it?"

"Don't put it like that."

"That's how it is."

"Lacey, honey, you said we'd work this out. You said you wouldn't give me up."

"That was when I thought there was a chance Philip would accept you. Now I know he *won't*." She gripped his arms. "Please, Seth, for all our sakes, try to see that."

"No, Lacey, no. It can't end this way."

"It has to."

Abruptly Seth let go of her and prowled the room once more. She watched him struggle to gain control, struggle to internalize—and accept—what she'd said. It took a long time, but she could tell when he did. He stopped pacing and studied her for long seconds. The realization that her words were true, her points accurate, dawned on his handsome, beloved face. "I can't believe this. I'm really going to lose you?" Seth walked to her and gently took her in his arms. "Lace, oh, Lord..."

She willed herself not to cry. She couldn't break down. She had to be strong. If she wasn't, Seth would never let her go.

So she concentrated on the strength of his muscles against her breasts. The silky texture of his hair. How his shoulders made her feel small and feminine. Drawing back, she raised her eyes to his. As she drew his head down, she whispered, "I stopped at the shop in the lobby downstairs. We're prepared tonight, Seth."

He closed his eyes. "You mean you want—"

"I want to make love for..." She didn't say the rest, but she knew he understood, *For the last time*.

The misery on his face, the utter desolation in those blue eyes she loved so much, almost undid her. She stood on tiptoe and brought her mouth to his.

As soon as his lips brushed across hers, she knew that this time their lovemaking would be as gentle as it had been out of control the last time. He barely touched her with his mouth; his hands skimmed over her arms, around her back, cradling her bottom and easing her close. She felt herself melt into him, be absorbed by him, steep in him. His lips were everywhere, but still gentle and tender.

Slowly, as if they had years together instead of hours, he shifted and tugged at the buttons on her jacket. Underneath, his teeth lightly grazed the black strap of her bra before seeking fingers came up to undo it. As he filled his hands with her breasts, he murmured, "So lovely," and kissed each one. "You are so, so lovely," he repeated.

He loosened her skirt, removed it and her panty hose along with her panties. His hands lingered over every curve. When she realized he was memorizing her body, she shivered with grief.

Mistaking her reaction, he led her to the bed, turned down the covers and gently pressed her down so she sat on the mattress. She reached out and pulled him to stand between her legs. The wool of his suit felt slightly rough on the skin of her inner thighs. She undid his belt as he shrugged out of his coat, pulled off his tie and unbuttoned his shirt. Her mouth sought his skin; her lips brushed back and forth across his stomach, and his arousal pressed insistently into her chest.

"I'll never forget how you taste, how you smell," she mumbled against his skin.

He groaned, from pain at her words, she realized, so she unzipped his pants to distract him.

Seth felt her take him into her hands, stroke him and kiss him lightly.

Arousal warred with rage inside him.

As she had meant it to, arousal won. He endured the caress as long as he could, then eased her back onto the sheets. He slid her up until she lay on the king-size bed. Quickly he shed the rest of his clothes and sheathed himself with one of the condoms she'd bought. His eyes locked on hers. Did she know how sad they looked? How he could tell she was crumbling inside? Somehow, he knew she needed this— so, dear God, did he—but the poignant sorrow on her face ate away at him.

When he covered her body with his, he said, "I love you, Lacey. I'll never love anyone like I love you."

"Come inside me now. I need to feel you there."

He obeyed. He was powerless to stop the gentle glide into her soft, welcoming body. Just as he was powerless to stop the arch of her hips against him. Instead, he helped her, inching his hands under her bottom to lift her to meet him more fully. He slid in and out of her, only twice before the spasms overtook her. She called out his name. Just before the final thrust, just before he emptied himself inside her, he saw the sparkle of tears in her eyes.

Seth surfaced from the depths of the most intense orgasm of his life to the sound of her sobs. Slowly, he edged to his side. Because she whimpered and said, "No, don't leave me," he moved her with him. He wasn't ready for the separation either.

Cradling her against him, he tugged up the blankets and held on to her. All she said was, "How will I ever bear watching you go on with your life— fall in love with someone else, have a child with her?"

"Shh," he said and smoothed her hair down.

She cried longer, but eventually the tears abated and dried on her face. Then she fell asleep.

But Seth didn't. He stayed awake, analyzing every facet of what she'd told him. He could get around losing his job. He'd find somewhere to teach, even if he had to donate his services in underprivileged areas. With Lacey, it would be worth the sacrifice of his reputation. But it was the fact that Philip could have another heart attack that Seth couldn't rationalize. If Philip died, Lacey would never be happy. She'd lost every other member of her family; she was still on the razor edge of grief because of Kevin's death. She would never survive losing Philip over something she'd precipitated.

Near 2:00 a.m., when it was time to wake her, Seth accepted that there was only one thing he could do for her now, one last gift he could give her.

And he'd do it, damn it, no matter what the cost to himself.

CHAPTER FOURTEEN

ON THE MONDAY before Christmas, at lunchtime, Philip dragged open his front door to find Seth Taylor on the porch. "What the hell are you doing here?"

Taylor scanned Philip's rumpled bathrobe and slippers. A frown creased his forehead. "Are you ill?"

"No," Philip said gruffly. "I overslept." In truth, Philip had roamed the downstairs most of the night, worrying about Lacey. He didn't have enough energy to get dressed yet. "What do you want?"

"Five minutes of your time." Philip started to shake his head, but Seth said, "I won't leave until I've spoken with you."

Hearing the steel in the man's voice, Philip stepped aside and motioned him in. He should have known Taylor wouldn't take this lying down. The only thing Lacey had told Philip yesterday was that she'd broken off with Taylor. He could still see her in the doorway of her bedroom, lifting her brown eyes—brimming with utter anguish—to him. "It's done," was all she'd said.

Philip hadn't experienced the sense of satisfaction he'd expected to feel when he heard those words.

Still in the foyer, Philip shivered with the cold

Taylor had brought with him. "We can go in the living room, if you're chilled," Taylor said, his tone concerned.

Anger kindled inside Philip. He refused to be susceptible to Taylor's phony solicitousness. "What do you want?"

"To give you these." Taylor held out an envelope in his gloved hand. His *unsteady* gloved hand.

Regarding him carefully, Philip snatched up the envelope. With a long glare at the man he hated more than anyone in the world, Philip ripped open the seal. Inside he found two letters, both written by Taylor. One to the Bayview Heights Board of Education. One to the State Education Department in Albany. Philip scanned them. "What's all this about?"

"You win, Philip. I'm leaving Bayview Heights High School."

Philip ignored the undiluted sadness in the other man's voice. "Running scared, Taylor?"

Taylor's face reddened and his hands fisted at his sides. "You just don't get it, do you?"

"What do you mean?"

"I'm not afraid of you. For myself, anyway. I'm only fearful of what you can do to your granddaughter. If I thought Lacey could handle a fight, I'd stay and give you the battle of your life. But she can't withstand one after all she's been through."

"I can take care of Lacey."

"You've done a *wonderful* job lately." Taylor gave him a scathing glance to accompany his sarcastic comment. "Tell me, Philip, how was she yesterday?"

Philip's heart plummeted. Lacey had come home Saturday night around 3:00 a.m. She'd stayed in bed all day Sunday. When he'd gone upstairs at noon to check on her, she came to the door disheveled and distraught. All she'd said was, "I'm tired, Grandpa. I need to sleep."

"She was tired. She slept most of the day."

A muscle tensed in Taylor's jaw. "That doesn't sound like Lacey."

No, of course it didn't. Philip had gone back up at four in the afternoon with soup, crackers and some milk. From the doorway again, she'd glanced at the meal; he was afraid she might vomit all over it. "Are you sick, honey?" he'd asked. "Should I call Doc Meyers?"

She'd shaken her head and returned to bed.

Philip shifted from one foot to the other. "It'll take her a while to get through this. First Kevin's death, now you. Her relationship with you has made her miserable."

Taylor's teeth clenched. "A fact I truly regret."

The other man's acceptance of his role in Lacey's pain pricked Philip's conscience. Especially in light of the fact that Philip was more concerned about Lacey than he was letting on. He'd gone back to her room at eight in the evening, with hot chocolate. She'd let him in then, but slid back in bed. She'd sipped a little cocoa, staring blindly into space. Then she'd looked at him with hollow eyes. "I need to go back to sleep, Grandpa."

Her dejected tone tore at him. "Honey, I..."

"No, please, just give me space."

He had, but he'd heard her sobs as he'd closed

the door, and twice when he'd checked on her during the night, she was crying again.

Taylor drew him out of the recollection. "My leaving Bayview Heights will help her get over me," Taylor said, nodding toward the papers he'd given Philip.

"How?"

"Bayview is too small a place for us to avoid seeing each other." He cleared his throat. "And eventually, if I dated...or she was with another man, neither of us could..." Taylor's voice trailed off and he strove visibly to get control of himself. "Suffice it to say that I love her too much to make her suffer any more than she has to. And she's ready to snap. It's best for her if I leave Bayview Heights." He indicated the envelope again. "I have the perfect vehicle to do it now. So I'm moving right after the new year."

Hardening his heart against Taylor, refusing to acknowledge the selfless gesture, Philip held up the letters. "You think I'm going to change my mind, tell you not to do this?"

Seth shook his head sadly. "I've already done it. By registered mail, this morning. I came here to tell you about it so you'll be prepared to deal with Lacey. She won't find out until after the holidays, but she'll need you then. You'll have to help her through it."

Philip remained silent.

Taylor straightened his shoulders. Against his will, Philip really looked at the man. His eyes were bloodshot and his skin drawn tight across his cheekbones.

Taylor broke the perusal by starting for the door. When he reached for the handle, he stopped and turned back to Philip. "You know, I feel sorry for you. If you love her half as much as I do, it'll kill you to watch her suffer through this." He looked Philip up and down. "I would never have asked her to choose between you and me, never forced her to accept another loss."

Again, Philip was speechless.

"I hope your heart's strong enough to take that." Then Taylor left, closing the door softly behind him.

Philip trudged into the den and sat down at his desk. He tried to busy himself with the *Herald,* planning how he'd get back into the business slowly, but he kept seeing Lacey's face, hearing her sobs and recalling Taylor's words, *I would never have asked her to choose...*

"Philip?" he heard from the doorway.

Celia. Good, she'd clarify things for him, make the situation better. She'd done a lot of that lately.

His housekeeper walked into the room. "Are you all right?"

"It's been a tough week."

Sitting down across from him, she got right to the point. "The party Saturday for Taylor must have been hard for you."

Philip's fist clenched. He'd heard about the party the school had given for that bastard. It strengthened his resolve. "Not as hard as you might guess." Succinctly, Philip told Celia what had transpired that weekend.

Instead of being happy for him, Celia shook her

head, her soft features transformed into a frown. "I was hoping you wouldn't go this far, Philip."

"What do you mean?"

"How can you put your own needs above your granddaughter's happiness?"

"I'm doing what's best for Lacey. I always have."

"Not this time." Celia straightened and held his gaze unblinkingly. "I've always admired you for coming back to Bayview to raise those kids when you were on your way to a Pulitzer Prize. After my Ken died, I think I was even a little in love with you. But not anymore." She stood and shrugged into the coat she carried. "I can't work for you any longer, Philip. I can't be a party to this selfish, unnecessary thing you're doing to those two young people. You'll have to find another housekeeper."

Before she reached the door, Philip rose from his chair. "Celia?" She turned. "I thought we were friends. More than just employer and employee."

"We were. But I don't want a friend who would do this awful thing. Goodbye, Philip."

The rest of the day passed in a blur. Philip managed to dress and eat some soup, but he waited anxiously for Lacey to return from work.

It was worth the wait. She burst through the door carrying a baby boy. "Mrs. Cornwall let me take him for supper, Grandpa." As she tugged off Josh's snowsuit, her eyes, still red, still swollen, at least had life in them. It was going to be all right. "I signed the papers for foster care today. They take effect in two days." She looked down at the boy. "Josh, meet your grandfather."

Philip was shocked to see tears in her eyes. "Lacey? Honey?"

She shook her head. "No, it's okay. Say hi to Josh."

They played with the baby, and ate sandwiches for supper. When Lacey asked about Celia, Philip made some excuse about her not coming in today. Lacey let it go. After she returned from taking Josh home, she went upstairs. Soon he heard scrapes along the floor above him and the blare of some ungodly rock music coming from her stereo.

He went to investigate.

She didn't answer his knock—probably didn't hear it—so he eased open the door. Her lovely room, the one he'd kept just as she'd had it fourteen years ago when she'd left home for good, was torn apart. The pictures had been taken off the wall. The bed had been moved across the room. Bed linen, curtains and other knickknacks were in piles on the floor.

He watched in silence as Lacey, her back to him, yanked on the middle drawer of her desk. It stuck. She yanked again. After three tries, it gave way. She pulled the drawer so hard it came off the track. She froze for a moment. Then, to his utter astonishment, she raised it up a foot and smashed it down onto the corner of the desk. Pens, paper went flying. The wood splintered. Lacey stared at it for a moment, then sank to her knees in a fit of weeping.

Philip rushed to her, knelt down and grasped her shoulders. Before he could say anything, she shook him off. "No, please, go. Leave me alone. I just want to be left alone."

After a long hesitation, Philip stumbled to his feet, crossed the room and left her crying on the floor.

ON TUESDAY, Philip was pleased when Leonard Small called him and invited him to lunch at Pepper's. As they sat in a small booth, Philip chatted aimlessly, grateful for the respite from worrying about Lacey.

After lunch, Leonard coughed and cleared his throat. "Philip, I've got something to say to you."

Philip's forehead creased.

"You know I'm glad the superintendent insisted I attend Taylor's party Saturday night." Leonard peered over at Philip, scowling. "In light of the dinner—and the registered letter yesterday notifying the school district of Taylor's resignation—I have to tell you that I don't like what you've done here. What *I've* helped you do. Taylor's made some mistakes, but if you could have heard all those people talk about him, seen all those kids and adults he helped—"

"I don't want to hear this!"

Leonard watched him quietly for a minute. "Well, you're going to have to hear it. We've been friends for almost fifty years. If I don't tell you this, no one will."

Don't bet on it, Philip thought, recalling Celia's comments.

"You're wrong about Seth Taylor. People make mistakes, particularly when they're young. I've made my share and you've made yours. What's more, you've no right to interfere in Taylor's life."

"When he's after my granddaughter, I do."

"No, Philip, you don't. Lacey's *thirty*-four, not four. If she's making a mistake with Taylor—which I don't think she is—it's her business. She has a right to make her own choices without your interference."

"She made her own choice."

Leonard shook his head. "She made *your* choice, Philip. Ultimately you know that." He put down his napkin and slid out of the booth. Standing over the table, his old friend finished, "I truly regret the part I played in this scheme of yours. I've got a lot of penance to do over it." After a pause, he added, "So do you. I hope you realize that before it's too late."

With a squeeze of Philip's shoulder, Leonard left him alone in the diner.

After supper that night, Philip was mulling over Leonard's words when Lacey appeared at the den doorway. "I'm going running, Grandpa."

He took in her heavy sweatshirt and sweatpants. "Over at the school?"

Her eyes were blank. "No, no, I'm not running at the school anymore. Outside."

Philip glanced at the window. The glass was frosted over. "It's freezing weather, honey. You can't run outdoors in the middle of winter."

She shrugged stiffly. "Of course I can. See you later."

And she was gone.

For too long.

Philip worried as the minutes ticked by. He lost track of how many times he opened the front door looking for her. After almost two hours, he was alarmed. *Lacey's ready to snap...*

Philip walked to the phone to call the Lansings. Mitch would go look for her. Oh, God, what if she'd tripped and was lying hurt somewhere? His heart thudded in his chest as he searched for the phone directory Lacey kept in the drawer. Clumsy hands made finding the number slow.

He was just dialing when the side door opened and closed. His body sagged with relief, and a wave of dizziness overcame him. He seized the edge of the desk to steady himself. When he was finally able to make his way out of the den, he found her climbing the stairs. "Lacey?"

She stopped. As he approached her, he said, "Are you all right?"

She wasn't. Her face was as white as the snow outside, her lips thinned, bluish. Her slender body shivered.

But it was her eyes that got to him. They were glazed, vacant. "All right?" she asked. The cold had made her voice hoarse.

He reached out and touched her hood, running his hand down it. Little bits of icicles beaded the fleece. For a minute, she stiffened then she leaned into his touch. "Honey, you've been gone two hours."

"I have?" Again the husky voice. "I ran...I don't know exactly where..." She stared at him with wide and hollow eyes. "I just kept running."

He didn't know to do. He studied her taut features, her rigid stance, and finally said, "Go take a warm bath, honey."

Wordlessly she nodded and trudged up the stairs, her steps made heavy by the snow that caked the sneakers she still wore. Philip was reminded of the night her father died. She'd been overwhelmed with grief and he'd insisted she take a hot bath, then had brought her and Kevin cocoa in bed.

Somehow Philip knew chocolate and warm water wouldn't be enough tonight.

Lacey went to bed soon after her bath. Philip lit a fire in the den and turned on the TV to distract himself.

Christmas movies were playing. He reached for the remote to shut off the TV, when he realized he'd tuned into his favorite film, *A Christmas Carol*. He wanted to turn it off, but something kept him from doing so. Instead, he watched Ebeneezer Scrooge systematically alienate all those he loved. *His partner.* Philip thought of Leonard Small. *Scrooge's fiancée.* Philip saw Celia's face, heard the condemnation in her voice. Philip remembered Lacey, half-frozen on the steps.

And, for the first time in his seventy-six years, Philip was ashamed of himself.

SETH SAT ALONE in church waiting for the annual Christmas Eve candlelight service to begin. Though they didn't attend church regularly, he and Joey always came to this particular service, as did half the town. It was a moving, poignant highlight of the Christmas season.

Joey was out in the narthex, talking with a girl Seth suspected his son had a crush on. He smiled at the thought. How many more years would the boy join Seth to participate in their annual holiday ritual?

Seth prayed for strength. God knew he'd been in despair for the last several days.

There'd been the excruciating process of resigning his job and accepting the State Ed. position.
He'd sat in his office, staring at the plaques on the
wall, wondering how he was ever going to live without Lacey *and* without the job.

Seth decided to think about all the good things he
had to be thankful for this Christmas Eve.

First, as always, there was Joey. He was working
at the *Herald,* and like a hungry man staring at a
banquet he'd been barred from, Seth waited every
day to hear about Lacey. *She's so cool Dad, she let
me copyedit one of the smaller stories… She signed
the papers today to give foster care to this little
boy… Why is Ms. Cartwright so sad? Is it because
of her brother?*

Despite having to hear about Lacey's suffering,
Joey's joy in working at the *Herald* was a blessing
Seth cherished.

When he turned around to look for his son, he
saw the Lansings, along with Johnny, enter the
church and sit in the back pew. Probably in case
Cassie had to leave. He smiled at them. She was due
any day. Another blessing in his life. Seth recalled
the dinner she'd organized, and all those people who
had come to tell him he'd done a good job at the
high school.

He *had* done good things there. The latest piece
of news was that Jerry Bosco had sent in his letter
of intent to retire, effective this June.

As Joey came down a side aisle and sat down on
his left, Seth saw Darcy McCormick and Nick Leonardi sidle into a pew next to Nick's parents. Yes,
Seth had done some good.

The church darkened and the minister began to light the candles assembled on the altar.

It was when their glow illuminated the church once again that he saw Lacey had slipped in and sat three rows up, on the opposite side of the sanctuary. On her right was Philip. On her left, little Josh, holding tightly to her hand.

As the congregation stood to sing "Away in a Manger," Seth feasted his eyes on her. She'd removed her coat and wore dark green, velvety-looking pants and an oversize shirt. Her lush flaxen hair was pulled back in a clip and, too vividly, he recalled what it felt like sliding through his fingers. He wished he could see her face, but it was too dim inside the church.

He tried to tear his gaze away from her, but he couldn't. When the lights came up for the choir to sing, Seth saw Josh climb up to stand on the pew. Lacey reached to heft him down, but the toddler got a glimpse of Seth.

Josh's features broke out in a huge grin. "Se…Se…Se," he said aloud, and before Lacey could stop him, he scrambled out of the pew—heading right for Seth. He raced down the aisle as Seth stepped out and scooped him up. "Hi, buddy," he whispered.

Josh patted Seth's face and gave him a sloppy kiss on the cheek. By then, the choir had begun a complex rendition of "It Came Upon a Midnight Clear," and Lacey came toward them. As he hugged the child to his chest, Seth met her eyes. The absolute love he saw in hers nearly leveled him. But God must have been watching over them, because

Seth found the strength to smile and she smiled back. Reluctantly, he handed the baby over to her, and squeezed her arm.

Be strong, he told her silently.

I will, she said with her eyes.

Seth sat through the rest of the service in a daze. He managed to make his way to the narthex without too much trouble, though he felt as if he was bleeding inside. He avoided Lacey and Josh, snatched his coat from the rack and was heading for the door when he felt a strong hand grasp his shoulder.

He turned to find Philip Cartwright behind him.

"GET THE DOOR, Lacey, will you?" Philip called from the den. "Before the bell wakes up Josh."

Lacey rose from her seat by the living-room fire, dreading a visit from whoever was here at nine o'clock on Christmas Eve. She wasn't up to company; the contact with Seth at the church had drained what little strength she had. All she wanted to do was look forward to tomorrow morning, when Mrs. Cornwall would join them to see Josh receive his presents.

Dragging open the door, the smile she'd pasted on her face vanished. Her jaw dropped. "Oh my God. What are you doing here?"

"I don't exactly know." Seth stood before her, looking so sexy in his tweed coat and holiday scarf that her knees buckled with longing. She grasped the door handle to steady herself. They stood there, devouring the sight of each other, while snow dusted his shoulders and a light wind whipped around Lacey's slippered feet.

"I don't understand," she told him.

"I'll explain it to you both," Philip said from behind them. "Now get that man inside, Lacey, before you catch cold."

Seth stepped into the foyer, a puzzled expression on his face. Lacey closed the door, numb with surprise.

"Come in here," they heard Philip order as he headed for the living room.

Silently Seth followed Lacey.

"Sit down." Philip went to stand by the hearth, looking grim.

Seth and Lacey exchanged glances then started for chairs opposite from each other.

"On the couch, together."

Oh, God, Lacey thought. *One more chance to be close to him.*

They sat, their thighs brushing. Both stared up at Philip. It was then that Lacey realized the tree lights glowed and flickered and soft Christmas carols crooned from the stereo. Both for the first time this season.

Philip dug his hands into his pants pockets and faced them squarely. He looked younger tonight, less weary, almost untroubled. Lacey was glad.

"I've been wrong," he said without preamble. "Very wrong. I should never have tried to force you to choose between him and me, honey. I've come to realize over the last few days that I've acted selfishly. I hope—" his voice shook, but he plowed ahead "—that some day you'll be able to forgive me."

Lacey's heart started beating faster. She chanced

a glimpse at Seth and saw him swallow hard, his face flush.

Then Philip turned to Seth. "And you, too. I've been wrong to be so obsessed with Kevin. I've been wrong to blame you for his problems. In my head, I know people are responsible for their own actions. It just might take a while for my heart to catch up." Her grandfather drew in a heavy breath and studied them both. "Meanwhile, you two belong together. I won't interfere. I won't make any more trouble." He looked at Seth again. "And I'll try to build some sort of relationship with you, Seth. If you're willing."

Briefly Lacey closed her eyes, realizing Philip had used Seth's given name for the first time. The lump in her throat only increased when Seth stood.

"I'm willing, Philip."

Then, Seth crossed the room halfway and extended his hand.

Her grandfather met him in the middle and shook that hand. Holding back the tears, she stood, too. Philip watched her, his gaze steady. Smiling, Lacey flew across the room into his arms. "I love you, Grandpa."

"I love you, too, girl. Be happy."

Before she could respond, a cry sounded from upstairs. Philip squeezed her once, then said, "I'll go tend to the boy. I feel like rocking him for a while."

With one last nod to Seth, Philip left the room.

Seth simply stared at Lacey, holding his breath, fearful that if he moved, or said anything, he'd awaken from this dream and none of what happened would be real.

Almost in slow motion, she moved toward him, the soft velour caressing her curves, her hair tumbling onto her shoulders. When she reached him and twined her arms around his neck, he let out his breath and crushed her to him. He wanted to weep with joy, shout out loud and dance in the streets. As "White Christmas" filled the silence around them, she said, "This is a miracle, Seth."

Burying his face in her neck, he inhaled deeply and tightened his grip. "It is."

"It's real, right?"

He slid his hands to her hips and pulled her closer. "Very real."

"I don't understand everything that's happened."

"I don't, either. But I'm willing to accept it on faith. You're in my arms on Christmas Eve. That's all that matters."

She drew back and looked up at him, her eyes sparkling brighter than the lights on the tree. "Merry Christmas, love."

"Mmm, it will be that," Seth said, lowering his head. "And so will our next fifty together."

EPILOGUE

"JOSH, go get your mother. Quick. She's on the phone in the den." Philip patted his five-year-old adopted great-grandson's bottom to send him on his way, then turned to the baby on his right, whose arm he held securely so the boy wouldn't fall. He spared a quick glance to the other side of the living room. "Celia, get the camcorder ready."

"It's ready, dear."

Over the musical sound of "Mo—om" as Josh ran through the house, Philip said, "You two just sit there and watch."

Out of the corner of his eye, Philip saw Seth give Joey an indulgent smile.

"Grandpa," Joey said. "He's only nine months old. He's too little to walk."

Ignoring the soft swell of emotion he experienced every time Joey called him grandpa, Philip said, "He's not too little. Kevin walked at nine months. This guy's ready." He caught Seth's gaze. "Isn't he, Dad?"

"I believe you." Seth's smile was genuine. "Miracles *do* happen on Christmas Eve."

Philip knew that Seth was remembering two years ago when he'd finally come to his senses the night before Christmas. The road had been rocky along the way for all of them, and there'd been some hard times, especially those first few months, but they'd made it. His voice gruff, he said, "Yes, they do."

"What's going on?" Lacey entered the room, Josh tugging her by the hand.

Joey said, "Grandpa says little Philip's gonna walk."

Lacey laughed and locked eyes with her husband. She rested her hands on her stomach and said, "Of course, it's Christmas Eve."

Philip backed up about three feet, leaving the boy anchored to the couch. He squatted and stretched out his arms.

The child turned, then teetered, his brown eyes glowing, his chubby cheeks rosy with delight. "Pa...Pa...Pa," he said as he took his first steps.

Tears clouded Philip's eyes. "Come on, boy. You can do it. Come to Papa."

One more...two more...three more steps, and the baby gripped his large hands.

Philip scooped up his great-grandson. "Good boy, Philip. Good boy."

Lacey watched the scene unfold, more content than she ever thought she'd be. The family cheered and talked at once about little Philip's accomplishment, and her motherly heart rejoiced in her son's triumph. A lot of things had brought this family together, and eased their grief over Kevin. But this little bundle of joy, born on her grandfather's seventy-eighth birthday, was the solidifier.

A loud blast of a horn sounded outside. "It's the fire trucks," Philip said, standing up, still clasping his namesake to him. "Come on, the baby's never seen this.'' The spring in Philip's step testifying to his good health, he gave orders. ''I'll get Philip into his snowsuit. Joe, you suit up Josh. Celia, don't forget the camera.''

Celia laughed. Lacey was so grateful to have Celia in their lives. In a move that surprised them all, Celia included, Philip had proposed to her the summer after the Christmas that had changed their lives. Her influence, along with some counseling Philip had gotten, had gone a long way to unite their family.

So had Seth's insistence last Christmas that Philip head up a senior citizens' group to work with the high-school students on the Good Deeds Project. Now Philip practically ran the whole project, leaving Seth free to oversee the rest of Bayview Heights High School as its principal.

Philip, Celia, Joey and the two little boys headed to the foyer. Loud honks sounded from outside their house. Philip's friends on the Bayview Heights Volunteer Fire Department knew about his attachment to his great-grandchildren and were waiting for him, as prearranged, with their seasonal tribute—a decorated fire truck making the rounds in the neighborhood.

''You coming?'' Joey appeared in the doorway a few minutes later, coat on, holding a bundled-up Josh's hand.

Seth raised an eyebrow at Lacey.

She shook her head. ''Not right now. I want a minute alone with your dad.''

Joey rolled his eyes and said to Josh in a stage whisper, ''Come on, buddy. They probably want to neck under Grandpa's mistletoe. Geez," he added with faked disgust. "That's all they ever do."

Lacey's eyes narrowed on Joey playfully. "Watch what you say, cub reporter, or I'll fire you from the paper."

"Grandpa would never allow that," Joey said haughtily. He zipped up his jacket, secured Josh's hat and disappeared.

Seth laughed, still amazed at the bizarre turns their lives had taken. Who would have thought two years ago that Joey would have gotten close to Philip Cartwright, helping to ease the tension between Seth and the older man.

Philip spent hours teaching Joey the ropes of newspaper reporting. So much so that, at the end of his sophomore year, Joey had transferred to Columbia School of Journalism to be near his family and do more work at the *Herald*. He now roomed in New York City with Johnny Battaglia but came home often. Philip frequently boasted that Joey—his protégé—was someday going to win the Pulitzer he himself had never gotten.

"Seth? Are you okay?"

He cleared his throat. "Couldn't be better."

"Don't bet on it," she said mysteriously. Going to the stereo, she put on Handel's *Messiah,* her favorite Christmas music, then came to cuddle next to him. They sat in silence, listening to the strains of the classical piece, staring at the tree filled with lop-sided ornaments and clumped tinsel that Joey and Josh had put on when they'd helped their grandpa decorate it last weekend.

"Sometimes," he whispered into her hair, "it all seems too good to be true."

He felt her smile against his chest. "That's what Cassie just said on the phone."

"Are they coming for dinner tomorrow?"

"Yes, Alexandra's cold is better."

"Oh no. Warn Josh. The little terror won't leave him alone." Mitch and Cassie's two-year-old daughter had turned out to be a handful, just like her mother.

Lacey laughed aloud. She did that often. As he hugged her, they heard Joey's voice from the foyer. "Dad, Lace, we're going on the truck with the firefighters. You guys want to come?"

"No thanks," Seth called out.

"It figures," Joey retorted, then slammed the door.

"I've got other plans," Seth whispered, pulling his wife onto his lap and unbuttoning her sweater. He nuzzled his face in her chest. "Mmm, this feels good."

As he said it, something niggled inside of him. Her breasts did feel good, but they also felt...

She slipped off his lap and crossed to the tree before he could finish the thought. When she returned, she handed him a small package and did up her shirt.

"What's this?" he asked, eyeing her suspiciously.

"A private Christmas present."

Stretching up, he gave her a quick but thorough kiss, then ripped open the package.

He held up the tiniest superhero pajamas he'd ever seen. "A little small for me, aren't they?"

She glanced back down at the wrapping. He tracked the look. Inside was another pair of pajamas, identical to the first.

"Lace? What's this all about?"

She gave him a Mona Lisa smile. "Guess."

He reached over and palmed her breast. "You're pregnant. We're going to have another baby."

"And another."

"Another? As in *two?*"

"Yep. Two boys."

"Two boys? Two *more* boys?"

Lacey giggled girlishly. "Uh-huh. Looks like I'm destined to spend my life with all men." Her eyes glowed. "I had amniocentesis, just like the last time, because of my age. I waited until I got the results to tell you. It killed me to keep this to myself, but I wanted to surprise you on Christmas Eve."

Seth hauled her into his arms, the small sets of pj's scrunched between them. "Two more sons…"

He held her tightly, almost overcome with his good fortune. After a moment, she drew back and framed his face with her hands. "Only fitting for a superhero. Are you happy?"

He grasped the back of her neck and pulled her to him. Just before his lips met hers, he whispered, "Happier than I ever thought I could be, Ace."

Around them, in the warmth of the fire and the good cheer of Christmas, the Boston Pops sang loud and clear, "Hallelujah!"

They're ranchers, cowboys, men of the West!

O LITTLE TOWN
OF GLORY

by Judith Bowen

**Visit the town of Glory in December 1998!
A good place to go for Christmas...**

Calgary lawyer Honor Templeman makes a shocking dis-
covery after her husband's death. Parker Templeman had
another wife—and two children—in the small town of
Glory. Two children left to the care of their uncle, Joe
Gallant, who has no intention of giving them up—to
Honor *or* her powerful father-in-law.

Available wherever Harlequin books are sold.

HARLEQUIN®
Makes any time special ™

G

Dangerous, powerful and passionate...

THE

AUSTRALIANS

Stories of romance Australian-style, guaranteed to
fulfill that sense of adventure!

This January 1999, look for

Her Outback Man

by **Margaret Way**

Logan Dangerfield, head of one of Australia's most affluent
families, had severe doubts about Dana Barry's motives.
Offering comfort to Logan's niece kept Dana on his cattle
station, but could she hide the fact that Logan was the only
Outback man she had ever loved?

*The Wonder from Down Under: where spirited women win
the hearts of Australia's most independent men!*

Available January 1999
at your favorite retail outlet.

HARLEQUIN®
*M*akes any time special ™